Although many great authors never wrote a novel on an occult theme, few did not write a short story about the supernatural. *Uncanny Tales* are collections of these short stories which cover the widest range of the works of well-loved writers.

The first selection consists of tales by authors whose fame has long outlived them and are still, to lovers of thrilling fiction, household words.

The Dennis Wheatley Library of the Occult

Dracula
Bram Stoker

The Werewolf of Paris
Guy Endore

Moonchild
Aleister Crowley

Studies in Occultism
Helena Blavatsky

Carnacki the Ghost-Finder
William Hope Hodgson

The Sorcery Club
Elliott O'Donnell

Harry Price: The Biography of a Ghost-Hunter
Paul Tabori

The Witch of Prague
F. Marion Crawford

The Prisoner in the Opal
A. E. W. Mason

Uncanny Tales 1
Selected by DENNIS WHEATLEY

SPHERE BOOKS LIMITED
30/32 Gray's Inn Road, London WC1X 8JL

First published in Great Britain by
Sphere Books Ltd 1974
Introduction copyright © Dennis Wheatley 1974

TRADE
MARK

This book is sold subject to the condition that
it shall not, by way of trade or otherwise, be lent,
re-sold, hired out or otherwise circulated without
the publisher's prior consent in any form of
binding or cover other than that in which it is
published and without a similar condition
including this condition being imposed on the
subsequent purchaser.

Set in Intertype Baskerville

Printed in Great Britain by
Hazell Watson & Viney Ltd
Aylesbury, Bucks

ISBN 0 7221 9036 0

CONTENTS

INTRODUCTION

CARMILLA by Sheridan Le Fanu	9
THE DREAM WOMAN by Wilkie Collins	83
THE TAPESTRIED CHAMBER by Sir Walter Scott	107
THE OPEN DOOR by Mrs Oliphant	121
THE SPECTRE BRIDEGROOM by Washington Irving	163
LIGEIA by Edgar Allan Poe	176
CLARIMONDE by Théophile Gautier	192

INTRODUCTION

It is an interesting fact that, although many great authors never wrote a novel with an occult theme, there are comparatively few who did not write a short story about some supernatural occurrence. To fail to include these in our library would be a serious omission, so we propose to publish collections of them every few months under the title of *Uncanny Tales*.

The first selection consists of tales by authors whose fame has long outlived them and are still, to lovers of thrilling fiction, household words.

Sheridan Le Fanu, an Irishman, provides the major piece. He was one of the most renowned of all Victorian authors who specialised in writing about ghosts, demons and such matters. His most famous novels, *Uncle Silas* and *The House by the Churchyard*, we hope to publish in due course. As a specimen of his work I have chosen *Carmilla*, a novelette which is nearly half the length of an average modern novel. Its plot, although having no resemblance to Bram Stoker's *Dracula*, is also set in Middle Europe and is about a vampire.

Wilkie Collins was equally famous and, in due course, we plan to publish his great novels. Meanwhile here is a story, *The Dream Woman*, which is typical of his work.

Sir Walter Scott's novels still stand high in compulsory reading for education. Personally, I always found their long descriptive passages terribly dull and, as an historical novelist, I think him incomparably inferior to Alexander Dumas, or even Stanley Weyman. But *The Tapestried Chamber* stands up well as one of his rare excursions into the occult.

Mrs Oliphant is another author who was also Scottish. She was an indefatigable writer, particularly of historical novels, and achieved great popularity. Before she died in 1897 she had published over a hundred books, and in *The Open Door* she gives us a splendid example of building up suspense in a really first class ghost story.

Washington Irving is known as the grandfather of American literature. He was born in New York in 1783 and died in 1859. The youngest of eleven children of a stern Protestant father he became, nevertheless, broad-minded which he probably owed to having studied and passed the examination for the American Bar. He is particularly famous for his short stories and his *The Spectre Bridegroom,* published here, is typical of what is known as the Gothic style of fiction.

Edgar Allan Poe first made his reputation with a poem called *The Raven*. His *Tales of Mystery and Imagination* is one of the best-known books in English literature. On re-reading them, however, it much surprised me to find that very few of them concerned the supernatural. From those that did I chose *Ligeia*; for in it the American master produces a finale that is beyond the uncanny. It is breath-takingly gruesome.

Théophile Gautier's *Clarimonde,* completes this collection. Gautier was a Gascon and also achieved celebrity as a young poet. Later he became a great traveller, and lived for a time in Spain, England, Algeria, Italy, Turkey, Greece and Russia. He is best known for his splendid novel *Mam'selle de Maupin,* and must be numbered among the greatest of French writers.

Dennis Wheatley

CARMILLA

Sheridan Le Fanu

PROLOGUE

Upon a paper attached to the Narrative which follows, Doctor Hesselius has written a rather elaborate note, which he accompanies with a reference to his Essay on the strange subject which the MS illuminates.

This mysterious subject he treats, in that Essay, with his usual learning and acumen, and with remarkable directness and condensation. It will form but one volume of the series of that extraordinary man's collected papers.

As I publish the case, in this volume, simply to interest the 'laity,' I shall forestall the intelligent lady, who writes it, in nothing; and after due consideration, I have determined, therefore, to abstain from presenting any *précis* of the learned Doctor's reasoning, or extract from his statement on a subject which he describes as 'involving, not improbably, some of the profoundest arcana of our dual existence, and its intermediates'.

I was anxious on discovering this paper, to reopen the correspondence commenced by Doctor Hesselius, so many years before, with a person so clever and careful as his informant seems to have been. Much to my regret, however, I found that she had died in the interval.

She, probably, could have added little to the Narrative which she communicates in the following pages, with, so far as I can pronounce, such a conscientious particularity.

1

AN EARLY FRIGHT

In Styria, we, though by no means magnificent people, inhabit a castle, or schloss. A small income, in that part of the world, goes a great way. Eight or nine hundred a year does wonders. Scantily enough ours would have answered among wealthy people at home. My father is English, and I bear an English name, although I never saw England. But here, in this lonely and primitive place, where everything is so marvellously cheap, I really don't see how ever so much more money would at all materially add to our comforts, or even luxuries.

My father was in the Austrian service, and retired upon a pension and his patrimony, and purchased this feudal residence, and the small estate on which it stands, a bargain.

Nothing can be more picturesque or solitary. It stands on a slight eminence in a forest. The road, very old and narrow, passes in front of its drawbridge, never raised in my time, and its moat, stocked with perch, and sailed over by many swans, and floating on its surface white fleets of water-lilies.

Over all this the schloss shows its many-windowed front, its towers, and its Gothic chapel.

The forest opens in an irregular and very picturesque glade before its gate, and at the right a steep Gothic bridge carries the road over a stream that winds in deep shadow through the wood.

I have said that this is a very lonely place. Judge whether I say truth. Looking from the hall door toward the road, the forest in which our castle stands extends fifteen miles to the right, and twelve to the left. The nearest inhabited village is about seven of your English miles to the left. The nearest inhabited schloss of any historic associations, is that of old General Spielsdorf, nearly twenty miles away to the right.

I have said 'the nearest *inhabited* village', because there is, only three miles westward, that is to say in the direction of General Spielsdorf's schloss, a ruined village, with its quaint little church, now roofless, in the aisle of which are the mouldering tombs of the proud family of Karnstein, now extinct, who once owned the equally-desolate château which, in the thick of the forest, overlooks the silent ruins of the town.

Respecting the cause of the desertion of this striking and melancholy spot, there is a legend which I shall relate to you another time.

I must tell you now, how very small is the party who constitute the inhabitants of our castle. I don't include servants, or those dependants who occupy rooms in the buildings attached to the schloss. Listen, and wonder! My father, who is the kindest man on earth, but growing old; and I, at the date of my story, only nineteen. Eight years have passed since then. I and my father constituted the family at the schloss. My mother, a Styrian lady, died in my infancy, but I had a good-natured governess, who had been with me from, I might almost say, my infancy. I could not remember the time when her fat, benignant face was not a familiar picture in my memory. This was Madame Perrodon, a native of Berne, whose care and good nature in part supplied to me the loss of my mother, whom I do not even remember, so early I lost her. She made a third at our little dinner party. There was a fourth, Mademoiselle De Lafontaine, a lady such as you term, I believe, a 'finishing governess'. She spoke French and German, Madame Perrodon French and broken English, to which my father and I added English, which, partly to prevent its becoming a lost language amongst us, and partly from patriotic motives, we spoke every day. The consequence was a Babel, at which strangers used to laugh, and which I shall make no attempt to reproduce in this narrative. And there were two or three young lady friends besides, pretty nearly of my own age, who were occasional visitors, for longer or shorter terms; and these visits I sometimes returned.

These were our regular social resources; but of course there were chance visits from 'neighbours' of only five or six leagues' distance. My life was, notwithstanding, rather a solitary one, I can assure you.

My gouvernantes had just so much control over me as you might conjecture such sage persons would have in this case of a rather spoiled girl, whose only parent allowed her pretty nearly her own way in everything.

The first occurrence in my existence, which produced a terrible impression upon my mind, which, in fact, never has been effaced, was one of the very earliest incidents of my life which I can recollect. Some people will think it so trifling that it should not be recorded here. You will see, however, by-and-by, why I mention it. The nursery, as it was called, though I had it all to myself, was a large room in the upper storey of the castle, with a steep oak roof. I can't have been more than six years old, when one night I awoke, and looking round the room from my bed, failed to see the nursery-maid. Neither was my nurse there; and I thought myself alone. I was not frightened, for I was one of those happy children who are studiously kept in ignorance of ghost stories, of fairy tales, and of all such lore as makes us cover up our heads when the door creaks suddenly, or the flicker of an expiring candle makes the shadow of a bed-post dance upon the wall, nearer to our faces. I was vexed and insulted at finding myself, as I conceived, neglected, and I began to whimper, preparatory to a hearty bout of roaring; when to my surprise, I saw a solemn, but very pretty face looking at me from the side of the bed. It was that of a young lady who was kneeling, with her hands under the coverlet. I looked at her with a kind of pleased wonder, and ceased whimpering. She caressed me with her hands, and lay down beside me on the bed, and drew me towards her, smiling; I felt immediately delightfully soothed, and fell asleep again. I was wakened by a sensation as if two needles ran into my breast very deep at the same moment, and I cried loudly. The lady started back, with her eyes fixed on me, and then slipped down upon the floor, and, as I thought, hid herself under the bed.

I was now for the first time frightened, and I yelled with all my might and main. Nurse, nursery-maid, housekeeper, all came running in, and hearing my story, they made light of it, soothing me all they could meanwhile. But, child as I was, I could perceive that their faces were pale with an unwonted look of anxiety, and I saw them look under the bed, and about the room, and peep under tables and pluck open cupboards; and the housekeeper whispered to the nurse; 'Lay your hand along that hollow in the bed; some one *did* lie there, so sure as you did not; the place is still warm.'

I remember the nursery-maid petting me, and all three examining my chest, where I told them I felt the puncture, and pronouncing that there was no sign visible that any such thing had happened to me.

The housekeeper and the two other servants who were in charge of the nursery, remained sitting up all night; and from that time a servant always sat up in the nursery until I was about fourteen.

I was very nervous for a long time after this. A doctor was called in, he was pallid and elderly. How well I remember his long saturnine face, slightly pitted with smallpox, and his chestnut wig. For a good while, every second day, he came and gave me medicine, which of course I hated.

The morning after I saw this apparition I was in a state of terror, and could not bear to be left alone, daylight though it was, for a moment.

I remember my father coming up and standing at the bedside, and talking cheerfully, and asking the nurse a number of questions, and laughing very heartily at one of the answers; and patting me on the shoulder, and kissing me, and telling me not to be frightened, that it was nothing but a dream and could not hurt me.

But I was not comforted, for I knew the visit of the strange woman was *not* a dream; and I was *awfully* frightened.

I was a little consoled by the nursery-maid's assuring me that it was she who had come and looked at me, and lain down beside me in the bed, and that I must have been half-dreaming not to have known her face. But this, though supported by the nurse, did not quite satisfy me.

I remember, in the course of that day, a venerable old man, in a black cassock, coming into the room with the nurse and housekeeper, and talking a little to them, and very kindly to me; his face was very sweet and gentle, and he told me they were going to pray, and joined my hands together, and desired me to say, softly, while they were praying, 'Lord, hear all good prayers for us, for Jesus' sake.' I think these were the very words, for I often repeated them to myself, and my nurse used for years to make me say them in my prayers.

I remember so well the thoughtful sweet face of that white-haired old man, in his black cassock, as he stood in that rude, lofty brown room, with the clumsy furniture of a fashion three hundred years old, about him, and the scanty light entering its shadowy atmosphere through the small lattice. He kneeled, and the three women with him, and he prayed aloud with an earnest quavering voice for, what appeared to me, a long time. I forget all my life preceding that event, and for some time after it is all obscure also; but the scenes I have just described stand out vivid as the isolated pictures of the phantasmagoria surrounded by darkness.

2

A QUEST

I am now going to tell you something so strange that it will require all your faith in my veracity to believe my story. It is not only true, nevertheless, but truth of which I have been an eye-witness.

It was a sweet summer evening, and my father asked me, as he sometimes did, to take a little ramble with him along that beautiful forest vista which I have mentioned as lying in front of the schloss.

'General Spielsdorf cannot come to us so soon as I had hoped,' said my father, as we pursued our walk.

He was to have paid us a visit of some weeks, and we had expected his arrival next day. He was to have brought with him a young lady, his niece and ward, Mademoiselle Rheinfeldt, whom I had never seen, but whom I had heard described as a very charming girl, and in whose society I had promised myself many happy days. I was more disappointed than a young lady living in a town, or a bustling neighbourhood can possibly imagine. This visit, and the new acquaintance it promised, had furnished my day dream for many weeks.

'And how soon does he come?' I asked.

'Not until autumn. Not for two months, I dare say,' he answered. 'And I am very glad now, dear, that you never knew Mademoiselle Rheinfeldt.'

'And why?' I asked, both mortified and curious.

'Because the poor young lady is dead,' he replied. 'I quite forgot I had not told you, but you were not in the room when I received the General's letter this evening.'

I was very much shocked. General Spielsdorf had mentioned in his first letter, six or seven weeks before, that she was not so well as he would wish her, but there was nothing to suggest the remotest suspicion of danger.

We sat down on a rude bench, under a group of magnificent lime trees. The sun was setting with all its melancholy splendour behind the sylvan horizon, and the stream that flows beside our home, and passes under the steep old bridge I have mentioned, wound through many a group of noble trees, almost at our feet, reflecting in its current the fading crimson of the sky. General Spielsdorf's letter was extraordinary, so vehement, and in some places so self-contradictory, that I read it twice over — the second time aloud to my father — and was still unable to account for it, except by supposing that grief had unsettled his mind.

It said, 'I have lost my darling daughter, for as such I loved her. During the last days of dear Bertha's illness I was not able to write to you. Before then I had no idea of her danger. I have lost her, and now learn *all*, too late. She died in the peace of innocence and in the glorious hope of a blessed futurity. The friend who betrayed our infatuated hospitality has done it all. I thought I was receiving into my house innocence, gaiety, a charming companion for my lost Bertha. Heavens! what a fool I have been! I thank God my child died without a suspicion of the cause of her sufferings. She is gone without so much as conjecturing the nature of her illness, and the accursed passion of the agent of all this misery. I devote my remaining days to tracking and extinguishing a monster. I am told I may hope to accomplish my righteous and merciful purpose. At present there is scarcely a gleam of light to guide me. I curse my conceited incredulity, my despicable affection of superiority, my blindness, my obstinacy — all — too late. I cannot write or talk collectedly now. I am distracted. So soon as I shall have a little recovered, I mean to devote myself for a time to inquiry, which may possibly lead me as far as Vienna. Some time in the autumn, two months hence, or earlier if I live, I will see you – that is, if you permit me; I will then tell you all that I scarce dare put upon paper now. Farewell. Pray for me, dear friend.'

In these terms ended this strange letter. Though I had never seen Bertha Rheinfeldt, my eyes filled with tears at the sudden intelligence; I was startled, as well as profoundly disappointed.

The sun had now set, and it was twilight by the time I had returned the General's letter to my father.

It was a soft clear evening, and we loitered, speculating upon the possible meanings of the violent and incoherent sentences which I had just been reading. We had nearly a mile to walk before reaching the road that passes the schloss in front, and by that time the moon was shining brilliantly. At the drawbridge we met Madame Perrodon and Mademoiselle de Lafontaine, who had come out, without their bonnets, to enjoy the exquisite moonlight.

We heard their voices gabbling in animated dialogue as we approached. We joined them at the drawbridge, and turned about to admire with them the beautiful scene.

The glade through which we had just walked lay before us. At our left the narrow road wound away under clumps of lordly trees, and was lost to sight amid the thickening forest. At the right the same road crosses the steep and picturesque bridge, near which stands a ruined tower, which once guarded that pass; and beyond the bridge an abrupt eminence rises, covered with trees, and showing in the shadow some grey ivy-clustered rocks.

Over the sward and low grounds, a thin film of mist was stealing, like smoke, marking the distances with a transparent veil; and here and there we could see the river faintly flashing in the moonlight.

No softer, sweeter scene could be imagined. The news I had just heard made it melancholy; but nothing could disturb its character of profound serenity, and the enchanted glory and vagueness of the prospect.

My father, who enjoyed the picturesque, and I, stood looking in the silence over the expanse beneath us. The two good governesses standing a little way behind us, discoursed upon the scene, and were eloquent upon the moon.

Madame Perrodon was fat, middle-aged, and romantic, and talked and sighed poetically. Mademoiselle de Lafontaine – in right of her father, who was a German, assumed to be psychological, metaphysical, and something of a mystic – now declared that when the moon shone with a light so intense it was well known that it indicated a special spiritual activity. The effect of the full moon in such a state of brilliancy was manifold. It acted on dreams, it acted on lunacy, it acted on nervous people; it had marvellous physical influences connected with life. Mademoiselle related that her cousin, who was mate of a merchant ship, having taken a nap on deck on such a night, lying on his back, with his face full in the light of the moon, had wakened, after a dream of an old woman clawing him by the cheek, with his features horribly drawn to one side; and his countenance had never quite recovered its equilibrium.

'The moon, this night,' she said, 'is full of odylic and magnetic influence – and see, when you look behind you at the front of the schloss, how all its windows flash and twinkle with that silvery splendour, as if unseen hands had lighted up the rooms to receive fairy guests.'

There are indolent states of the spirits in which, indisposed to talk ourselves, the talk of others is pleasant to our listless ears; and I gazed on, pleased with the tinkle of the ladies' conversation.

'I have got into one of my moping moods tonight,' said my father, after a silence, and quoting Shakespeare, whom, by way of keeping up our English, he used to read aloud, he said :—

> In truth I know not why I am so sad :
> It wearies me; you say it wearies you;
> But how I got it – came by it.

'I forget the rest. But I feel as if some great misfortune were hanging over us. I suppose the poor general's afflicted letter had something to do with it.'

At this moment the unwonted sound of carriage wheels and many hoofs upon the road, arrested our attention.

They seemed to be approaching from the high ground overlooking the bridge, and very soon the equipage emerged from that point. Two horsemen first crossed the bridge, then came a carriage drawn by four horses, and two men rode behind.

It seemed to be the travelling carriage of a person of

rank; and we were all immediately absorbed in watching that very unusual spectacle. It became, in a few moments, greatly more interesting, for just as the carriage had passed the summit of the steep bridge, one of the leaders, taking fright, communicated his panic to the rest, and, after a plunge or two, the whole team broke into a wild gallop together, and dashing between the horsemen who rode in front, came thundering along the road towards us with the speed of a hurricane.

The excitement of the scene was made more painful by the clear, long-drawn screams of a female voice from the carriage window.

We all advanced in curiosity and horror; my father in silence, the rest with various ejaculations of terror.

Our suspense did not last long. Just before you reach the castle drawbridge, on the route they were coming, there stands by the roadside a magnificent lime tree, on the other side stands an ancient stone cross, at sight of which the horses, now going at a pace that was perfectly frightful, swerved so as to bring the wheel over the projecting roots of the tree.

I knew what was coming. I covered my eyes, unable to see it out, and turned my head away; at the same moment I heard a cry from my lady-friends, who had gone on a little.

Curiosity opened my eyes, and I saw a scene of utter confusion. Two of the horses were on the ground, the carriage lay upon its side, with two wheels in the air; the men were busy removing the traces, and a lady, with a commanding air and figure had got out, and stood with clasped hands, raising the handkerchief that was in them every now and then to her eyes. Through the carriage door was now lifted a young lady, who appeared to be lifeless. My dear old father was already beside the elder lady, with his hat in his hand, evidently tendering his aid and the resources of his schloss. The lady did not appear to hear him, or to have eyes for anything but the slender girl who was being placed against the slope of the bank.

I approached; the young lady was apparently stunned, but she was certainly not dead. My father, who picqued himself on being something of a physician, had just had his fingers to her wrist and assured the lady, who declared herself her mother, that her pulse, though faint and irregular, was undoubtedly still distinguishable. The lady clasped her hands and looked upward, as if in a momentary transport of gratitude; but immediately she broke out again in that theatrical way which is, I believe, natural to some people.

She was what is called a fine-looking woman for her time of life, and must have been handsome; she was tall but not thin, and dressed in black velvet, and looked rather pale, but with a proud and commanding countenance, though now agitated strangely.

'Was ever being so born to calamity?' I heard her say, with clasped hands, as I came up. 'Here am I, on a journey of life and death, in prosecuting which to lose an hour is possibly to lose all. My child will not have recovered sufficiently to resume her route for who can say how long. I must leave her; I cannot, dare not, delay. How far on, sir, can you tell, is the nearest village? I must leave her there; and shall not see my darling, or even hear of her till my return, three months hence.'

I plucked my father by the coat, and whispered earnestly in his ear, 'Oh! papa, pray ask her to let her stay with us – it would be so delightful. Do, pray.'

'If Madame will entrust her child to the care of my daughter, and her good gouvernante, Madame Perrodon, and permit her to remain as our guest, under my charge, until her return, it will confer a distinction and an obligation upon us, and we shall treat her with all the care and devotion which so sacred a trust deserves.'

'I cannot do that, sir, it would be to task your kindness and chivalry too cruelly,' said the lady, distractedly.

'It would, on the contrary, be to confer on us a very great kindness at the moment when we most need it. My daughter has just been disappointed by a cruel misfortune, in a visit from which she had long anticipated a great deal of happiness. If you confide this young lady to our care it will be her best consolation. The nearest village on your route is distant, and affords no such inn as you could think of placing your daughter at; you cannot allow her to continue her journey for any considerable distance without danger. If, as you say, you cannot suspend your journey, you must part with her tonight, and nowhere could you do so with more honest assurances of care and tenderness than here.'

There was something in this lady's air and appearance so distinguished, and even imposing, and in her manner so engaging, as to impress one, quite apart from the dignity of her equipage, with a conviction that she was a person of consequence.

By this time the carriage was replaced in its upright position, and the horses, quite tractable, in the traces again.

The lady threw on her daughter a glance which I fancied was not quite so affectionate as one might have anticipated from the beginning of the scene; then she beckoned slightly to my father, and withdrew two or three steps with him out of hearing; and talked to him with a fixed and stern countenance; not at all like that with which she had hitherto spoken.

I was filled with wonder that my father did not seem to perceive the change, and also unspeakably curious to learn what it could be that she was speaking, almost in his ear, with so much earnestness and rapidity.

Two or three minutes at most, I think, she remained thus employed, then she turned, and a few steps brought her to where her daughter lay, supported by Madame Perrodon. She kneeled beside her for a moment and whispered, as Madame supposed, a little benediction in her ear; then hastily kissing her, she stepped into her carriage, the door was closed, the footmen in stately liveries jumped up behind, the outriders spurred on, the postilions cracked their whips, the horses plunged and broke suddenly into a furious canter that threatened soon again to become a gallop, and the carriage whirled away, followed at the same pace by the two horsemen in the rear.

3

WE COMPARE NOTES

We followed the cortège with our eyes until it was swiftly lost to sight in the misty wood; and the very sound of the hoofs and wheels died away in the silent air.

Nothing remained to assure us that the adventure had not been an illusion of a moment but the young lady, who just at that moment opened her eyes. I could not see, for her face was turned from me, but she raised her head, evidently looking about her, and I heard a very sweet voice ask complainingly, 'Where is mamma?'

Our good Madame Perrodon answered tenderly, and added some comfortable assurances.

I then heard her ask:

'Where am I? What is this place?' and after that she said, 'I don't see the carriage; and Matska, where is she?'

Madame answered all her questions in so far as she understood them; and gradually the young lady remembered how the misadventure came about, and was glad to hear that no one in, or in attendance on, the carriage was hurt; and on learning that her mamma had left her here, till her return in about three months, she wept.

I was going to add my consolations to those of Madame Perrodon when Mademoiselle de Lafontaine placed her hand upon my arm, saying:

'Don't approach, one at a time is as much as she can at present converse with; a very little excitement would possibly overpower her now.'

As soon as she is comfortably in bed, I thought, I will run up to her room and see her.

My father in the meantime had sent a servant on horseback for the physician, who lived about two leagues away; and a bedroom was being prepared for the young lady's reception.

The stranger now rose, and leaning on Madame's arm, walked slowly over the drawbridge and into the castle gate.

In the hall, servants waited to receive her, and she was conducted forthwith to her room.

The room we usually sat in as our drawing-room is long, having four windows, that looked over the moat and drawbridge, upon the forest scene I have just described.

It is furnished in old carved oak, with large carved cabinets, and the chairs are cushioned with crimson Utrecht velvet. The walls are covered with tapestry, and surrounded with great gold frames, the figures being as large as life, in ancient and very curious costume, and the subjects represented are hunting, hawking, and generally festive. It is not too stately to be extremely comfortable; and here we had our tea, for with his usual patriotic leanings he insisted that the national beverage should make its appearance regularly with our coffee and chocolate.

We sat here this night, and with candles lighted, were talking over the adventure of the evening.

Madame Perrodon and Mademoiselle de Lafontaine were both of our party. The young stranger had hardly lain down in her bed when she sank into a deep sleep; and those ladies had left her in the care of a servant.

'How do you like our guest?' I asked, as soon as Madame entered. 'Tell me all about her?'

'I like her extremely,' answered Madame, 'she is, I almost think the prettiest creature I ever saw; about your age, and so gentle and nice.'

'She is absolutely beautiful,' threw in Mademoiselle, who had peeped for a moment into the stranger's room.

'And such a sweet voice!' added Madame Perrodon.

'Did you remark a woman in the carriage, after it was set up again, who did not get out,' inquired Mademoiselle, 'but only looked from the window?'

No, we had not seen her.

Then she described a hideous black woman, with a sort of coloured turban on her head, who was gazing all the time from the carriage window, nodding and grinning derisively towards the ladies, with gleaming eyes and large white eye-balls, and her teeth set as if in fury.

'Did you remark what an ill-looking pack of men the servants were?' asked Madame.

'Yes,' said my father, who had just come in, 'ugly, hang-dog looking fellows, as ever I beheld in my life. I hope they mayn't rob the poor lady in the forest. They are clever rogues, however: they got everything to rights in a minute.'

'I dare say they are worn out with too long travelling,' said Madame. 'Besides looking wicked, their faces were so strangely lean, and dark, and sullen. I am very curious, I own; but I dare say the young lady will tell us all about it tomorrow, if she is sufficiently recovered.'

'I don't think she will,' said my father, with a mysterious smile, and a little nod of his head, as if he knew more about it than he cared to tell us.

This made me all the more inquisitive as to what had

passed between him and the lady in black velvet, in the brief but earnest interview that had immediately preceded her departure.

We were scarcely alone, when I entreated him to tell me. He did not need much pressing.

'There is no particular reason why I should not tell you. She expressed a reluctance to trouble us with the care of her daughter, saying she was in delicate health, and nervous, but not subject to any kind of seizure – she volunteered that – nor to any illusion; being, in fact, perfectly sane.'

'How very odd to say all that!' I interpolated. 'It was so unnecessary.'

'At all events it *was* said,' he laughed, 'and as you wish to know all that passed, which was indeed very little, I tell you. She then said, "I am making a long journey of *vital* importance" – she emphasised the word— "rapid and secret; I shall return for my child in three months; in the meantime, she shall be silent as to who we are, whence we come, and whither we are travelling." That is all she said. She spoke very pure French. When she said the word "secret", she paused for a few seconds, looking sternly, her eyes fixed on mine. I fancy she makes a great point of that. You saw how quickly she was gone. I hope I have not done a very foolish thing, in taking charge of the young lady.'

For my part, I was delighted. I was longing to see and talk to her; and only waiting till the doctor should give me leave. You, who live in towns, can have no idea how great an event the introduction of a new friend is, in such a solitude as surrounded us.

The doctor did not arrive till nearly one o'clock; but I could no more have gone to my bed and slept, than I could have overtaken, on foot, the carriage in which the princess in black velvet had driven away.

When the physician came down to the drawing-room, it was to report very favourably upon his patient. She was now sitting up, her pulse quite regular, apparently perfectly well. She had sustained no injury, and the little shock to her nerves had passed away quite harmlessly. There could be no harm certainly in my seeing her, if we both wished it; and with this permission, I sent, forthwith, to know whether she would allow me to visit her for a few minutes in her room.

The servant returned immediately to say that she desired nothing more.

You may be sure I was not long in availing myself of this permission.

Our visitor lay in one of the handsomest rooms in the schloss. It was, perhaps, a little stately. There was a sombre piece of tapestry opposite the foot of the bed, representing Cleopatra with the asps to her bosom; and other classic scenes were displayed, a little faded, upon the other walls. But there was gold carving, and rich and varied colour enough in the other decorations of the room, to more than redeem the gloom of the old tapestry.

There were candles at the bed side. She was sitting up; her slender pretty figure enveloped in the soft silk dressing-gown, embroidered with flowers, and lined with thick quilted silk, which her mother had thrown over her feet as she lay upon the ground.

What was it that, as I reached the bed side and had just begun my little greeting, struck me dumb in a moment, and made me recoil a step or two from before her? I will tell you.

I saw the very face which had visited me in my childhood at night, which remained so fixed in my memory, and on which I had for so many years so often ruminated with horror, when no one suspected of what I was thinking.

It was pretty, even beautiful; and when I first beheld it, wore the same melancholy expression.

But this almost instantly lighted into a strange fixed smile of recognition.

There was a silence of fully a minute, and then at length *she* spoke; *I* could not.

'How wonderful!' she exclaimed. 'Twelve years ago, I saw your face in a dream, and it has haunted me ever since.'

'Wonderful indeed!' I repeated, overcoming with an effort the horror that had for a time suspended my utterances. 'Twelve years ago, in vision or reality, *I* certainly saw you. I could not forget your face. It has remained before my eyes ever since.'

Her smile had softened. Whatever I had fancied strange

in it, was gone, and it and her dimpling cheeks were now delightfully pretty and intelligent.

I felt reassured, and continued more in the vein which hospitality indicated, to bid her welcome, and to tell her how much pleasure her accidental arrival had given us all, and especially what a happiness it was to me.

I took her hand as I spoke. I was a little shy, as lonely people are, but the situation made me eloquent, and even bold. She pressed my hand, she laid hers upon it, and her eyes glowed, as looking hastily into mine, she smiled again, and blushed.

She answered my welcome very prettily. I sat down beside her, still wondering; and she said:

'I must tell you my vision about you; it is so very strange that you and I should have had, each of the other, so vivid a dream, that each should have seen, I you and you me, looking as we do now, when of course we both were mere children. I was a child about six years old, and I awoke from a confused and troubled dream, and found myself in a room, unlike my nursery, wainscoted clumsily in some dark wood, and with cupboards and bedsteads, and chairs and benches placed about it. The beds were, I thought, all empty, and the room itself without any one but myself in it; and I, after looking about me for some time, and admiring especially an iron candlestick, with two branches, which I should certainly know again, crept under one of the beds to reach the window; but as I got from under the bed, I heard some one crying; and looking up, while I was still upon my knees, I saw *you* –most assuredly you – as I see you now; a beautiful young lady, with golden hair and large blue eyes, and lips – your lips – you, as you are here. Your looks won me; I climbed on the bed and put my arms about you, and I think we both fell asleep. I was aroused by a scream; you were sitting up screaming. I was frightened, and slipped down upon the ground, and, it seemed to me, lost consciousness for a moment; and when I came to myself, I was again in my nursery at home. Your face I have never forgotten since. I could not be misled by mere resemblance. You *are* the lady whom I then saw.'

It was now my turn to relate my corresponding vision, which I did, to the undisguised wonder of my new acquaintance.

'I don't know which should be more afraid of the other,' she said, again smiling. 'If you were less pretty, I think I should be very much afraid of you, but being as you are, and you and I both so young, I feel only that I have made your acquaintance twelve years ago, and have already a right to your intimacy; at all events, it does seem as if we were destined, from our earliest childhood, to be friends, I wonder whether you feel as strangely drawn towards me as I do to you; I have never had a friend – shall I find one now?' She sighed, and her fine dark eyes gazed passionately on me.

Now the truth is, I felt rather unaccountably towards the beautiful stranger. I did feel, as she said, 'drawn towards her,' but there was also something something of repulsion. In this ambiguous feeling, however, the sense of attraction immensely prevailed. She interested and won me; she was so beautiful and so indescribably engaging.

I perceived now something of languor and exhaustion stealing over her, and hastened to bid her good night.

'The doctor thinks,' I added, 'that you ought to have a maid to sit up with you tonight; one of ours is waiting, and you will find her a very useful and quiet creature.'

'How kind of you, but I could not sleep. I never could with an attendant in the room. I shan't require any assistance – and shall I confess my weakness, I am haunted with a terror of robbers. Our house was robbed once, and two servants murdered, so I always lock my door. It has become a habit – and you look so kind I know you will forgive me. I see there is a key in the lock.'

She held me close in her pretty arms for a moment and whispered in my ear, 'Good-night, darling, it is very hard to part with you, but goodnight; tomorrow, but not early, I shall see you again.'

She sank back on the pillow with a sigh, and her fine eyes followed me with a fond and melancholy gaze, and she murmured again, 'Good-night, dear friend.'

Young people like, and even love on impulse. I was flattered by the evident, though as yet undeserved, fondness she showed me. I liked the confidence with which she at once received me. She was determined that we should be very dear friends.

Next day came and we met again. I was delighted with my companion; that is to say, in many respects.

Her looks lost nothing in daylight – she was certainly the most beautiful creature I had ever seen, and the unpleasant remembrance of the face presented in my early dream, had lost the effect of the first unexpected recognition.

She confessed that she had experienced a similar shock on seeing me, and precisely the same faint antipathy that had mingled with my admiration of her. We now laughed together over our momentary horrors.

4

HER HABITS – A SAUNTER

I told you that I was charmed with her in most particulars.

There were some that did not please me so well.

She was above the middle height of women. I shall begin by describing her. She was slender, and wonderfully graceful. Except that her movements were languid – *very* languid – indeed, there was nothing in her appearance to indicate an invalid. Her complexion was rich and brilliant; her features were small and beautifully formed; her eyes large, dark, and lustrous; her hair was quite wonderful, I never saw hair so magnificently thick and long when it was down about her shoulders; I have often placed my hands under it, and laughed with wonder at its weight. It was exquisitely fine and soft, and in colour a rich very dark brown, with something of gold. I loved to let it down, tumbling with its own weight, as, in her room, she lay back in her chair talking in her sweet low voice, I used to fold and braid it, and spread it out and play with it. Heavens! If I had but known all!

I said there were particulars which did not please me. I have told you that her confidence won me the first night I saw her; but I found that she exercised with respect to herself, her mother, her history, everything in fact connected with her life, plans, and people, an ever-wakeful reserve. I dare say I was unreasonable, perhaps I was wrong; I dare say I ought to have respected the solemn injunction laid upon my father by the stately lady in black velvet. But curiosity is a restless and unscrupulous passion, and no one girl can endure, with patience, that hers should be baffled by another. What harm could it do anyone to tell me what I so ardently desired to know? Had she no trust in my good sense or honour? Why would she not believe me when I assured her, so solemnly, that I would not divulge one syllable of what she told me to any mortal breathing?

There was a coldness, it seemed to me, beyond her years, in her smiling melancholy persistent refusal to afford me the least ray of light.

I cannot say we quarrelled upon this point, for she would not quarrel upon any. It was, of course, very unfair of me to press her, very ill-bred, but I really could not help it; and I might just as well have left it alone.

What she did tell me amounted, in my unconscionable estimation – to nothing.

It was all summed up in three very vague disclosures.

First. – Her name was Carmilla.

Second. – Her family was very ancient and noble.

Third. – Her home lay in the direction of the west.

She would not tell me the name of her family, nor their armorial bearings, nor the name of their estate, nor even that of the country they lived in.

You are not to suppose that I worried her incessantly on these subjects. I watched opportunity, and rather insinuated than urged my inquiries. Once or twice, indeed, I did attack her more directly. Reproaches and caresses were all lost upon her. But I must add this, that her evasion was conducted with so pretty a melancholy and deprecation, with so many, and even passionate declarations of her liking for me, and trust in my honour, and with so many promises that I should at last know all, that I could not find it in my heart long to be offended with her.

She used to place her pretty arms about my neck, draw me to her, and laying her cheek to mine, murmur with her lips near my ear, 'Dearest, your little heart is wounded; think me not cruel because I obey the irresistible law of my strength and weakness; if your dear heart is wounded, my wild heart bleeds with yours. In the rapture of my enormous humiliation I live in your warm life, and you shall die – die, sweetly die – into mine. I cannot help it; as I draw near to you, you, in your turn, will draw near to others, and learn the rapture of that cruelty, which yet is love; so, for a while, seek to know no more of me and mine, but trust me with all your loving spirit.'

And when she had spoken such a rhapsody, she would press me more closely in her trembling embrace, and her lips in soft kisses gently glow upon my cheek.

Her agitations and her language were unintelligible to me.

From these foolish embraces, which were not of very frequent occurrence, I must allow, I used to wish to extricate myself; but my energies seemed to fail me. Her murmured words sounded like a lullaby in my ear, and soothed my resistance into a trance, from which I only seemed to recover myself when she withdrew her arms.

In these mysterious moods I did not like her. I experienced a strange tumultous excitement that was pleasurable, ever and anon, mingled with a vague sense of fear and disgust. I had no distinct thoughts about her while such scenes lasted, but I was conscious of a love growing into adoration, and also of abhorrence. This I know is paradox, but I can make no other attempt to explain the feeling.

I now write, after an interval of more than ten years, with a trembling hand, with a confused and horrible recollection of certain occurrences and situations, in the ordeal through which I was unconsciously passing; though with a vivid and very sharp remembrance of the main current of my story. But, I suspect, in all lives there are certain emotional scenes, those in which our passions have been most wildly and terribly roused, that are of all others the most vaguely and dimly remembered.

Sometimes after an hour of apathy, my strange and beautiful companion would take my hand and hold it with a fond pressure, renewed again and again; blushing softly, gazing in my face with languid and burning eyes, and breathing so fast that her dress rose and fell with the tumultuous respiration. It was like the ardour of a lover; it embarrassed me; it was hateful and yet overpowering; and with gloating eyes she drew me to her, and her hot lips travelled along my cheek in kisses; and she would whisper, almost in sobs, 'You are mine, you *shall* be mine, and you and I are one for ever.' Then she has thrown herself back in her chair, with her small hands over her eyes, leaving me trembling.

'Are we related,' I used to ask; 'what can you mean by all this? I remind you perhaps of some one whom you love; but you must not, I hate it; I don't know you – I don't know myself when you look so and talk so.'

She used to sigh at my vehemence, then turn away and drop my hand.

Respecting these very extraordinarily manifestations I strove in vain to form any satisfactory theory – I could not refer them to affectation or trick. It was unmistakably the momentary breaking out of suppressed instinct and emotion. Was she, notwithstanding her mother's volunteered denial, subject to brief visitations of insanity; or was there here a disguise and a romance? I had read in old story books of such things. What if a boyish lover had found his way into the house, and sought to prosecute his suit in masquerade, with the assistance of a clever old adventuress? But there were many things against this hypothesis, highly interesting as it was to my vanity.

I could boast of no little attentions such as masculine gallantry delights to offer. Between these passionate moments there were long intervals of common-place, of gaiety, of brooding melancholy fire, following me, at times I might have been as nothing to her. Except in these brief periods of mysterious excitement her ways were girlish; and there was always a languor about her, quite incompatible with a masculine system in a state of health.

In some respects her habits were odd. Perhaps not so singular in the opinion of a town lady like you, as they appeared to us rustic people. She used to come down very late, generally not till one o'clock, she would then take a cup of chocolate, but eat nothing; we then went out for a walk, which was a mere saunter, and she seemed, almost immediately, exhausted, and either returned to the schloss or sat on one of the benches that were placed, here and there, among the trees. This was a bodily languor in which her mind did not sympathise. She was always an animated talker, and very intelligent.

She sometimes alluded for a moment to her own home, or mentioned an adventure or situation, or an early recollection, which indicated a people of strange manners, and described customs of which we knew nothing. I gathered from these chance hints that her native country was much more remote than I had at first fancied.

As we sat thus one afternoon under the trees a funeral passed us by. It was that of a pretty young girl, whom I had often seen, the daughter of one of the rangers of the forest. The poor man was walking behind the coffin of his darling; she was his only child, and he looked quite heart-broken. Peasants walking two-and-two came behind, they were singing a funeral hymn.

I rose to mark my respect as they passed, and joined in the hymn they were very sweetly singing.

My companion shook me a little roughly, and I turned surprised.

She said brusquely, 'Don't you perceive how discordant that is?'

'I think it very sweet, on the contrary,' I answered, vexed at the interruption, and very uncomfortable, lest the people who composed the little procession should observe and resent what was passing.

I resumed, therefore, instantly, and was again interrupted. 'You pierce my ears,' said Carmilla, almost angrily, and stopping her ears with her tiny fingers. 'Besides, how can you tell that your religion and mine are the same; your forms wound me, and I hate funerals. What a fuss! Why, *you* must die – *everyone* must die; and all are happier when they do. Come home.'

'My father has gone on with the clergyman to the churchyard. I thought you knew she was to be buried to-day.'

'*She?* I don't trouble my head about peasants. I don't know who she is,' answered Carmilla, with a flash from her fine eyes.

'She is the poor girl who fancied she saw a ghost a fortnight ago, and has been dying ever since, till yesterday, when she expired.'

'Tell me nothing about ghosts. I shan't sleep to-night if you do.'

'I hope there is no plague or fever coming; all this looks very like it,' I continued. 'The swineherd's young wife died only a week ago, and she thought something seized her by the throat as she lay in her bed, and nearly strangled her. Papa says such horrible fancies do accompany some forms of fever. She was quite well the day before. She sank afterwards, and died before a week.'

'Well, *her* funeral is over, I hope, and *her* hymn sung; and our ears shan't be tortured with that discord and jargon. It has made me nervous. Sit down here, beside me; sit close; hold my hand; press it hard – hard – harder.'

We had moved a little back, and had come to another seat.

She sat down. Her face underwent a change that alarmed and even terrified me for a moment. It darkened, and became horribly livid; her teeth and hands were clenched, and she frowned and compressed her lips, while she stared down upon the ground at her feet, and trembled all over with a continued shudder as irrepressible as ague. All her energies seemed strained to suppress a fit, with which she was then breathlessly tugging; and at length a low convulsive cry of suffering broke from her, and gradually the hysteria subsided. 'There! That comes of strangling people with hymns!' she said at last. 'Hold me, hold me still. It is passing away.'

And so gradually it did; and perhaps to dissipate the sombre impression which the spectacle had left upon me, she became unusually animated and chatty; and so we got home.

This was the first time I had seen her exhibit any definable symptoms of that delicacy of health which her mother had spoken of. It was the first time, also, I had seen her exhibit anything like temper.

Both passed away like a summer cloud; and never but once afterwards did I witness on her part a momentary sign of anger. I will tell you how it happened.

She and I were looking out of one of the long drawing-room windows, when there entered the court-yard, over the drawbridge, a figure of a wanderer whom I knew very well. He used to visit the schloss generally twice a year.

It was the figure of a hunchback, with the sharp lean features that generally accompany deformity. He wore a pointed black beard, and he was smiling from ear to ear, showing his white fangs. He was dressed in buff, black and scarlet, and crossed with more straps and belts than I could count, from which hung all manner of things.

Behind he carried a magic lantern, and two boxes, which I well knew, in one of which was a salamander, and in the other a mandrake. These monsters used to make my father laugh. They were compounded of parts of monkeys, parrots, squirrels, fish, and hedgehogs, dried and stitched together with great neatness and startling effect. He had a fiddle, a box of conjuring apparatus, a pair of foils and masks attached to his belt, several other mysterious cases dangling about him, and a black staff with copper ferrules in his hand. His companion was a rough spare dog, that followed at his heels, but stopped short, suspiciously at the drawbridge, and in a little while began to howl dismally.

In the meantime, the mountebank, standing in the midst of the courtyard, raised his grotesque hat, and made us a very ceremonious bow, paying his compliments very volubly in execrable French, and German not much better. Then, disengaging his fiddle, he began to scrape a lively air, to which he sang with a merry discord, dancing with ludicrous airs and activity, that made me laugh, in spite of the dog's howling.

Then he advanced to the window with many smiles and salutations, and his hat in his left hand, his fiddle under his arm, and with a fluency that never took breath, he gabbled a long advertisement of all his accomplishments, and the resources of the various arts which he placed at our service, and the curiosities and entertainments which it was in his power, at our bidding to display.

'Will your ladyships be pleased to buy an amulet against the oupire, which is going like the wolf, I hear, through these woods,' he said, dropping his hat on the pavement. 'They are dying of it right and left, and here is a charm that never fails; only pinned to the pillow; and you may laugh in his face.'

These charms consisted of oblong slips of vellum with cabalistic ciphers and diagrams upon them.

Carmilla instantly purchased one and so did I.

He was looking up, and we were smiling down upon him, amused; at least, I could answer for myself. His piercing black eye, as he looked up in our faces, seemed to detect something that fixed for a moment his curiosity.

In an instant he unrolled a leather case, full of all manner of odd little steel instruments.

'See here, my lady,' he said, displaying it, and addressing me, 'I profess, among other things less useful, the art of dentistry. Plague take the dog!' he interpolated. 'Silence, beast! He howls so that your ladyships can scarcely hear a word. Your noble friend, the young lady at your right, has the sharpest tooth – long, thin, pointed, like an awl, like a needle; ha, ha. With my sharp and long sight, as I look up, I have seen it distinctly; now if it happens to hurt the young lady, and I think it must, here am I, here are my file, my punch, my nippers; I will make it round and blunt, if her ladyship pleases; no longer the tooth of a fish, but of a beautiful young lady as she is. Hey? Is the young lady displeased? Have I been too bold? Have I offended her?'

The young lady, indeed, looked very angry as she drew back from the window.

'How dare that mountebank insult us so? Where is your father? I shall demand redress from him. My father would have had the wretch tied up to the pump, and flogged with a cart-whip, and burnt to the bones with the castle brand!'

She retired from the window a step or two, and sat down, and had hardly lost sight of the offender, when her wrath subsided as suddenly as it had risen, and she gradually recovered her usual tone, and seemed to forget the little hunchback and his follies.

My father was out of spirits that evening. On coming in he told us that there had been another case very similar to the two fatal ones which had lately occurred. The sister of a young peasant on his estate, only a mile away, was very ill, had been, as she described it, attacked very nearly in the same way, and was now slowly but steadily sinking.

'All this,' said my father, 'is strictly referable to natural causes. These poor people infect one another with their superstitions, and so repeat in imagination the images of terror that have infested their neighbours.'

'But that very circumstances frightens one horribly,' said Carmilla.

'How so?' inquired my father.

'I am so afraid of fancying I see such things; I think it would be as bad as reality.'

'We are in God's hands; nothing can happen without His permission, and all will end well for those who love

Him. He is our faithful creator; He has made us all, and will take care of us.'

'Creator! *Nature!*' said the young lady in answer to my gentle father. 'And this disease that invades the country is natural. Nature. All things proceed from Nature – don't they? All things in the heaven, in the earth, and under the earth, act and live as Nature ordains? I think so.'

'The doctor said he would come here to-day,' said my father, after a silence. 'I want to know what he thinks about it, and what he thinks we had better do.'

'Doctors never did me any good,' said Carmilla.

'Then you have been ill?' I asked.

'More ill than ever you were,' she answered.

'Long ago?'

'Yes, a long time. I suffered from this very illness; but I forget all but my pain and weakness, and they were not so bad as are suffered in other diseases.'

'You were very young then?'

'I dare say; let us talk no more of it. You would not wound a friend?' She looked languidly in my eyes, and passed her arm round my waist lovingly, and led me out of the room. My father was busy over some papers near the window.

'Why does your papa like to frighten us?' said the pretty girl, with a sigh and a little shudder.

'He doesn't, dear Carmilla, it is the very furthest thing from his mind.'

'Are you afraid, dearest?'

'I should be very much if I fancied there was any real danger of my being attacked as those poor people were.'

'You are afraid to die?'

'Yes, everyone is.'

'But to die as lovers may – to die together, so that they may live together. Girls are caterpillars while they live in the world, to be finally butterflies when the summer comes; but in the meantime there are grubs and larvae, don't you see – each with their peculiar propensities, necessities and structure. So says Monsieur Buffon, in his big book, in the next room.'

Later in the day the doctor came, and was closeted with papa for some time. He was a skilful man, of sixty upwards, he wore powder, and shaved his pale face smooth as a pumpkin. He and papa emerged from the room together, and I heard papa laugh, and say as they came out:

'Well, I do wonder at a wise man like you. What do you say to hippogriffs and dragons?'

The doctor was smiling, and made answer, shaking his head—

'Nevertheless, life and death are mysterious states, and we know little of the resources of either.'

And so they walked on, and I heard no more. I did not then know what the doctor had been broaching, but I think I guess it now.

5

A WONDERFUL LIKENESS

This evening there arrived from Gratz the grave, dark-faced son of the picture-cleaner, with a horse and cart laden with two large packing-cases, having many pictures in each. It was a journey of ten leagues, and whenever a messenger arrived at the schloss from our little capital of Gratz, we used to crowd about him in the hall, to hear the news.

This arrival created in our secluded quarters quite a sensation. The cases remained in the hall, and the messenger was taken care of by the servants till he had eaten his supper. Then with assistants, and armed with hammer, ripping chisel, and turnscrew, he met us in the hall, where we had assembled to witness the unpacking of the cases.

Carmilla sat looking listlessly on, while one after the other the old pictures, nearly all portraits, which had undergone the process of renovation, were brought to light. My mother was of an old Hungarian family, and most of these pictures, which were about to be restored to their places, had come to us through her.

My father had a list in his hand, from which he read, as the artist rummaged out the corresponding numbers. I don't know that the pictures were very good, but they were, undoubtedly, very old, and some of them very curious also. They had, for the most part, the merit of being now seen by me, I may say, for the first time; for the smoke and dust of time had all but obliterated them.

'There is a picture that I have not seen yet,' said my father. 'In one corner, at the top of it, is the name, as well as I could read, "Marcia Karnstein," and the date "1698"; and I am curious to see how it has turned out.'

I remembered it; it was but a small picture, about a foot and a half high, and nearly square, without a frame; but it was so blackened by age that I could not make it out.

The artist now produced it with evident pride. It was quite beautiful; it was startling; it seemed to live. It was the effigy of Carmilla!

'Carmilla, dear, here is an absolute miracle. Here you are, living, smiling, ready to speak, in this picture. Isn't it beautiful, papa? And see, even the mole on her throat.'

My father laughed, and said, 'Certainly it is a wonderful likeness,' but he looked away, and to my surprise seemed but little struck by it, and went on talking to the picture-cleaner, who was also something of an artist, and discoursed with intelligence about the portraits or other works, which his art had just brought into light and colour, while I was more and more lost in wonder the more I looked at the picture.

'Will you let me hang this picture in my room, papa?' I asked.

'Certainly, dear,' said he, 'I'm very glad you think it so like. It must be prettier even than I thought, if it is.'

The young lady did not acknowledge this pretty speech, did not seem to hear it. She was leaning back in her seat, her fine eyes under her long lashes gazing on me in contemplation, and she smiled in a kind of rapture.

'And now you can read quite plainly the name that is written in the corner. It is not Marcia; it looks as if it was done in gold. The name is Mircalla, Countess Karnstein, and this is a little coronet over it, and underneath A.D. 1698. I am descended from the Karnsteins; that is, mama was.'

'Ah!' said the lady, languidly, 'so am I, I think, a very long descent, very ancient. Are there any Karnsteins living now?'

'None who bear the name, I believe. The family were ruined, I believe, in some civil wars, long ago but the ruins of the castle are only about three miles away.'

'How interesting!' she said languidly. 'But see what beautiful moonlight!' She glanced through the hall door, which stood a little open. 'Suppose you take a little ramble round the court, and look down at the road and river.'

'It is so like the night you came to us,' I said.

She sighed, smiling.

She rose, and each with her arm about the other's waist, we walked out upon the pavement.

In silence, slowly we walked down to the drawbridge, where the beautiful landscape opened before us.

'And so you were thinking of the night I came here?' she almost whispered. 'Are you glad I came?'

'Delighted, dear Carmilla,' I answered.

'And you ask for a picture you think like me, to hang in your room,' she murmured with a sigh, as she drew her arms closer about my waist, and let her pretty head sink upon my shoulder.

'How romantic you are, Carmilla,' I said. 'Whenever you tell me your story, it will be made up chiefly of some one great romance.'

She kissed me silently.

'I am sure, Carmilla, you have been in love; that there is, at this moment, an affair of the heart going on.'

'I have been in love with no one, and never shall,' she whispered, 'unless it should be you.'

How beautiful she looked in the moonlight.

Shy and strange was the look with which she quickly hid her face in my neck and hair, with tumultuous sighs, that seemed almost to sob, and pressed in mine a hand that trembled.

Her soft cheek was glowing against mine. 'Darling, darling,' she murmured, 'I live in you; and you would die for me, I love you so.'

I started from her.

She was gazing on me with eyes from which all fire, all meaning had flown, and a face colourless and apathetic.

'Is there a chill in the air, dear?' she said drowsily. 'I almost shiver; have I been dreaming? Let us come in. Come, come; come in.'

'You look ill, Carmilla; a little faint. You certainly must take some wine,' I said.

'Yes, I will. I'm better now. I shall be quite well in a

few minutes. Yes, do give me a little wine,' answered Carmilla, as we approached the door. 'Let us look again for a moment; it is the last time, perhaps, I shall see the moonlight with you.'

'How do you feel now, dear Carmilla? Are you really better?' I asked.

I was beginning to take alarm, lest she should have been stricken with the strange epidemic that they said had invaded the country about us.

'Papa would be grieved beyond measure,' I added, 'if he thought you were ever so little ill, without immediately letting us know. We have a very skilful doctor near this, the physician who was with papa to-day.'

'I'm sure he is. I know how kind you all are: but, dear child, I am quite well again. There is nothing ever wrong with me, but a little weakness. People say I am languid; I am incapable of exertion; I can scarcely walk as far as a child of three years old; and every now and then the little strength I have falters, and I become as you have just seen me. But after all I am very easily set up again; in a moment I am perfectly myself. See how I have recovered.'

So, indeed, she had; and she and I talked a great deal, and very animated she was; and the remainder of that evening passed without any recurrence of what I called her infatuations. I mean her crazy talk and looks, which embarrassed, and even frightened me.

But there occurred that night an event which gave my thoughts quite a new turn, and seemed to startle even Carmilla's languid nature into momentary energy.

6

A VERY STRANGE AGONY

When we got into the drawing-room, and had sat down to our coffee and chocolate, although Carmilla did not take any, she seemed quite herself again, and Madame, and Mademoiselle De Lafontaine, joined us, and made a little card party, in the course of which papa came in for what he called his 'dish of tea'.

When the game was over he sat down beside Carmilla on the sofa, and asked her, a little anxiously, whether she had heard from her mother since her arrival.

She answered 'No.'

He then asked her whether she knew where a letter would reach her at present.

'I cannot tell,' she answered, ambiguously, 'but I have been thinking of leaving you; you have been already too hospitable and too kind to me. I have given you an infinity of trouble, and I should wish to take a carriage tomorrow, and post in pursuit of her; I know where I shall ultimately find her, although I dare not yet tell you.'

'But you must not dream of such a thing,' exclaimed my father, to my great relief. 'We can't afford to lose you so, and I won't consent to your leaving us, except under the care of your mother, who was so good as to consent to your remaining with us till she should herself return. I should be quite happy if I knew that you heard from her; but this evening the accounts of the progress of the mysterious disease that has invaded our neighbourhood, grow even more alarming; and my beautiful guest, I do feel the responsibility, unaided by advice from your mother, very much. But I shall do my best; and one thing is certain, that you must not think of leaving us without her distinct direction to that effect. We should suffer too much in parting from you to consent to it easily.'

'Thank you, sir, a thousand times for your hospitality,' she answered, smiling bashfully. 'You have all been too kind to me. I have seldom been so happy in all my life before, as in your beautiful chateau, under your care, and in the society of your dear daughter.'

So he gallantly, in his old-fashioned way, kissed her hand, smiling, and pleased at her little speech.

I accompanied Carmilla as usual to her room, and sat and chatted to her while she was preparing for bed.

'Do you think,' I said, at length, 'that you will ever confide fully in me?'

She turned around smiling, but made no answer, only continued to smile on me.

'You won't answer that?' I said. 'You can't answer pleasantly; I ought not to have asked you.'

'You were quite right to ask me that, or anything. You do not know how dear you are to me, or you could not think any confidence too great to look for. But I am under vows, no nun half so awfully, and I dare not tell my story yet, even to you. The time is very near when you shall know everything. You will think me cruel, very selfish, but love is always selfish; the more ardent the more selfish. How jealous I am you cannot know. You must come with me, loving me, to death; or else hate me, and still come with me, and *hating* me through death and after. There is no such word as indifference in my apathetic nature.'

'Now, Carmilla, you are going to talk your wild nonsense again,' I said hastily.

'Not I, silly little fool as I am, and full of whims and fancies; for your sake I'll talk like a sage. Were you ever at a ball?'

'No; how you do run on. What is it like? How charming it must be.'

'I almost forget, it is years ago.'

I laughed.

'You are not so old. Your first ball can hardly be forgotten yet.'

'I remember everything about it – with an effort. I see it all, as divers see what is going on above them, through a medium, dense, rippling, but transparent. There occurred that night, what has confused the picture, and made its colours faint. I was all but assassinated in my bed, wounded *here*,' she touched her breast, 'and never was the same since.'

'Were you near dying?'

'Yes, a very – cruel love – strange love, that would have taken my life. Love will have its sacrifices. No sacrifice without blood. Let us go to sleep now; I feel lazy. How can I get up just now and lock my door?'

She was lying with her tiny hands buried in her rich wavy hair, under her cheek, her little head upon the pillow, and her glittering eyes followed me everywhere I moved, with a kind of shy smile that I could not decipher.

I bid her good-night, and crept from the room with an uncomfortable sensation.

I often wondered whether our pretty guest ever said her prayers. *I* certainly had never seen her upon her knees. In the morning she never came down until long after our family prayers were over, and at night she never left the drawing-room to attend our brief evening prayers in the hall.

If it had not been that it had casually come out in one of our careless talks that she had been baptised, I should have doubted her being a Christian. Religion was a subject on which I had never heard her speak a word. If I had known of the world better, this particular neglect or antipathy would not have so much surprised me.

The precautions of nervous people are infectious, and persons of a like temperament are pretty sure, after a time, to imitate them. I had adopted Carmilla's habit of locking her bed-room door, having taken into my head all her whimsical alarms about midnight invaders, and prowling assassins. I had also adopted her precaution of making a brief search through her room, to satisfy herself that no lurking assassin or robber was 'ensconced.'

These wise measures taken, I got into my bed and fell asleep. A light was burning in my room. This was an old habit, of very early date, and which nothing could have tempted me to dispense with.

Thus fortified I might take my rest in peace. But dreams come through stone walls, light up dark rooms, or darken light ones, and their persons make their exits and their entrances as they please, and laugh at locksmiths.

I had a dream that night that was the beginning of a very strange agony.

I cannot call it a nightmare, for I was quite conscious of being asleep. But I was equally conscious of being in my room, and lying in bed, precisely as I actually was. I saw, or fancied I saw, the room and its furniture just as I had seen it last, except that it was very dark, and I saw something moving round the foot of the bed. which at first I could not accurately distinguish. But I soon saw that it was a sooty black animal that resembled a monstrous cat. It appeared to me about four or five feet long, for it measured fully the length of the hearth rug as it passed over it; and continued to-ing and fro-ing with the lithe sinister restlessness of a beast in a cage. I could not cry out, although as you may suppose, I was terrified. Its pace was growing faster, and the room rapidly darker and darker, and at length so dark that I could no longer see anything of it but its eyes. I felt it spring lightly on the bed. The two broad eyes approached my face, and suddenly I felt a stinging pain as if two large needles darted, an inch of two apart, deep into my breast. I waked with a scream. The room was lighted by the candle that burnt there all through the night, and I saw a female figure standing at the foot of the bed, a little at the right side. It was in a dark loose dress, and its hair was down and covered its shoulders. block of stone could not have been more still. There was not the slightest air of respiration. As I stared at it, the figure appeared to have changed its place, and was now nearer the door; then, close to it, the door opened and it passed out.

I was now relieved, and able to breathe and move. My first thought was that Carmilla had been playing me a trick, and that I had forgotten to secure my door. I hastened to it, and found it locked as usual on the inside. I was afraid to open it – I was horrified. I sprang into my bed and covered my head up in the bedclothes, and lay there more dead than alive till morning.

7

DESCENDING

It would be vain my attempting to tell you of the horror with which, even now, I recall the occurrence of that night. It was no such transitory terror as a dream leaves behind it. It seemed to deepen by time, and communicated itself to the room and the very furniture that had encompassed the apparition.

I could not bear the next day to be alone for a moment. I should have told papa, but for two opposite reasons. At one time I thought he would laugh at my story, and I could not bear its being treated as a jest; and at another, I thought he might fancy that I had been attacked by the mysterious complaint which had invaded our neighbourhood. I had myself no misgivings of the kind, and as he had been rather an invalid for some time, I was afraid of alarming him.

I was comfortable enough with my good-natured companions, Madame Perrodon, and the vivacious Mademoiselle De Lafontaine. They both perceived that I was out of spirits and nervous, and at length I told them what lay so heavy at my heart.

Mademoiselle laughed, but I fancied that Madame Perrodon looked anxious.

'By-the-by,' said Mademoiselle, laughing, 'the long lime tree walk, behind Carmilla's bedroom window, is haunted!'

'Nonsense!' exclaimed Madame, who probably thought the theme rather inopportune, 'and who tells that story, my dear?'

'Martin says that he came up twice, when the old yard-gate was being repaired before sunrise, and twice saw the same female figure walking down the lime tree avenue.'

'So he well might, as long as they have cows to milk in the river fields,' said Madame.

'I daresay; but Martin chooses to be frightened, and never did I see fool more frightened.'

'You must not say a word about it to Carmilla, because she can see down the walk from her room window,' I interposed, 'and she is, if possible, a greater coward than I.'

Carmilla came down rather later than usual that day.

'I was so frightened last night,' she said, so soon as we were together, 'and I am sure I should have seen something dreadful if it had not been for that charm I bought from the poor little hunch-back whom I called such hard names. I had a dream of something black coming round my bed, and I awoke in a perfect horror, and I really thought, for some seconds, I saw a dark figure near the chimney piece, but I felt under my pillow for my charm, and the moment my fingers touched it, the figure disappeared, and I felt quite certain, only that I had it by me, that something frightful would have made its appearance, and, perhaps, throttled me, as it did those poor people we heard of.'

'Well, listen to me,' I began, and recounted my adventure, at the recital of which she appeared horrified.

'And had you the charm near you?' she asked earnestly.

'No, I had dropped it into a china vase in the drawing-room, but I shall certainly take it with me to-night, as you have so much faith in it.'

At this distance of time I cannot tell you, or even understand, how I overcame my horror so effectually as to lie alone in my room that night. I remember distinctly that

I pinned the charm to my pillow. I fell asleep almost immediately, and slept even more soundly than usual all night.

Next night I passed as well. My sleep was delightfully deep and dreamless. But I wakened with a sense of lassitude and melancholy, which, however, did not exceed a degree that was almost luxurious.

'Well, I told you so,' said Carmilla, when I described my quiet sleep, 'I had such delightful sleep myself last night; I pinned the charm to the breast of my nightdress. It was too far away the night before. I am quite sure it was all fancy, except the dreams, I used to think that evil spirits made dreams, but our doctor told me it is no such thing. Only a fever passing by, or some other malady, as they often do, he said, knocks at the door, and not being able to get in, passes on, with that alarm.'

'And what do you think the charm is?' said I.

'It has been fumigated or immersed in some drug, and is an antidote against the malaria,' she answered.

'Then it acts only on the body.'

'Certainly; you don't suppose that evil spirits are frightened by bits of ribbon, or the perfumes of a druggist's shop? No, these complaints, wandering in the air, begin by trying the nerves, and so infect the brain; but before they can seize upon you, the antidote repels them. That I am sure is what the charm has done for us. It is nothing magical, it is simply natural.'

I should have been happier if I could quite have agreed Carmilla, but I did my best, and the impression was a little losing its force.

For some nights I slept profoundly; but still every morning I felt the same lassitude, and a languor weighed upon me all day. I felt myself a changed girl. A strange melancholy was stealing over me, a melancholy that I would not have interrupted. Dim thoughts of death began to open, and an idea that I was slowly sinking took gentle, and, somehow, not unwelcome possession of me. If it was sad, the tone of mind which this induced was also sweet. Whatever it might be, my soul acquiesced in it.

I would not admit that I was ill, I would not consent to tell my papa, or to have the doctor sent for.

Carmilla became more devoted to me than ever, and her strange paroxysms of languid adoration more frequent. She used to gloat on me with increasing ardour the more my strength and spirits waned. This always shocked me like a momentary glare of insanity.

Without knowing it, I was now in a pretty advanced stage of the strangest illness under which mortal ever suffered. There was an unaccountable fascination in its earlier symptoms that more than reconciled me to the incapacitating effect of that stage of the malady. This fascination increased for a time, until it reached a certain point, when gradually a sense of the horrible mingled itself with it, deepening, as you shall hear, until it discoloured and perverted the whole state of my life.

The first change I experienced was rather agreeable. It was very near the turning point from which began the descent of Avernus.

Certain vague and strange sensations visited me in my sleep. The prevailing one was of that pleasant, peculiar cold thrill which we feel in bathing, when we move against the current of a river. This was soon accompanied by dreams that seemed interminable, and were so vague that I could never recollect their scenery and persons, or any one connected portion of their action. But they left an awful impression, and a sense of exhaustion, as if I had passed through a long period of great mental exertion and danger. After all these dreams there remained on waking a remembrance of having been in a place very nearly dark, and of having spoken to people whom I could not see; and especially of one clear voice, of a female's, very deep, that spoke as if at a distance, slowly, and producing always the same sensation of indescribable solemnity and fear. Sometimes there came a sensation as if a hand was drawn softly along my cheek and neck. Sometimes it was as if warm lips kissed me, and longer and more lovingly as they reached my throat, but there the caress fixed itself. My heart beat faster, my breathing rose and fell rapidly and full drawn; a sobbing, that rose into a sense of strangulation, supervened, and turned into a dreadful convulsion, in which my senses left me, and I became unconscious.

It was now three weeks since the commencement of this unaccountable state. My sufferings had, during the last week, told upon my appearance. I had grown pale, my eyes were dilated and darkened underneath, and the languor which I had long felt began to display itself in my countenance.

My father asked me often whether I was ill; but, with an obstinacy which now seems to me unaccountable, I persisted in assuring him that I was quite well.

In a sense this was true. I had no pain, I could complain of no bodily derangement. My complaint seemed to be one of the imagination, or the nerves, and, horrible as my sufferings were, I kept them, with a morbid reserve, very nearly to myself.

It could not be that terrible complaint which the peasants call the oupire, for I had now been suffering for three weeks, and they were seldom ill for more than three days, when death put an end to their miseries.

Carmilla complained of dreams and feverish sensations, but by no means of so alarming a kind as mine. I say that mine were extremely alarming. Had I been capable of comprehending my condition, I would have invoked aid and advice upon my knees. The narcotic of an unsuspected influence was acting upon me, and my perceptions were benumbed.

I am going to tell you now of a dream that led immediately to an odd discovery.

One night, instead of the voice I was accustomed to hear in the dark, I heard one, sweet and tender, and at the same time terrible, which said, 'Your mother warns you to beware of the assassin.' At the same time a light unexpectedly sprang up, and I saw Carmilla, standing, near the foot of my bed, in her white nightdress, bathed, from her chin to her feet, in one great stain of blood.

I wakened with a shriek, possessed with the one idea that Carmilla was being murdered. I remember springing from my bed, and my next recollection is that of standing on the lobby, crying for help.

Madame and Mademoiselle came scurrying out of their rooms in alarm; a lamp burned always on the lobby, and seeing me, they soon learned the cause of my terror.

I insisted on our knocking at Carmilla's door. Our knocking was unanswered. It soon became a pounding and an uproar. We shrieked her name, but all was in vain.

We all grew frightened, for the door was locked. We hurried back, in panic, to my room. There we rang the bell long and furiously. If my father's room had been at that side of the house, we would have called him up at once to our aid. But, alas! he was quite out of hearing, and to reach him involved an excursion for which we none of us had the courage.

Servants, however, soon came running up the stairs; I had got on my dressing-gown and slippers meanwhile, and companions were already similarly furnished. Recognizing the voices of the servants on the lobby, we sallied out together; and having renewed, as fruitlessly, our summons at Carmilla's door, I ordered the men to force the lock. They did so, and we stood, holding our lights aloft, in the doorway, and so stared into the room.

We called her by name; but there was still no reply. We looked round the room. Everything was undisturbed. It was exactly in the state in which I left it on bidding her good night. But Carmilla was gone.

8

SEARCH

At sight of the room, perfectly undisturbed except for our violent entrance, we began to cool a little, and soon recovered our senses sufficiently to dismiss the men. It had struck Mademoiselle that possibly Carmilla had been wakened by the uproar at her door, and in her first panic had jumped from her bed, and hid herself in a press, or behind a curtain, from which she could not, of course, emerge until the majordomo and his myrmidons had withdrawn. We now recommenced our search, and began to call her by name again.

It was all to no purpose. Our perplexity and agitation increased. We examined the windows, but they were secured. I implored of Carmilla, if she had concealed herself, to play this cruel trick no longer – to come out, and to end our anxieties. It was all useless. I was by this time convinced that she was not in the room, nor in the dressing-room, the door of which was still locked on this side. She could not have passed it. I was utterly puzzled. Had Carmilla discovered one of those secret passages which the old housekeeper said were known to exist in the schloss, although the tradition of their exact situation had been lost? A little time would, no doubt, explain all – utterly perplexed as, for the present, we were.

It was past four o'clock, and I preferred passing the remaining hours of darkness in Madame's room. Daylight brought no solution of the difficulty.

The whole household, with my father at its head, was in a state of agitation next morning. Every part of the chateau was searched. The grounds were explored. Not a trace of the missing lady could be discovered. The stream was about to be dragged; my father was in distraction; what a tale to have to tell the poor girl's mother on her return. I, too, was almost beside myself, though my grief was quite of a different kind.

The morning was passed in alarm and excitement. It was now one o'clock, and still no tidings. I ran up to Carmilla's room, and found her standing at her dressing-table. I was astounded. I could not believe my eyes. She beckoned me to her with her pretty finger, in silence. Her face expressed extreme fear.

I ran to her in an ecstasy of joy; I kissed and embraced her again and again. I ran to the bell and rang it vehemently, to bring others to the spot, who might at once relieve my father's anxiety.

'Dear Carmilla, what has become of you all this time? We have been in agonies of anxiety about you,' I exclaimed. 'Where have you been? How did you come back?'

'Last night has been a night of wonders,' she said.

'For mercy's sake, explain all you can.'

'It was past two last night,' she said, 'when I went to sleep as usual in my bed, with my doors locked, that of the dressing-room, and that opening upon the gallery. My sleep was uninterrupted, and, so far as I know, dreamless; but I awoke just now on the sofa in the dressing-room there, and I found the door between the rooms open, and the other door forced. How could all this have happened without my being wakened? It must have been accompanied with a great deal of noise, and I am particularly easily wakened; and how could I have been carried out of my bed without my sleep having being interrupted, I whom the slightest stir startles?'

By this time, Madame, Mademoiselle, my father, and a

number of servants were in the room. Carmilla, was, of course, overwhelmed with inquiries, congratulations, and welcomes. She had but one story to tell, and seemed the least able of all the party to suggest any way of accounting for what had happened.

My father took a turn up and down the room, thinking. I saw Carmilla's eye follow him for a moment with a sly, dark glance.

When my father had sent the servants away, Mademoiselle having gone in search of a little bottle of valerian and sal-volatile, and there being no one in the room with Carmilla except my father, Madame, and myself, he came to her thoughtfully, took her hand very kindly, led her to the sofa, and sat down beside her.

'Will you forgive me, my dear, if I risk a conjecture, and ask a question?'

'Who can have a better right?' she said. 'Ask what you please, and I will tell you everything. But my story is simply one of bewilderment and darkness. I know absolutely nothing. Put any question you please. But you know, of course, the limitations mama has placed me under.'

'Perfectly, my dear child. I need not approach the topics on which she desires our silence. Now, the marvel of last nights consists in your having been removed from your bed and your room without being wakened, and this removal having occurred apparently while the windows were still secured, and the two doors locked upon the inside. I will tell you my theory, and first ask you a question.'

Carmilla was leaning on her hand dejectedly; Madame and I were listening breathlessly.

'Now, my question is this. Have you ever been suspected of walking in your sleep?'

'Never since I was very young indeed.'

'But you did walk in your sleep when you were very young?'

'Yes; I know I did. I have been told so often by my old nurse.'

My father smiled and nodded.

'Well, what has happened is this. You got up in your sleep, unlocked the door, not leaving the key, as usual, in the lock, but taking it out and locking it on the outside; you again took the key out, and carried it away with you to some one of the five-and-twenty rooms on this floor, or perhaps upstairs or downstairs. There are so many rooms and closets, so much heavy furniture, and such accumulations of lumber, that it would require a week to search this old house thoroughly. Do you see, now, what I mean?'

'I do, but not all,' she answered.

'And how, papa, do you account for her finding herself on the sofa in the dressing-room, which we had searched so carefully?'

'She came there after you had searched, still in her sleep, and at last awoke spontaneously, and was as much surprised to find herself where she was as any one else. I wish all mysteries were as easily and innocently explained as yours, Carmilla,' he said, laughing. 'And so we may congratulate ourselves on the certainty that the most natural explanation of the occurrence is one that involves no drugging, no tampering with locks, no burglars, or poisoners, or witches – nothing that need alarm Carmilla, or any one else, for our safety.'

Carmilla was looking charmingly. Nothing could be more graceful than her tints. Her beauty was, I think, enhanced by that graceful languor that was peculiar to her. I think my father was silently contrasting her looks with mine, for he said:—

'I wish my poor Laura was looking more like herself;' and he sighed.

So our alarms were happily ended, and Carmilla restored to her friends.

9

THE DOCTOR

As Carmilla would not hear of an attendant sleeping in her room, my father arranged that a servant should sleep outside her door, so that she could not attempt to make another such excursion without being arrested at her own door.

That night passed quickly; and next morning early, the doctor, whom my father had sent for without telling me a word about it, arrived to see me.

Madame accompanied me to the library; and there the

grave little doctor, with white hair and spectacles, whom I mentioned before, was waiting to receive me.

I told him my story, and as I proceeded he grew graver and graver.

We were standing, he and I, in the recess of one of the windows, facing one another. When my statement was over, he leaned with his shoulders against the wall, and with his eyes fixed on me earnestly, with an interest in which was a dash of horror.

After a minute's reflection, he asked Madame if he could see my father.

He was sent for accordingly, and as he entered, smiling, he said:

'I dare say, doctor, you are going to tell me that I am an old fool for having brought you here; I hope I am.'

But his smile faded into shadow as the doctor, with a very grave face beckoned him to him.

He and the doctor talked for some time in the same recess where I had just conferred with the physician. It seemed an earnest and argumentative conversation. The room is very large, and I and Madame stood together, burning with curiosity, at the further end. Not a word could we hear, however, for they spoke in a very low tone, and the deep recess of the window quite concealed the doctor from view, and very nearly my father, whose foot, arm and shoulder only could we see: and the voices were, I suppose, all the less audible for the sort of closet which the thick wall and window formed.

After a time my father's face looked into the room; it was pale, thoughtful, and, I fancied, agitated.

'Laura, dear, come here for a moment. Madame, we shan't trouble you, the doctor says, at present.'

Accordingly I approached, for the first time a little alarmed; for, although I felt very weak, I did not feel ill; and strength, one always fancies, is a thing that may be picked up when we please.

My father held out his hand to me as I drew near, but he was looking at the doctor, and he said:

'It certainly *is* very odd; I don't understand it quite. Laura, come here, dear; now attend to Doctor Spielsberg, and recollect yourself.'

'You mentioned a sensation like that of two needles piercing the skin, somewhere about your neck, on the night when you experienced your first horrible dream. Is there still any soreness?'

'None at all,' I answered.

'Can you indicate with your finger about the point at which you think this occurred?'

'Very little below my throat – *here*,' I answered.

I wore a morning dress, which covered the place I pointed to.

'Now you can satisfy yourself,' said the doctor. 'You won't mind your papa's lowering your dress a very little. It is necessary, to detect a symptom of the complaint under which you have been suffering.'

I acquiesced. It was only an inch or two below the edge of my collar.

'God bless me! – so it is,' exclaimed my father, growing pale.

'You see it now with your own eyes,' said the doctor, with a gloomy triumph.

'What is it?' I exclaimed, beginnig to be frightened.

'Nothing, my dear young lady, but a small blue spot, about the size of the tip of your little finger; and now,' he continued, turning to papa, 'the question is what is the best to be done?'

'Is there any danger?' I urged, in great trepidation.

'I trust not, my dear,' answered the doctor. 'I don't see why you should not recover. I don't see why you should not begin *immediately* to get better. That is the point at which the sense of strangulation begins?'

'Yes,' I answered.

'And – recollect as well as you can – the same point was a kind of centre of that thrill which you described just now like the current of a cold stream running against you?'

'It may have been; I think it was.'

'Ay, you see?' he added, turning to my father. 'Shall I say a word to Madame?'

He called Madame to him, and said:

'I find my young friend here far from well. It won't be of any great consequence, I hope; but it will be necessary that some steps be taken, which I will explain by-and-by; but in the meantime, Madame, you will be so good as not to let Miss Laura be alone for one moment. That is the only direction I need give for the present. It is indispensable.'

'We may rely upon your kindness, Madame, I know,' added my father.

Madame satisfied him eagerly.

'And you, dear Laura. I know you will observe the doctor's direction.'

'I shall have to ask your opinion upon another patient, whose symptoms slightly resemble those of my daughter, that have just been detailed to you – very much milder in degree, but I believe quite of the same sort. She is a young lady – our guest; but as you say you will be passing this way again this evening, you can't do better than take your supper here, and you can then see her. She does not come down till the afternoon.'

'I thank you,' said the doctor. 'I shall be with you, then, at about seven this evening.'

And then they repeated their directions to me and to Madame, and with this parting charge my father left us, and walked out with the doctor; and I saw them pacing together up and down between the road and the moat, on the grassy platform in front of the castle, evidently absorbed in earnest conversation.

The doctor did not return. I saw him mount his horse there, take his leave, and ride away eastward through the forest. Nearly at the same time I saw the man arrive from Dranfeld with the letters, and dismount and hand the bag to my father.

In the meantime, Madame and I were both busy, lost in conjecture, as to the reasons of the singular and earnest direction which the doctor and my father had concurred in imposing. Madame. as she afterwards told me, was afraid the doctor apprehended a sudden seizure, and that, without prompt assistance, I might either lose my life in a fit, or at least be seriously hurt.

This interpretation did not strike me; and I fancied, perhaps luckily for my nerves, that the arrangement was prescribed simply to secure a companion, who would prevent my taking too much exercise, or eating unripe fruit, or doing any of the fifty foolish things to which young people are supposed to be prone.

After about half-an-hour my father came in – he had a letter in his hand – and said :

'This letter has been delayed; it is from General Spielsdorf. He might have been here yesterday, he may not come till to-morrow, or he may be here to-day.'

He put the open letter into my hand; but he did not look pleased, as he used when a guest, especially one so much loved as the General, was coming. On the contrary, he looked as if he wished him at the bottom of the Red Sea. There was plainly something on his mind which he did not choose to divulge.

'Papa, darling, will you tell me this?' said I, suddenly laying my hand on his arm, and looking, I am sure, imploringly in his face.

'Perhaps,' he answered, smoothing my hair caressingly over my eyes.

'Does the doctor think me very ill?'

'No dear; he thinks, if right steps are taken, you will be quite well again, at least on the high road to a complete recovery, in a day or two,' he answered, a little drily. 'I wish our good friend, the General, had chosen any other time; that is, I wish you had been perfectly well to receive him.'

'But do tell me papa,' I insisted, '*what* does he think is the matter with me?'

'Nothing; you must not plague me with questions,' he answered, with more irritation than I ever remember him to have displayed before; and seeing that I looked wounded, I suppose, he kissed me, and added, 'You shall know all about it in a day or two; that is, all that *I* know. In the meantime, you are not to trouble your head about it.'

He turned and left the room, but came back before I had done wondering and puzzling over the oddity of all this; it was merely to say that he was going to Karnstein, and had ordered the carriage to be ready at twelve, and that I and Madame should accompany him; he was going to see the priest who lived near those picturesque grounds, upon business, and as Carmilla had never seen them, she could follow, when she came down, with Mademoiselle, who would bring materials for what you call a pic-nic, which might be laid for us in the ruined castle.

At twelve o'clock, accordingly, I was ready, and not long after, my father, Madame and I set out upon our projected drive. Passing the drawbridge we turn to the right, and follow the road over the steep Gothic bridge, westward, to reach the deserted village and ruined castle of Karnstein.

No sylvan drive can be fancied prettier. The ground breaks into gentle hills and hollows, all clothed with beautiful wood, totally destitute of the comparative formality which artificial planting and early culture and pruning impart.

The irregularities of the ground often lead the road out of its course, and cause it to wind beautifully round the sides of broken hollows and the steeper sides of the hills, among varieties of ground almost inexhaustible.

Turning one of these points, we suddenly encountered our old friend, the General, riding towards us, attended by a mounted servant. His portmanteaux were following in a hired waggon, such as we term a cart.

The General dismounted as we pulled up, and, after the usual greetings, was easily persuaded to accept the vacant seat in the carriage, and send his horse on with his servant to the schloss.

10

BEREAVED

It was about ten months since we had last seen him; but that time had sufficed to make an alteration of years in his appearance. He had grown thinner; something of gloom and anxiety had taken the place of that cordial serenity which used to characterise his features. His dark blue eyes, always penetrating, now gleamed with a sterner light from under his shaggy eyebrows. It was not such a change as grief alone usually induces, and angrier passions seemed to have had their share in bringing it about.

We had not long resumed our drive, when the General began to talk, with his usual soldierly directness, of the bereavement, as he termed it, which he had sustained in the death of his beloved niece and ward; and then he broke out in a tone of intense bitterness and fury, inveighing against the 'hellish arts' to which she had fallen a victim, and expressing with more exasperation than piety, his wonder that Heaven should tolerate so monstrous an indulgence of the lusts and malignity of hell.

My father, who saw at once that something very extraordinary had befallen, asked him, if not too painful to him, to detail the circumstances which he thought justified the strong terms in which he expressed himself.

'I should tell you with all pleasure,' said the General, 'but you would not believe me.'

'Why should I not?' he asked.

'Because,' he answered testily, 'you believe in nothing but what consists with your own prejudices and illusions. I remember when I was like you, but I have learned better.'

'Try me,' said my father; 'I am not such a dogmatist as you suppose. Besides which, I very well know that you generally require proof for what you believe, and am, therefore, very strongly predisposed to respect your conclusions.'

'You are right in supposing that I have not been led lightly into a belief in the marvellous – for what I have experienced *is* marvellous – and I have been forced by extraordinary evidence to credit that which ran counter, diametrically, to all my theories. I have been made the dupe of a preternatural conspiracy.'

Notwithstanding his profession of confidence in the General's penetration, I saw my father, at this point, glance at the General, with, as I thought, a marked suspicion of his sanity.

The General did not see it, luckily. He was looking gloomily and curiously into the glades and vistas of the woods that were opening before us.

'You are going to the Ruins of Karnstein?' he said. 'Yes, it is a lucky coincidence; do you know I was going to ask you to bring me there to inspect them. I have a special object in exploring. There is a ruined chapel, ain't there, with a great many tombs of that extinct family?'

'So there are – highly interesting,' said my father, 'I hope you are thinking of claiming the title and estates.'

My father said this gaily, but the General did not recollect the laugh, or even smile, which courtesy exacts for a friend's joke; on the contrary, he looked grave and even fierce, ruminating on a matter that stirred his anger and horror.

'Something very different,' he said gruffly. 'I mean to unearth some of those fine people. I hope by God's blessing, to accomplish a pious sacrilege here, which will relieve our earth of certain monsters, and enable honest people to sleep in their beds without being assailed by murderers. I have strange things to tell you, my dear friend, such as I myself would have scouted as incredible a few months since.'

My father looked at him again, but this time not with a glance of suspicion – with an eye, rather, of keen intelligence and alarm.

'The house of Karnstein,' he said, 'has been long extinct: a hundred years at least. My dear wife was maternally descended from the Karnsteins. But the name and title have long ceased to exist. The castle is a ruin; the very village deserted; it is fifty years since the smoke of a chimney was seen there; not a roof left.'

'Quite true. I have heard a great deal about that since I last saw you; a great deal that will astonish you. But I had better relate everything in the order in which it occurred,' said the General. 'You saw my dear ward – my child, I may call her. No creature could have been more beautiful, and only three months ago none more blooming.'

'Yes, poor thing! when I saw her last she certainly was quite lovely,' said my father. 'I was grieved and shocked more than I can tell you, my dear friend; I knew what a blow it was to you.'

He took the General's hand, and they exchanged a kind pressure. Tears gathered in the old soldier's eyes. He did not seek to conceal them. He said:

'We have been very old friends; I know you would feel for me, childless as I am. She had become an object of very dear interest to me, and repaid my care by an affection that cheered my home and made my life happy. That is all gone. The years that remain to me on earth may not be very long; but by God's mercy I hope to accomplish a service to mankind before I die, and to subserve the vengeance of Heaven upon the fiends who have murdered my poor child in the spring of her hopes and beauty!'

'You said, just now, that you intend relating everything

as it occurred,' said my father. 'Pray do; I assure you that it is not mere curiosity that prompts me.'

By this time we had reached the point at which the Drunstall road, by which the General had come, diverges from the road which we were travelling to Karnstein.

'How far is it to the ruins?' inquired the General, looking anxiously forward.

'About half a league,' answered my father. 'Pray let us hear the story you were so good as to promise.'

11

THE STORY

'With all my heart,' said the General, with an effort; and after a pause in which to arrange his subject, he commenced one of the strangest narratives I ever heard.

'My dear child was looking forward with great pleasure to the visit you had been so good as to arrange for her to your charming daughter.' Here he made me a gallant but melancholy bow. 'In the meantime we had an invitation to my old friend the Count Carlsfeld, whose schloss is about six leagues to the other side of Karnstein. It was to attend the series of fêtes which, you remember, were given by him in honour of his illustrious visitor, the Grand Duke Charles.'

'Yes; and very splendid, I believe they were,' said my father.

'Princely! But then his hospitalities are quite regal. He has Aladdin's lamp. The night from which my sorrow dates was devoted to a magnificent masquerade. The grounds were thrown open, the trees hung with coloured lamps. There was such a display of fireworks as Paris itself had never witnessed. And such music – music, you know, is my weakness – such ravishing music! The finest instrumental band, perhaps, in the world, and the finest singers who could be collected from all the great operas in Europe. As you wandered through those fantastically illuminated grounds, the moon-lighted château throwing a rosy light from its long rows of windows, you would suddenly hear these ravishing voices stealing from the silence of some grove, or rising from boats upon the lake. I felt myself, as I looked and listened, carried back into the romance and poetry of my early youth.

'When the fireworks were ended, and the ball beginning, we returned to the noble suite of rooms that were thrown open to the dancers. A masked ball, you know, is a beautiful sight; but so brilliant a spectacle of the kind I never saw before.

'It was a very aristocratic assembly. I saw myself almost the only "nobody" present.

'My dear child was looking quite beautiful. She wore no mask. Her excitement and delight added an unspeakable charm to her features, always lovely. I remarked a young lady, dressed magnificently, but wearing a mask, who appeared to me to be observing my ward with extraordinary interest. I had seen her, earlier in the evening, in the great hall, and again, for a few minutes, walking near us, on the terrace under the castle windows, similarly employed. A lady, also masked, richly and gravely dressed, and with stately air, like a person of rank accompanied her as a chaperon. Had the young lady not worn a mask, I could of course, have been much more certain upon the question whether she was really watching my poor darling. I am now well assured that she was.

'We were in one of the *salons*. My poor dear child had been dancing, and was resting a little in one of the chairs near the door; I was standing near. The two ladies I have mentioned had approached, and the younger took the chair next my ward; while her companion stood beside me and for a little time addressed herself, in a low tone, to her charge.

'Availing herself of the privilege of her mask, she turned to me, and in the tone of an old friend, and calling me by my name, opened a conversation with me, which picqued my curiosity a good deal. She referred to many scenes where she had met me – at Court, and at distinguished houses. She alluded to little incidents which I had long ceased to think of, but which, I found, had only lain in abeyance to my memory, for they instantly started into life at her touch.

'I became more and more curious to ascertain who she was, every moment. She parried my attempts to discover very adroitly and pleasantly. The knowledge she showed of many passages in my life seemed to me all but unaccountable; and she appeared to take a not unnatural pleasure in foiling my curiosity, and in seeing me flounder, in my eager perplexity, from one conjecture to another.

'In the meantime the young lady, whom her mother called by the odd name of Millarca, when she once or twice addressed her, had, with the same ease and grace, got into conversation with my ward.

'She introduced herself by saying that her mother was a very old acquaintance of mine. She spoke of the agreeable audacity which a mask rendered practicable; she talked like a friend; she admired her dress, and insinuated very prettily her adoration of her beauty. She amused her with laughing criticisms upon the people who crowded the ballroom, and laughed at my poor child's fun. She was very witty and lively when she pleased, and after a time they had grown very good friends, and the young stranger lowered her mask, displaying a remarkably beautiful face. I had never seen it before, neither had my dear child. But though it was new to us, the features were so engaging, as well as lovely, that it was impossible not to feel the attraction powerfully. My poor girl did so. I never saw anyone more taken with another at first sight, unless, indeed, it was the stranger herself, who seemed quite to have lost her heart to her.

'In the meantime, availing myself of the licence of a masquerade, I put not a few questions to the elder lady.

' "You have puzzled me utterly," I said, laughing. "Is that not enough? Won't you now consent to stand on equal terms, and do me the kindness to remove your mask?"

' "Can any request be more unreasonable?" she replied. "Ask a lady to yield an advantage! Besides, how do you know you should recognise me? Years make changes."

' "As you see," I said, with a bow, and I suppose, a rather melancholy little laugh.

' "As philosophers will tell us," she said; "and how do you know that a sight of my face would help you?"

' "I should take chance for that,' I answered. "It is vain trying to make yourself out an old woman; your figure betrays you."

' "Years nevertheless have passed since I saw you, rather you saw me, for that is what I am considering. Millarca, there, is my daughter; I cannot then be young, even in the opinion of people whom time has taught to be indulgent, and I may not like to be compared with what you remember me. You have no mask to remove. You can offer me nothing in exchange."

' "My petition is to your pity, to remove it."

' "And mine to yours, to let is stay where it is," she replied.

' "Well, then, at least you will tell me whether you are French or German; you speak both languages perfectly."

' "I don't think I shall tell you that, General; you intend a surprise, and are meditating the particular point of attack."

' "At all events, you won't deny this," I said, "that being honoured by your permission to converse, I ought to know how to address you. Shall I say Madame la Comtesse?"

'She laughed, and she would, no doubt, have met me with another evasion — if, indeed, I can treat any occurrence in an interview every circumstance was pre-arranged, as I now believe, with the profoundest cunning, as liable to be modified by accident.

' "As to that," she began; but she was interrupted, almost as she opened her lips, by a gentleman, dressed in black, who looked particularly elegant and distinguished, with this drawback, that his face was the most deadly pale I ever saw, except in death. He was in no masquerade — in the plain evening dress of a gentleman; and he said, without a smile, but with a courtly and unusually low bow:—

' "Will Madame la Comtesse permit me to say a very few words which may interest her?"

'The lady turned quickly to him, and touched her lips in token of silence; she then said to me, "Keep my place for me, General; I shall return when I have said a few words."

'And with this injunction, playfully given, she walked a little aside with the gentleman in black, and talked for some minutes, apparently very earnestly. They then walked away slowly together in the crowd, and I lost them for some minutes.

'I spent the interval in cudgelling my brains for conjecture as to the identity of the lady who seemed to remember me so kindly, and I was thinking of turning about and joining in the conversation between my pretty ward and the Countess's daughter, and trying whether, by the time she returned, I might not have a surprise in store for her, by having her name, title, château, and estates at my fingers' ends. But at this moment she returned, accompanied by the pale man in black, who said:

"I shall return and inform Madame la Comtesse when her carriage is at the door."

'He withdrew with a bow.'

12

A PETITION

' "Then we are to lose Madame la Comtesse, but I hope only for a few hours," I said with a low bow.

' "It may be that only, or it may be for a few weeks. It was very unlucky his speaking to me just now as he did. Do you now know me?"

'I assured her I did not.

' "You shall know me," she said, "but not at present. We are older and better friends than, perhaps, you suspect. I cannot yet declare myself. I shall in three weeks pass your beautiful schloss about which I have been making enquiries. I shall then look in upon you for an hour or two, and renew a friendship which I never think of without a thousand pleasant recollections. This moment a piece of news has reached me like a thunderbolt. I must set out now, and travel by a devious route, nearly a hundred miles, with all the dispatch I can possibly make. My perplexities multiply. I am only deterred by the compulsory reserve I practise as to my name from making a very singular request of you. My poor child has not quite recovered her strength. Her horse fell with her, at a hunt which she had ridden out to witness, her nerves have not yet recovered the shock, and our physician says that she must on no account exert herself for some time to come. We came here, in consequence, by very easy stages – hardly six leagues a day. I must now travel day and night, on a mission of life and death – a mission the critical and momentous nature of which I shall be able to explain to you when we meet, as I hope we shall, in a few weeks, without the necessity of any concealment."

'She went on to make her petition, and it was in the tone of a person from whom such a request amounted to conferring, rather than seeking a favour. This was only in manner, and, as it seemed, quite unconsciously. It was simply that I would consent to take charge of her daughter during her absence.

'This was, all things considered, a strange, not to say, an audacious request. She in some sort disarmed me, by stating and admitting everything that could be urged against it, and throwing herself entirely upon my chivalry. At the same moment, by a fatality that seems to have pre-determined all that happened, my poor child came to my side, and, in an undertone, besought me to invite her new friend, Millarca, to pay us a visit. She had just been sounding her, and thought, if her mamma would allow her, she would like it extremely.

'At another time I should have told her to wait a little, until at least, we knew who they were. But I had not a moment to think in. The two ladies assailed me together, and I must confess the refined and beautiful face of the young lady, about which there was something extremely engaging, as well as the elegance and fire of high birth, determined me; and quite overpowered, I submitted, and undertook, too easily, the care of the young lady, whom her mother called Millarca.

'The Countess beckoned to her daughter, who listened with grave attention while she told her, in general terms, how suddenly and peremptorily she had been summoned, and also of the arrangement she had made for her under my care, adding that I was one of her earliest and most valued friends.

'I made, of course, such speeches as the case seemed to call for, and found myself, on reflection, in a position which I did not half like.

'The gentleman in black returned, and very ceremoniously conducted the lady from the room.

'The demeanour of this gentleman was such as to impress me with the conviction that the Countess was a lady of very much more importance than her modest title alone might have led me to assume.

'Her last charge to me was that no attempt was to be

made to learn more about her than I might have already guessed, until her return. Our distinguished host, whose guest she was, knew her reasons.

' "But here," she said, "neither I nor my daughter could safely remain more than a day. I removed my mask imprudently for a moment, about an hour ago, and, too late, I fancied you saw me. So I have resolved to seek an opportunity of talking a little to you. Had I found that you *had* seen me I should have thrown myself on your high sense of honour to keep my secret for some weeks. As it is, I am satisfied that you did not see; but if you *now suspect, or,* on reflection, *should* suspect, who I am, I commit myself in like manner, entirely to your honour. My daughter will observe the same secrecy, and I well know that you will, from time to time, remind her, lest she should thoughtlessly disclose it."

'She whispered a few words to her daughter, kissed her hurriedly twice, and went away, accompanied by the pale gentleman in black, and disappeared in the crowd.

' "In the next room," said Millarca, "there is a window that looks upon the hall door. I should like to see the last of mamma, and to kiss my hand to her."

'We assented, of course, and accompanied her to the window. We looked out, and saw a handsome old-fashioned carriage, with a troop of couriers and footmen. We saw the slim figure of the pale gentleman in black, as he held a thick velvet cloak, and placed it about her shoulders and threw the hood over her head. She nodded to him, and just touched his hand with hers. He bowed low repeatedly as the door closed, and the carriage began to move.

' "She is gone," said Millarca with a sigh.

' "She is gone," I repeated to myself, for the first time – in the hurried moments that elapsed since my consent – reflecting upon the folly of my act.

' "She did not look up," said the young lady plaintively.

' "The Countess had taken off her mask, perhaps, and did not care to show her face," I said; "and she could not know if you were in the window."

'She sighed and looked in my face. She was so beautiful that I relented. I was sorry I had for a moment repented of my hospitality, and I determined to make amends for the unavowed churlishness of my reception.

'The young lady, replacing her mask, joined my ward in persuading me to return to the grounds, where the concert was soon to be renewed. We did so, and walked up and down the terrace that lies under the castle windows. Millarca became very intimate with us, and amused us with lively descriptions and stories of most of the great people whom we saw upon the terrace. I liked her more and more every minute. Her gossip, without being ill-natured, was extremely diverting to me, who had been so long out of the great world. I thought what life she would give to our sometimes lonely evenings at home.

'This ball was not over until the morning sun had almost reached the horizon. It pleased the Grand Duke to dance till then, so loyal people could not go away, or think of bed.

'We had just got through a crowded saloon, when my ward asked me what had become of Millarca. I thought she had been by her side, and she fancied she was by mine. The fact was, we had lost her.

'All my efforts to find her were in vain. I feared that she had mistaken, in the confusion of the momentary separation from us, other people for her new friends, and had, possibly, pursued and lost them in the extensive grounds which were thrown open to us.

'Now, in its full force, I recognised a new folly in my having undertaken the charge of a young lady without so much as knowing her name; and fettered as I was by promises, of the reasons for imposing which I knew nothing, I could not even point my inquiries by saying that the missing young lady was the daughter of the Countess who had taken her departure a few hours before.

'Morning broke. It was clear by daylight before I gave up my search. It was not until near two o'clock the next day that we heard anything of my missing charge.

'At about that time a servant knocked at my niece's door, to say that he had been earnestly requested by a young lady, who appeared to be in great distress, to make out where she could find the General Baron Spielsdorf and the young lady, his daughter, in whose charge she had been left by her mother.

'There could be no doubt, notwithstanding, the slight

inaccuracy, that our young friend had turned up; and so she had. Would to Heaven we had lost her!

'She told my poor child a story to account for her having failed to recover us for so long. Very late, she said, she had got into the housekeeper's bedroom in despair of finding us, and had then fallen into a deep sleep which, long as it was, had hardly sufficed to recruit her strength after the fatigues of the ball.

'That day Millarca came home with us. I was only too happy, after all, to have secured so charming a companion for my dear girl.'

13

THE WOOD-MAN

'There soon, however, appeared some drawbacks. In the first place, Millarca complained of extreme langour – the weakness that remained after her late illness – and she never emerged from her room till the afternoon was pretty far advanced. In the next place it was accidentally discovered, although she always locked her door on the inside, and never disturbed the key from its place, till she admitted the maid to assist at her toilet, that she was undoubtedly sometimes absent from her room in the very early morning, and at various times later in the day, before she wished it to be understood that she was stirring. She was repeatedly seen from the windows of the schloss, in the first faint grey of the morning, walking through the trees, in an easterly direction, and looking like a person in a trance. This convinced me that she walked in her sleep. But this hypothesis did not solve the puzzle. How did she pass out from her room, leaving the door locked on the inside. How did she escape from the house without unbarring door or window?

'In the midst of my perplexities, an anxiety of far more urgent kind presented itself.

'My dear child began to lose her looks and health, and that in a manner so mysterious, and even horrible, that I became thoroughly frightened.

'She was at first visited by appalling dreams; then, as

she fancied by a spectre, sometimes resembling Millarca, sometimes in the shape of a beast, indistinctly seen, walking round the foot of her bed, from side to side. Lastly came sensations. One, not unpleasant, but very peculiar, she said, resembled the flow of an icy pair of large needles pierce her, a little below the throat, with a very sharp pain. A few nights after, followed a gradual and convulsive sense of strangulation; then came unconsciousness.'

I could hear distinctly every word the kind old General was saying, because this time we were driving upon the short grass that spreads on either side of the road as you approach the roofless village which had not shown the smoke of a chimney for more than half a century.

You may guess how strangely I felt as I heard my own symptoms so exactly described in those which had been experienced by the poor girl who, but for the catastrophe that followed, would have been at that moment a visitor at my father's château. You may suppose, also, how I felt as I heard him detail habits and mysterious peculiarities which were, in fact, those of our beautiful guest, Carmilla!

A vista opened in the forest; we were on a sudden under the chimneys and gables of the ruined village, and the towers and battlements of the dismantled castle, round which gigantic trees are grouped, overhung us from a slight eminence.

In a frightened dream I got down from the carriage, and in silence, for we had each abundant matter for thinking; we soon mounted the ascent, and were among the spacious chambers, winding stairs, and dark corridors of the castle.

'And this was once the palatial residence of the Karnsteins!' said the old General at length, as from a great window he looked out across the village, and saw the wide, undulating expanse of forest. 'It was a bad family, and here it's bloodstained annals were written,' he continued. 'It is hard that they should, after death, continue to plague the human race with their atrocious lusts. That is the chapel of the Karnsteins, down there.'

He pointed down to the grey walls of the Gothic building, partly visible through the foliage, a little way down the steep. 'And I hear the axe of the woodman,' he added, 'busy among the trees that surround it; he possibly may give us the information of which I am in search, and point out the grave of Mircalla, Countess of Karnstein. These rustics preserve the local traditions of great families, whose stories die out among the rich and titled so soon as the families themselves become extinct.'

'We have a portrait, at home, of Mircalla, the Countess Karnstein; should you like to see it?' asked my father.

'Time enough, dear friend,' replied the General. 'I believe that I have seen the original; and one motive which has led me to you earlier than I at first intended, was to explore the chapel which we are now approaching.'

'What! See the Countess Mircalla,' exclaimed my father; 'why, she has been dead more than a century!'

'Not so dead as you fancy, I am told,' answered the General.

'I confess, General, you puzzle me utterly,' replied my father, looking at him, I fancied for a moment with a return of the suspicion I detected before. But although there was anger and detestation, at times, in the old General's manner, there was nothing flighty.

'There remains to me,' he said, as we passed under the heavy arch of the Gothic church – for its dimensions would have justified its being so styled – 'but one object which can interest me during the few years that remain to me on earth, and that is to wreak on her the vengeance which, I thank God, may still be accomplished by a mortal arm.'

'What vengeance can you mean?' asked my father, in increasing amazement.

'I mean to decapitate the monster,' he answered, with a fierce flush, and a stamp that echoed mournfully through the hollow ruin, and his clenched hand was at the same moment raised, as if it grasped the handle of an axe, while he shook it ferociously in the air.

'What!' exclaimed my father, more than ever bewildered.

'To strike her head off.'

'Cut her head off!'

'Aye, with a hatchet, with a spade, or with anything that can cleave through her murderous throat. You shall hear,' he answered, trembling with rage. And hurrying forward he said:

'That beam will answer for a seat; your dear child is

fatigued; let her be seated, and I will, in a few sentences, close my dreadful story.'

The squared block of wood, which lay on the grass-grown pavement of the chapel, formed a bench on which I was very glad to seat myself, and in the meantime the General called to the wood-man, who had been removing some boughs which leaned upon the old walls; and, axe in hand, the hardy old fellow stood before us.

He could not tell us anything of these monuments; but there was an old man, he said, a ranger of this forest, at present sojourning in the house of the priest, about two miles away, who could point out every monument of the old Karnstein family; and, for a trifle, he undertook to bring back with him, if we would lend him one of our horses, in little more than half-an-hour.

'Have you been long employed about this forest?' asked my father of the old man.

'I have been a woodman here,' he answered in his *patois*, 'under the forester, all my days; so has my father before me, and so on, as many generations as I can count up. I could show you the very house in the village here, in which my ancestors lived.'

'How came the village to be deserted?' asked the General.

'It was troubled by *revenants,* sir; several were tracked to their graves, there detected by the usual tests, and extinguished in the usual way, by decapitation, by the stake, and by burning; but not until many of the villagers were killed.

'But after all these proceedings according to law,' he continued – 'so many graves opened, and so many vampires deprived of their horrible animation – the village was not relieved. But a Moravian nobleman, who happened to be travelling this way, heard how matters were, and being skilled – as many people are in his country – in such affairs, he offered to deliver the village from its tormentor. He did so thus : There being a bright moon that night, he ascended, shortly after sunset, the tower of the chapel here, from whence he could distinctly see the churchyard beneath him; you can see it from the window. From this point he watched until he saw the vampire come out of his grave, and place near it the linen clothes in which he had been folded, and glide away towards the village to plague its inhabitants.

'The stranger, having seen all this, same down from the steeple, took the linen wrappings of the vampire, and carried them up to the top of the tower, which he again mounted. When the vampire returned from his prowlings and missed his clothes, he cried furiously to the Moravian, whom he saw at the summit of the tower, and who, in reply, beckoned him to ascend and take them. Whereupon the vampire, accepting his invitation, began to climb the steeple, and so soon as he had reached the battlements, the Moravian, with a stroke of his sword, clove his skull in twain, hurling him down to the churchyard, whither, descending by the winding stairs, the stranger followed and cut his head off, and next day delivered it and the body to the villagers, who duly impaled and burnt them.

'This Moravian nobleman had the authority from the then head of the family to remove the tomb of Mircalla, Countess Karnstein, which he did effectually, so that in a little while its site was quite forgotten.'

'Can you point out where it stood?' asked the General, eagerly.

The forester shook his head and smiled.

'Not a living soul could tell you that now,' he said; 'besides, they say her body was removed; but no one is sure of that either.'

Having thus spoken, as time pressed, he dropped his axe and departed, leaving us to hear the remainder of the General's strange story.

14

THE MEETING

'My beloved child,' he resumed, 'was now growing rapidly worse. The physician who attended her had failed to produce the slightest impression upon her disease, for such I then supposed it to be. He saw my alarm, and suggested a consultation. I called in an abler physician, from Gratz. Several days elapsed before he arrived. He was a good and pious, as well as a learned man. Having seen my poor ward together, they withdrew to my library to confer and discuss. I, from the adjoining room, where I awaited their summons, heard these two gentlemen's voices raised in something sharper than a strictly philosophical discussion. I knocked at the door and entered. I found the old physician from Gratz maintaining his theory. His rival was combating it with undisguised ridicule, accompanied with bursts of laughter. This unseemly manifestation subsided and the altercation ended on my entrance.

' "Sir", said my first physician, "my learned brother seems to think that you want a conjuror, and not a doctor."

' "Pardon me," said the old physician from Gratz, looking displeased, "I shall state my own view on the case in my own way another time. I grieve, Monsieur le Général, that by my skill and science I can be of no use. Before I go I shall do myself the honour to suggest something to you."

'He seemed thoughtful, and sat down at a table, and began to write. Profoundly disappointed, I made my bow, and as I turned to go, the other doctor pointed over his shoulder to his companion who was writing, and then, with a shrug, significantly touched his forehead.

'This consultation, then, left me precisely where I was. I walked out into the grounds, all but distracted. The doctor from Gratz, in ten or fifteen minutes, overtook me. He apologised for having followed me, but said that he could not conscientiously take his leave without a few words more. He told me that he could not be mistaken; no natural disease exhibited the same symptoms; and that death was already very near. There remained, however, a day, or possibly two, of life. If the fatal seizure were at once arrested, with great care and skill her strength might possibly return. But all hung now upon the confines of the irrevocable. One more assault might extinguish the last spark of vitality which is, every moment, ready to die.

' "And what is the nature of the seizure you speak of?" I entreated.

' "I have stated all fully in this note, which I place in your hands, upon the distinct condition that you send for the nearest clergyman, and open my letter in his presence, and on no account read it till he is with you; you would despise it else, and it is a matter of life and death. Should the priest fail you, then, indeed, you may read it."

'He asked me, before taking his leave finally, whether I would wish to see a man curiously learned upon the very subject, which, after I had read his letter, would probably interest me above all others, and he urged me earnestly to invite him to visit him there; and so took his leave.

'The ecclesiastic was absent, and I read the letter by myself. At another time, or in another case, it might have excited my ridicule. But into what quackeries will people rush for a last chance, where all accustomed means have failed, and the life of a beloved object is at stake?

'Nothing, you will say, could be more absurd than the learned man's letter. It was monstrous enough to have consigned him to a madhouse. He said that the patient was suffering from the visits of a vampire! The punctures which she described as having occurred near the throat, were, he insisted, the insertion of those two long, thin, sharp teeth which, it is well known, are peculiar to vampires; and there could be no doubt, he added, as to the well defined presence of the small livid mark which all concurred in describing as that induced by the demon's lips, and every symptom described by the sufferer was in exact conformity with those recorded in every case of a similar visitation.

'Being myself wholly sceptical as to the existence of any such portent as the vampire, the supernatural theory of the good doctor furnished, in my opinion, but another instance of learning and intelligence oddly associated with some one hallucination. I was so miserable, however, that, rather than try nothing, I acted upon the instructions of the letter.

'I concealed myself in the dark dressing-room, that opened upon the poor patient's room, in which a candle was burning, and watched there until she was fast asleep. I stood at the door, peeping through the small crevice, my sword laid on the table beside me, as my directions prescribed, until a little after one, I saw a large black object, very ill-defined, crawl, as it seemed to me, over the foot of the bed, and swiftly spread itself up to the poor girl's throat, where it swelled, in a moment, into a great palpitating mass.

'For a few moments I stood petrified. I now sprang forward, with my sword in my hand. The black creature suddenly contracted toward the foot of the bed, glided over it, and, standing on the floor about a yard or so below the foot of the bed, with a glare of sulking ferocity and horror fixed on me, I saw Millarca. Speculating I know not what, I struck at her instantly with my sword; but I saw her standing near the door, unscathed. Horrified, I pursued, and struck again. She was gone! and my sword flew to shivers against the door.

'I can't describe to you all that passed on that horrible night. The whole house was up and stirring. The spectre Millarca was gone. But her victim was sinking fast, and before the morning dawned, she died.'

The old General was agitated. We did not speak to him. My father walked to some little distance, and began reading the inscriptions on the tombstones; and thus occupied, he strolled into the door of a side chapel to prosecute his researches. The General leaned against the wall, dried his eyes, and sighed heavily. I was relieved on hearing the voices of Carmilla and Madame, who were at that moment approaching. The voices died away.

In this solitude, having just listened to so strange a story, connected as it was with the great and titled dead, whose monuments were mouldering among the dust and ivy round us, and every incident of which bore so awfully upon my own mysterious case – in this haunted spot, darkened by the towering foliage that rose on every side, dense and high above its noiseless walls – a horror began to steal over me, and my heart sank as I thought that my friends were, after all, now about to enter and disturb this triste and ominous scene.

The old General's eyes were fixed on the ground, as he leaned with his hand upon the basement of a shattered monument.

Under a narrow, arched doorway, surmounted by one of those demoniacal grotesques in which the cynical and ghastly fancy of old Gothic carving delights, I saw very gladly the beautiful face and figure of Carmilla enter the shadowy chapel.

I was just about to rise and speak, and nodded smilingly, in answer to her pecularily engaging smile; when with a cry the old man by my side caught up the woodman's hatchet, and started forward. On seeing him a brutalised change came over her features. It was an instantaneous and horrible transformation, as she made a crouching step backwards. Before I could utter a scream, he struck at her with all his force, but she dived below his blow, and unscathed, caught him in her tiny grasp by the wrist. He struggled for a moment to release his arm, but his hand opened, the axe fell to the ground, and the girl was gone.

He staggered against the wall. His grey hair stood upon his head, and a moisture shone over his face, as if he were at the point of death.

The frightful scene had passed in a moment. The first thing I recollect after, is Madame standing before me, and impatiently repeating again and again, the question, 'Where is Mademoiselle Carmilla?'

I answered at length, 'I don't know – I can't tell – she went there,' and I pointed to the door through which Madame had just entered; 'only a minute or two since.'

'But I have been standing there, in the passage, ever since Mademoiselle Carmilla entered; and she did not return.'

She then began to call 'Carmilla' through every door and passage and from the windows, but no answer came.

'She called herself Carmilla?' asked the General, still agitated.

'Carmilla, yes,' I answered.

'Aye,' he said, 'that is Millarca. That is the same person who long ago was called Mircalla, Countess Karnstein. Depart from this accursed ground, my poor child, as quickly as you can. Drive to the clergyman's house, and stay there till we come. Begone! May you never behold Carmilla more; you will not find her here.'

15

ORDEAL AND EXECUTION

As he spoke one of the strangest-looking men I ever beheld, entered the chapel at the door through which Carmilla had made her entrance and her exit. He was tall, narrow-chested, stooping, with high shoulders, and dressed in black. His face was brown and dried in with deep furrows; he wore an oddly-shaped hat with a broad leaf. His hair, long and grizzled, hung on his shoulders. He wore a pair of gold spectacles, and walked slowly with an odd shambling gait, with his face sometimes turned up to the sky, and sometimes bowed down toward the ground, seemed to wear a perpetual smile; his long thin arms were swinging, and his lank hands, in old black gloves ever so much too wide for them, waving and gesticulating in utter abstraction.

'The very man!' exclaimed the General, advancing with manifest delight. 'My dear Baron, how happy I am to see you. I had no hope of meeting you so soon.' He signed to my father, who had by this time returned, and leading the fantastic old gentleman, whom he called the Baron, to meet him. He introduced him formally, and they at once entered into earnest conversation. The stranger took a roll of paper from his pocket, and spread it on the worn surface of a tomb that stood by. He had a pencil case in his fingers, with which he traced imaginary lines from point to point on the paper, which from their often glancing from it, together, at certain points of the building, I concluded to be a plan of the chapel. He accompanied, what I may term his lecture, with occasional readings from a dirty little book, whose yellow leaves were closely written over.

They sauntered together down the side aisle, opposite to the spot where I was standing, conversing as they went; then they begun measuring distances by paces, and finally they all stood together, facing a piece of the side wall, which they began to examine with great minuteness; pulling off the ivy that clung to it, and rapping the plaster with the ends of their sticks, scraping here, and knocking there. At length they ascertained the existence of a broad marble tablet, with letters carved in relief upon it.

With the assistance of the woodman, who soon returned, a monumental inscription, and carved escutcheon, were disclosed. They proved to be of those of the long lost monument of Mircalla, Countess Karnstein.

The old General, though not I fear given to the praying mood, raised his hands and eyes to heaven, in mute thanksgiving for some moments.

Then turning to the old man with the gold spectacles, whom I have described, he shook him warmly by both hands and said:

'Baron, how can I thank you? How can we all thank you? You will have delivered this region from a plague that has scourged its inhabitants for more than a century. The horrible enemy, thank God, is at last tracked.'

My father led the stranger aside, and the General followed. I knew that he had led them out of hearing, that he might relate my case, and I saw them glance often quickly at me, as the discussion proceeded.

My father came to me, kissed me again and again, and leading me from the chapel said:

'It is time to return, but before we go home, we must add to our party the good priest, who lives but a little way from this; and persuade him to accompany us to the schloss.'

In this quest we were successful: and I was glad, being unspeakably fatigued when we reached home. But my satisfaction was changed to dismay, on discovering that there were no tidings of Carmilla. Of the scene that occurred in the ruined chapel, no explanation was offered to me, and it was clear that it was a secret which my father for the present determined to keep from me.

The sinister absence of Carmilla made the remembrance of the scene more horrible to me. The arrangements for the night were singular. Two servants and Madame were to sit up in my room that night; and the ecclesiastic with my father kept watch in the adjoining dressing-room.

The priest had performed certain solemn rights that night, the purport of which I did not understand any more than I comprehended the reason of this extraordinary precaution taken for my safety during sleep.

I saw all clearly a few days later.

The disappearance of Carmilla was followed by the discontinuance of my nightly sufferings.

You have heard no doubt, of the appalling superstition that prevails in Upper Styria, in Moravia, Silesia, in Turkish Servia, in Poland, even in Russia; the superstition, so we must call it, of the vampire.

If human testimony, taken with every care and solemnity, judicially before commissions innumerable, each consisting of many members, all chosen for integrity and intelligence, and constituting reports more voluminous perhaps than exist upon any one other class of case, is worth anything, it is difficult to deny, or even to doubt the existence of such a phenomenon as the vampire.

For my part I have heard no theory by which to explain what I myself have witnessed and experienced, other than that supplied by the ancient and well-attested belief of the country.

The next day the formal proceedings took place in the Chapel of Karnstein. The grave of the Countess Mircalla was opened; and the General and my father recognised each his perfidious and beautiful guest, in the face now disclosed to view. The features, though a hundred and fifty years had passed since her funeral, were tinted with the warmth of life. Her eyes were open; no cadaverous smell exhaled from the coffin. The two medical men, one officially present, the other on the part of the promoter of the inquiry, attested the marvellous fact, that there was a faint, but appreciable respiration, and a corresponding action of the heart. The limbs were perfectly flexible, the flesh elastic; and the leaden coffin floated with blood, in which to a depth of seven inches, the body lay immersed. Here then, were all the admitted signs and proofs of vampirism. The body, therefore, in accordance with the ancient practice, was raised, and a sharp stake driven through the heart of the vampire, who uttered a piercing shriek at the moment, in all respects such as might escape from a living person in the last agony. Then the head was struck off, and a torrent of blood flowed from the severed neck. The body and head were next placed on a pile of wood, and reduced to ashes, which were thrown upon the river and borne away, and that territory has never since been plagued by the visits of a vampire.

My father has a copy of the report of the Imperial Commission, with the signatures of all who were present at these proceedings, attached in verification of the statement. It is from this official paper that I have summarised my account of this last shocking scene.

16

CONCLUSION

I write all this you suppose with composure. But far from it; I cannot think of it without agitation. Nothing but your earnest desire so repeatedly expressed, could have induced me to sit down to a task that has unstrung my nerves for months to come, and reinduced a shadow of the unspeakable horror which years after my deliverance continued to make my days and nights dreadful, and solitude insupportably terrifying.

Let me add a word or two about that quaint Baron Vordenburg, to whose curious lore we were indebted for the discovery of the Countess Mircalla's grave.

He had taken up his abode in Gratz, where, living upon a mere pittance, which was all that remained to him of the once princely estates of his family, in Upper Styria, he devoted himself to the minute and laborious investigation of the marvellously authenticated tradition of vampirism. He had at his fingers' ends all the great and little known works upon the subject. 'Magia Posthuma,' 'Phlegon de Mirabilibus,' 'Augustinus de cura pro Mortuis,' 'Philosophicae et Christianae Cogitationes de Vampiris,' by John Christopher Harenberg; and a thousand others, among which I remember only a few of those which he lent to my father. He had a voluminous digest of all the judicial cases, from which he had extracted a system of principles that appear to govern – some always, and others occasionally only – the condition of the vampire. I may mention, in passing, that the deadly pallor attributed to that sort of *revenant,* is a mere melodramatic fiction. They present in the grave, and when they show themselves in human society, the appearance of healthy life. When disclosed to light in their coffins, they exhibit all the symptoms that are enumerated as those which proved the vampire life of the long-dead Countess Karnstein.

How they escape from their graves and return to them for certain hours every day, without displacing the clay or leaving any trace of disturbance in the state of the coffin or the cerements, has always been admitted to be utterly inexplicable. The amphibious existence of the vampire is sustained by daily renewed slumber in the grave. Its horrible lust for living blood supplies the vigour of its waking existence. The vampire is prone to be fascinated with an engrossing vehemence, resembling the passion of love, by particular persons. In pursuit of these it will exercise inexhaustible patience and stratagem, for access to a particular object may be obstructed in a hundred ways. It will never desist until it has satiated its passion, and drained the very life of its coveted victim. But it will, in these cases, husband and protract its murderous enjoyment with the refinement of an epicure, and heighten it by the gradual approaches of an artful courtship. In these cases it seems to yearn for something like sympathy and consent. In ordinary ones it goes direct to its object, overpowers with violence, and strangles and exhausts often at a single feast.

The vampire, is apparently, subject, in certain situations, to special conditions. In the particular instance of which I have given you a relation, Mircalla seemed to be limited to a name which, if not her real one, should at least reproduce, without the omission or addition of a single letter, those, as we say, anagrammatically, which compose it. *Carmilla* did this; so did *Millarca*.

My father related to the Baron Vordenburg, who remained with us for two or three weeks after the expulsion of Carmilla, the story about the Moravian nobleman and the vampire at Karnstein churchyard, and then he asked the Baron how he had discovered the exact position of the long-concealed tomb of the Countess Millarca? The Baron's grotesque features puckered into a mysterious smile; he looked down, still smiling, on his worn spectacle-case and fumbled with it. Then looking up, he said:

'I have many journals, and other papers, written by that remarkable man; the most curious among them is one treating of the visit of which you speak, to Karnstein. The tradition, of course, discolours and distorts a little. He might have been termed a Moravian nobleman, for he had changed his abode to that territory, and was, beside, a noble. But he was, in truth, a native of Upper Styria. Is enough to say that in very early youth he had been a passionate and favoured lover of the beautiful Mircalla, Countess Karnstein. Her early death plunged him into inconsolable grief. It is the nature of vampires to increase and multiply, but according to an ascertained and ghostly law.

'Assume, at starting, a territory perfectly free from that pest. How does it begin, and how does it multiply itself? I will tell you. A person, more or less wicked, puts an end to himself. A suicide, under certain circumstances, becomes a vampire. That spectre visits living people in their slumbers; *they* die, and almost invariably, in the grave, develop into vampires. This happened in the case of the beautiful Mircalla, who was haunted by one of those demons. My ancestor, Vordenburg, whose title I still bear, soon discovered this, and in the course of the studies to which he devoted himself, learned a great deal more.

'Among other things, he concluded that suspicion of vampirism would probably fall, sooner, or later, upon the dead Countess, who in life had been his idol. He conceived a horror, be she what she might, of her remains being profaned by the outrage of a posthumous execution. He has left a curious paper to prove that the vampire, on its expulsion from its amphibious existence, is projected into a far more horrible life; and he resolved to save his once beloved Mircalla from this.

'He adopted the stratagem of a journey here, a pretended removal of her remains, and a real obliteration of her monument. When age had stolen upon him, and from the vale of years he looked back on the scenes he was leaving, he considered, in a different spirit, what he had done; and a horror took possession of him. He made the tracings and notes which have guided me to the very spot, and drew up a confession of the deception that he had practised. If he had intended any further action in this matter, death prevented him; and the hand of a remote descendant has, too late for many, directed the pursuit to the lair of the beast.'

We talked a little more, and among other things he said was this:

'One sign of the vampire is the power of the hand. The slender hand of Mircalla closed like a vice of steel on the General's wrist when he raised the hatchet to strike. But its power is not confined to its grasp; it leaves a numbness in the limb it seizes, which is slowly, if ever, recovered from.'

The following Spring my father took me a tour through Italy. We remained away for more than a year. It was long before the terror of recent events subsided; and to this hour the image of Carmilla returns to my memory with ambiguous alternations – sometimes the playful, languid, beautiful girl; sometimes the writhing fiend I saw in the ruined church; and often from a reverie I have started, fancying I heard the light step of Carmilla at the drawing-room door.

THE DREAM WOMAN

Wilkie Collins

1

I had not been settled much more than six weeks in my country practice, when I was sent for to a neighbouring town, to consult with the resident medical man there, on a case of very dangerous illness.

My horse had come down with me, at the end of a long ride the night before, and had hurt himself, luckily much more than he had hurt his master. Being deprived of the animal's services, I started for my destination by the coach (there were no railways at that time); and I hoped to get back again, towards the afternoon, in the same way.

After the consultation was over I went to the principal inn of the town to wait for the coach. When it came up, it was full inside and out. There was no resource left me but to get home as cheaply as I could, by hiring a gig. The price asked for this accommodation struck me as being so extortionate, that I determined to look out for an inn of inferior pretentions, and to try if I could not make a better bargain with a less prosperous establishment.

I soon found a likely-looking house, dingy and quiet, with an old-fashioned sign, that had evidently not been repainted for many years past. The landlord, in this case, was not above making a small profit; and as soon as we came to terms, he rang the yard bell to order the gig.

'Has Robert not come back from that errand?' asked the landlord, appealing to the waiter, who answered the bell.

'No, sir, he hasn't.'

'Well, then, you must wake up Isaac.'

'Wake up Isaac?' I replied; 'that sounds rather odd. Do your ostlers go to bed in the day-time?'

'This one does,' said the landlord, smiling to himself in rather a strange way.

'And dreams, too,' added the waiter.

'Never you mind about that,' retorted his master; 'you

go and rouse Isaac up. The gentleman's waiting for his gig.'

The landlord's manner and the waiter's manner expressed a great deal more than they either of them said. I began to suspect that I might be on the trace of something professionally interesting to me, as a medical man; and I thought I should like to look at the ostler, before the waiter awakened him.

'Stop a minute,' I interposed; 'I have rather a fancy for seeing this man before you wake him up. I am a doctor; and if this queer sleeping and dreaming of his comes from anything wrong in his brain, I may be able to tell you what to do with him.'

'I rather think you will find his complaint past all doctoring, sir,' said the landlord. 'But if you would like to see him, you're welcome, I'm sure.'

He led the way across a yard and down a passage to the stables; opened one of the doors; and waiting outside himself, told me to look in.

I found myself in a two-stall stable. In one of the stalls a horse was munching his corn. In the other, an old man was lying asleep on the litter.

I stooped and looked at him attentively. It was a withered, woe-begone face. The eyebrows were painfully contracted; the mouth was set fast, and drawn down at the corners. The hollow, wrinkled cheeks, and the scanty, grizzled hair, told their own tale of past sorrow or suffering. He was drawing his breath convulsively when I first looked at him; and in a moment more he began to talk in his sleep.

'Wake up!' I heard him say in a quick whisper, through his clenched teeth. 'Wake up there! Murder!'

He moved one lean arm slowly till it rested over his throat, shuddered a little, and turned on the straw. Then the arm left his throat, the hand stretched itself out, and clutched at the side towards which he had turned, as if he fancied himself to be grasping at the edge of something. I saw his lips move, and bent lower over him. He was still talking in his sleep.

'Light grey eyes,' he murmured, 'and a droop in the left eyelid – flaxen hair, with a gold-yellow streak in it – all right, mother – fair white arms, with a down on them – little lady's hand, with a reddish look under the finger-nails. The knife – always the cursed knife – first on one side, then on the other. Aha! you she-devil, where's the knife?'

At the last word his voice rose, and he grew restless on a sudden. I saw him shudder on the straw; his withered face became distorted, and he threw up both hands with a quick, hysterical gasp. They struck against the bottom of the manger under which he lay, and the blow awakened him. I had just time to slip through the door, and close it, before his eyes were fairly open, and his senses his own again.

'Do you know anything about that man's past life?' I said to the landlord.

'Yes, sir. I know pretty well all about it,' was the answer, 'and an uncommon queer story it is. Most people don't believe it. It's true, though, for all that. Why, just look at him,' continued the landlord, opening the stable door again. 'Poor devil! He's so worn out with his restless nights that he's dropped back into his sleep already.'

'Don't wake him,' I said; 'I'm in no hurry for the gig. Wait till the other man comes back from his errand. And, in the meantime, suppose I have some lunch, and a bottle of sherry; and suppose you come and help me to get through it.'

The heart of mine host, as I had anticipated, warmed to me over his own wine. He soon became communicative on the subject of the man asleep in the stable; and by little and little, I drew the whole story out of him. Extravagant and incredible as the events must appear to everybody, they are related here just as I heard them, and just as they happened.

2

Some years ago there lived in the suburbs of a large seaport town, on the west coast of England, a man in humble circumstances, by name Isaac Scatchard. His means of subsistence were derived from any employment he could get as an ostler, and occasionally, when times went well with him, from temporary engagements in service as stable-helper in private houses. Though a faithful, steady, and honest man, he got on badly in his calling. His ill-luck was proverbial among his neighbours. He was always missing good opportunities by no fault of his own; and always living longest in service with amiable people who were not punctual payers of wages. 'Unlucky Isaac' was his nickname in his own neighbourhood – and no-one could say that he did not richly deserve it.

With far more than one man's fair share of adversity to endure, Isaac had but one consolation to support him –and that was of the dreariest and most negative kind. He had no wife and children to increase his anxieties and add to the bitterness of his various failures in life. It might have been from mere insensibility, or it might have been from generous unwillingness to involve another in his own unlucky destiny – but the fact undoubtedly was, that he had arrived at the middle term of life without marrying; and, what is much more remarkable, without once exposing himself from eighteen to eight-and-thirty, to the genial imputation of ever having had a sweetheart.

When he was out of service, he lived alone with his widowed mother. Mrs. Scatchard was a woman above the average in her lowly station, as to capacity and manners. She had seen better days, as the phrase is; but she never referred to them in the presence of curious visitors; and though perfectly polite to everyone who approached her, never cultivated any intimacies among her neighbours. She contrived to provide, hardly enough for her simple wants, by doing rough work for the tailors; and always managed to keep a decent home for her son to return to, whenever his ill-luck drove him out helpless into the world.

One bleak Autumn, when Isaac was getting fast towards forty, and when he was, as usual, out of place through no fault of his own, he set forth from his mother's cottage on a long walk inland to a gentleman's seat, where he had heard that a stable-helper was required.

It wanted then but two days of his birthday; and Mrs. Scatchard, with her usual fondness, made him promise before he started, that he would be back in time to keep that anniversary with her in as festive a way as their poor means would allow. It was easy for him to comply with her request, even supposing he slept a night each way on the road.

He rose to start from home on Monday morning; and whether he got the new place or not, he was to be back for his birthday dinner on Wednesday at two o'clock.

Arriving at his destination too late on the Monday night to make application for the stable-helper's place, he slept at the village inn, and, in good time on the Tuesday morning, presented himself at the gentleman's house to fill the vacant situation. Here, again, his ill-luck pursued him as inexorably as ever. The excellent written testimonials to his character which he was able to produce, availed him nothing; his long walk had been taken in vain – only the day before, the stable-helper's place had been given to another man.

Isaac accepted this new disappointment resignedly, and as a matter of course. Naturally slow in capacity, he had the bluntness of sensibility and phlegmatic patience of disposition which frequently distinguish men with sluggishly-working mental powers. He thanked the gentleman's steward with his usual quiet civility, for granting him an interview, and took his departure with no appearance of unusual depression in his face or manner.

Before starting on his homeward walk, he made some inquiries at the inn, and ascertained that he might save a few miles, on his return, by following a new road. Furnished with full instructions, several times repeated, as to the various turnings he was to take, he set forth on his homeward journey, and walked on all day with only one stoppage for bread and cheese. Just as it was getting towards dark, the rain came on and the wind began to rise; and he found himself, to make matters worse, in a part of the country with which he was entirely unacquainted, though he knew himself to be some fifteen miles from home. The first house he found to inquire at was a lonely roadside inn, standing on the outskirts of a thick wood. Solitary as the place looked, it was welcome to a lost man who was also hungry, thirsty, footsore, and wet. The landlord was civil and respectable-looking; and the price he asked for a bed was reasonable enough. Isaac, therefore, decided on stopping comfortably at the inn for that night.

He was constitutionally a temperate man. His supper simply consisted of two rashers of bacon, a slice of home-made bread, and a pint of ale. He did not go to bed immediately after this moderate meal, but sat up with the landlord, talking about his bad prospects and his long run of ill-luck, and diverging from these topics to the subjects of horse-flesh and racing. Nothing was said, either by himself, his host, or the few labourers who strayed into the tap-room, which could, in the slightest degree, excite the small and very dull imaginative faculty which Isaac Scatchard possessed.

At a little after eleven the house was closed. Isaac went round with the landlord, and held the candle while the doors and lower windows were being secured. He noticed, with surprise, the strength of the bolts, bars, and iron-sheathed shutters.

'You see, we are rather lonely here,' said the landlord. 'We never have had any attempts made to break in yet, but it's always as well to be on the safe side. When nobody is sleeping here I am the only man in the house. My wife and daughter are timid, and the servant-girl takes after her missuses. Another glass of ale before you turn in? – No! – Well, how such a sober man as you comes to be out of a place is more than I can make out, for one. . . . Here's where you're to sleep. You're the only lodger to-night, and I think you'll say my missus has done her best to make you comfortable. You're quite sure you won't have another glass of ale? – Very well. Good night.'

It was half-past eleven by the clock in the passage as they went upstairs to the bedroom, the window of which looked on to the wood at the back of the house.

Isaac locked the door, set his candle on the chest of drawers, and wearily got ready for bed. The bleak autumn wind was still blowing, and the solemn, surging moan of it in the wood was dreary and awful to hear through the night-silence. Isaac felt strangely wakeful. He resolved, as he lay down in bed, to keep the candle alight until he began to grow sleepy; for there was something unendurably depressing in the bare idea of lying awake in the darkness, listening to the dismal, ceaseless moan of the wind in the wood.

Sleep stole on him before he was aware of it. His eyes closed, and he fell off insensibly to rest, without having so much as thought of extinguishing the candle.

The first sensation of which he was conscious, after sinking into slumber, was a strange shivering that ran through him suddenly from head to foot, and a dreadful sinking pain at the heart, such as he had never felt before. The shivering only disturbed his slumbers – the pain woke him instantly. In one moment he passed from a state of sleep to a state of wakefulness – his eyes wide open – his mental perceptions cleared on a sudden as if by a miracle.

The candle had burnt down nearly to the last morsel of tallow, but the top of the unsnuffed wick had just fallen off, and the light in the little room was, for the moment, fair and full.

Between the foot of his bed and the closed door, there stood a woman with a knife in her hand, looking at him.

He was stricken speechless with terror, but he did not lose the preternatural clearness of his faculties; and he never took his eyes off the woman. She said not a word as they stared each other in the face; but she began to move slowly towards the left-hand side of the bed.

His eyes followed her. She was a fair, fine woman, with yellowish flaxen hair, and light grey eyes, with a droop in the left eyelid. He noticed these things, and fixed them on his mind, before she was round at the side of the bed. Speechless, with no expression in her face, with no noise following her footfall, she came closer and closer – stopped – and slowly raised the knife. He laid his right arm over his throat to save it; but, as he saw the knife coming down, threw his hand across the bed to the right side, and jerked his body over that way, just as the knife descended on the mattress within an inch of his shoulder.

His eyes fixed on her arm and hand, as she slowly drew her knife out of the bed. A white, well-shaped arm, with a pretty down lying lightly over the fair skin. A delicate, lady's hand, with the crowning beauty of a pink flush under and round the fingernails.

She drew the knife out, and passed back again slowly to the foot of the bed; stopped there for a moment looking at him; then came on – still speechless, still with no expression on the beautiful face, still with no sound following the stealthy footfalls – came on to the right side of the bed where he now lay.

As she approached, she raised the knife again, and he drew himself away to the left side. She struck, as before, right into the mattress, with a deliberate, perpendicularly downward action of the arm. This time his eyes wandered from her to the knife. It was like the large clasp-knives which he had often seen labouring men use to cut their bread and bacon with. Her delicate little fingers did not conceal more than two-thirds of the handle; he noticed that it was made of buckhorn, clean and shining as the blade was, and looking like new.

For the second time she drew the knife out, concealed it in the wide sleeve of her gown, then stopped by the bedside, watching him. For an instant he saw her standing in that position – then the wick of the spent candle fell over into the socket. The flame diminished to a little blue point, and the room grew dark.

A moment, or less if possible, passed so – and then the wick flamed up, smokily, for the last time. His eyes were still looking eagerly over the right-hand side of the bed when the final flash came, but they discerned nothing. The fair woman with the knife was gone.

The conviction that he was alone again, weakened the hold of the terror that had struck him dumb up to this time. The preternatural sharpness which the very intensity of his panic had mysteriously imparted to his faculties, left them suddenly. His brain grew confused – his heart beat wildly – his ears opened, for the first time since the appearance of the woman, to a sense of the woeful, ceaseless moaning of the wind among the trees. With the dreadful conviction of the reality of what he had seen still strong within him, he leapt out of bed, and screaming – 'Murder! – Wake up there, wake up!' – dashed headlong through the darkness to the door.

It was fact locked, exactly as he had left it on going to bed.

His cries, on starting up, had alarmed the house. He heard the terrified, confused exclamations of women; he saw the master of the house approaching along the passage, with his burning rush-candle in one hand and his gun in the other.

'What is it?' asked the landlord, breathlessly.

Isaac could only answer in a whisper. 'A woman, with a knife in her hand,' he gasped out. 'In my room – a fair, yellow-haired woman; she jabbed at me with the knife, twice over.'

The landlord's pale cheek grew paler. He looked at

Isaac eagerly by the flickering light of his candle; and his face began to get red again – his voice altered, too, as well as his complexion.

'She seems to have missed you twice,' he said.

'I dodged the knife as it came down,' Isaac went on, in the same scared whisper. 'It struck the bed each time.'

The landlord took his candle into the bedroom immediately. In less than a minute he came out again into the passage in a violent passion.

'The devil fly away with you and your woman with the knife! There isn't a mark in the bed-clothes anywhere. What do you mean by coming into a man's place and frightening his family out of their wits by a dream?'

'I'll leave your house,' said Isaac, faintly. 'Better out on the road, in rain and dark, on my way home, than back again in that room, after what I've seen in it. Lend me a light to get my clothes by, and tell me what I'm to pay.'

'Pay!' cried the landlord, leading the way with his light sulkily into the bedroom. 'You'll find your score on the slate when you go downstairs. I wouldn't have taken you in for all the money you've got about you, if I'd known your dreaming, screeching ways beforehand. Look at the bed. Where's the cut of a knife in it? Look at the window – is the lock bursted? Look at the door (which I heard you fasten yourself) is it broke in? A murdering woman with a knife in my house! You ought to be ashamed of yourself!'

Isaac answered not a word. He huddled on his clothes: and then they went downstairs together.

'Nigh on twenty minutes past two!' said the landlord, as they passed the clock. 'A nice time in the morning to frighten honest people out of their wits!'

Isaac paid his bill, and the landlord let him out at the front door, asking, with a grin of contempt, as he undid the strong fastenings, whether 'the murdering woman got in that way?'

They parted without a word on either side. The rain had ceased; but the night was dark, and the wind bleaker than ever. Little did the darkness, or the cold, or the uncertainty about the way home matter to Isaac. If he had been turned out into a wilderness in a thunderstorm, it would have been a relief, after what he had suffered in the bedroom of the inn.

What was the fair woman with the knife? The creature of a dream, or that other creature from the unknown world, called among men by the name of ghost? He could make nothing of the mystery – had made nothing of it, even when it was midday on Wednesday, and when he stood, at last, after many times missing his road, once more on the doorstep of home.

3

His mother came out eagerly to receive him. His face told her in a moment that something was wrong.

'I've lost the place; but that's my luck. I dreamed an ill dream last night, mother – or, maybe, I saw a ghost. Take it either way, it scared me out of my senses, and I'm not my own man again yet.'

'Isaac! your face frightens me. Come in to the fire. Come in, and tell mother all about it.'

He was as anxious to tell as she was to hear; for it had been his hope, all the way home, that his mother, with her quicker capacity and superior knowledge, might be able to throw some light on the mystery which he could not clear up for himself. His memory of the dream was still mechanically vivid, though his thoughts were entirely confused by it.

His mother's face grew paler and paler as he went on. She never interrupted him by so much as a single word; but when he had done, she moved her chair close to his, put her arm round his neck, and said to him:

'Isaac, you dreamed your ill dream on this Wednesday morning. What time was it when you saw the fair woman with the knife in her hand?'

Isaac reflected on what the landlord had said when they had passed by the clock on his leaving the inn – allowed as nearly as he could for the time that must have elapsed between the unlocking of his bedroom door and the paying of his bill just before going away, and answered:

'Somewhere about two o'clock in the morning.'

His mother suddenly quitted her hold of his neck, and struck her hands together with a gesture of despair.

'This Wednesday is your birthday, Isaac; and two o'clock in the morning is the time when you were born!'

Isaac's capacities were not quick enough to catch the infection of his mother's superstitious dread. He was amazed, and a little startled also, when she suddenly rose from her chair, opened her old writing-desk, took pen, ink and paper, and then said to him:

'Your memory is but a poor one, Isaac, and now I'm an old woman, mine's not much better. I want all about this dream of yours to be as well known to both of us, years hence, as it is now. Tell me over again all you told me a minute ago, when you spoke of what the woman with the knife looked like.'

Isaac obeyed, and marvelled much as he saw his mother carefully set down on paper the very words that he was saying.

'Light grey eyes,' she wrote as they came to the descriptive part, 'with a droop in the left eyelid. Flaxen hair, with a gold-yellow streak in it. White arms, with a down upon them. Little lady's hand, with a reddish look about the finger-nails. Clasp-knife with a buckhorn handle, that seemed as good as new.' To these particulars, Mrs. Scatchard added the year, month, day of the week, and time in the morning, when the woman of the dream appeared to her son. She then locked up the paper carefully in her writing-desk.

Neither on that day, nor on any day after, could her son induce her to return to the matter of the dream. She obstinately kept her thoughts about it to herself, and even refused to refer again to the paper in her writing-desk. Ere long, Isaac grew weary of attempting to make her break her resolute silence; and time, which sooner or later wears out all things, gradually wore out the impression produced on him by the dream. He began by thinking of it carelessly, and he ended by not thinking of it at all.

This result was the more easily brought about by the advent of some important changes for the better in his prospects, which commenced not long after his terrible night's experience at the inn. He reaped at last the reward of his long and patient suffering under adversity, by getting an excellent place, keeping it for seven years, and leaving it, on the death of his master, not only with an excellent character, but also with a comfortable annuity bequeathed to him as a reward for having saved his mistress's life in a carriage accident. Thus it happened that Isaac Scatchard returned to his old mother, seven years after the time of the dream at the inn, with an annual sum of money at his disposal, sufficient to keep them both in ease and independence for the rest of their lives.

The mother, whose health had been bad of late years, profited so much by the care bestowed on her and by freedom from money anxieties, that when Isaac's birthday came round she was able to sit up comfortably at table and dine with him.

On that day, as the evening drew on, Mrs. Scatchard discovered that a bottle of tonic medicine – which she was accustomed to take, and in which she had fancied that a dose or more was still left – happened to be empty. Isaac immediately volunteered to go to the chemist's, and get it filled again. It was as rainy and bleak an autumn night as on the memorable past occasion when he lost his way and slept at the roadside inn.

On going into the chemist's shop, he was passed hurriedly by a poorly-dressed woman coming out of it. The glimpse he had of her face struck him, and he looked back after her as she descended the door-steps.

'You're noticing that woman?' said the chemist's apprentice behind the counter. 'It's my opinion there's something wrong with her. She's been asking for laudanum to put to a bad tooth. Master's out for half an hour; and I told her I wasn't allowed to sell poison to strangers in his absence. She laughed in a queer way, and said she would come back in half an hour. If she expects master to serve her, I think she'll be disappointed. It's a case of suicide, sir, if ever there was one yet.'

These words added immeasurably to the sudden interest in the woman which Isaac had felt at the first sight of her face. After he had got the medicine bottle filled, he looked about anxiously for her, as soon as he was out in the street. She was walking slowly up and down on the opposite side of the road. With his heart, very much to his own surprise, beating fast, Isaac crossed over and spoke to her.

He asked if she was in any distress. She pointed to her

torn shawl, her scanty dress, her crushed, dirty bonnet – then moved under a lamp so as to let the light fall on her stern, pale, but still most beautiful face.

'I look like a comfortable, happy woman – don't I?' she said, with a bitter laugh.

She spoke with a purity of intonation which Isaac had never heard before from other than ladies' lips. Her slightest actions seemed to have the easy, negligent grace of a thorough-bred woman. Her skin, for all its poverty-stricken paleness, was as delicate as if her life had been passed in the enjoyment of every social comfort that wealth can purchase. Even her small, finely-shaped hands, gloveless as they were, had not lost their whiteness.

Little by little, in answer to his questions, the sad story of the woman came out. There is no need to relate it here; it is told over and over again in police reports and paragraphs descriptive of Attempted Suicides.

'My name is Rebecca Murdoch,' said the woman, as she ended. 'I have ninepence left, and I thought of spending it at the chemist's over the way in securing a passage to the other world. Whatever it is, it can't be worse to me than this – so why should I stop here?'

Besides the natural compassion and sadness moved in his heart by what he heard, Isaac felt within him some mysterious influence at work all the time the woman was speaking, which utterly confused his ideas and almost deprived him of his powers of speech. All that he could say in answer to her last reckless words was, that he would prevent her from attempting her own life, if he followed her about all night to do it. His rough, trembling earnestness seemed to impress her.

'I won't occasion you that trouble,' she answered, when he repeated his threat. 'You have given me a fancy for living by speaking kindly to me. No need for the mockery of protestations and promises. You may believe me without them. Come to Fuller's Meadow to-morrow at twelve, and you will find me alive, to answer for myself. No! – no money. My ninepence will do to get me as good a night's lodgings as I want.'

She nodded and left him. He made no attempt to follow – he felt no suspicion that she was deceiving him.

'It's strange, but I can't help believing her,' he said to himself, and walked away bewildered towards home.

On entering the house, his mind was still so completely absorbed by its new subject of interest, that he took no notice of what his mother was doing when he came in with the bottle of medicine. She had opened her old writing-desk in his absence, and was now reading a paper attentively that lay inside it. On every birthday of Isaac's since she had written down the particulars of his dream from his own lips, she had been accustomed to read that same paper, and ponder over it in private.

The next day he went to Fuller's Meadow.

He had done only right in believing her so implicitly – she was there, punctual to a minute, to answer for herself. The last-left faint defences in Isaac's heart, against the fascination which a word or look from her began inscrutably to exercise over him, sank down and vanished before her for ever on that memorable morning.

When a man, previously insensible to the influence of women, forms an attachment in middle life, the instances are rare indeed, let the warning circumstances be what they may, in which he is found capable of freeing himself from the tyranny of the new ruling passion. The charm of being spoken to familiarly, fondly, and gratefully by a woman whose language and manners still retained enough of their early refinement to hint at the high social station that she had lost, would have been a dangerous luxury to a man of Isaac's rank at the age of twenty. But it was far more than that – it was certain ruin to him – now that his heart was opening unworthily to a new influence at that middle time of life when strong feelings of all kinds, once implanted, strike root most stubbornly in a man's moral nature. A few more stolen interviews after that first morning in Fuller's Meadow completed his infatuation. In less than a month from the time when he first met her, Isaac Scatchard had consented to give Rebecca Murdoch a new interest in existence, and a chance of recovering the character she had lost, by promising to make her his wife.

She had taken possession not of his passions only, but of his faculties as well. All the mind he had he put into her keeping. She directed him on every point, even instructing him how to break the news of his approaching marriage in the safest manner to his mother.

'If you tell her how you met me, and who I am at

first,' said the cunning woman, 'she will move heaven and earth to prevent our marriage. Say I am the sister of one of your fellow-servants – ask her to see me before you go into any more particulars – and leave it to me to do the rest. I mean to make her love me next best to you, Isaac, before she knows anything of who I really am.'

The motive of the deceit was sufficient to sanctify it to Isaac. The stratagem proposed relieved him of his one great anxiety, and quieted his uneasy conscience on the subject of his mother. Still, there was something wanting to perfect his happiness, something that he could not realize, something mysteriously untraceable, and yet something that perpetually made itself felt – not when he was absent from Rebecca Murdoch, but, strange to say, when he was actually in her presence! She was kindness itself with him; she never made him feel his inferior capacities and inferior manners – she showed the sweetest anxiety to please him in the smallest trifles; but, in spite of all these attractions, he never could feel quite at ease with her. At their first meeting, there had mingled with his admiration, when he looked in her face, a faint, involuntary feeling of doubt whether that face was entirely strange to him. No after-familiarity had the slightest effect on this inexplicable, wearisome uncertainty.

Concealing the truth, as he had been directed, he announced his marriage engagement precipitately and confusedly to his mother, on the day when he contracted it. Poor Mrs. Scatchard showed her perfect confidence in her son by flinging her arms round his neck, and giving him joy of having found at last, in the sister of one of his fellow-servants, a woman to comfort and care for him after his mother was gone. She was all eagerness to see the woman of her son's choice, and the next day was fixed for the introduction.

It was a bright, sunny morning, and the little cottage parlour was full of light, as Mrs. Scatchard, happy and expectant, dressed for the occasion in her Sunday gown, sat waiting for her son and her future daughter-in-law.

Punctual to the appointed time, Isaac hurriedly and nervously led his promised wife into the room. His mother rose to receive her – advanced a few steps, smiling – looked Rebecca full in the eyes – and suddenly stopped. Her face, which had been flushed the moment before, turned white in an instant – her eyes lost their expression of softness and kindness, and assumed a blank look of terror – her outstretched hands fell to her sides, and she staggered back a few steps with a low cry to her son.

'Isaac!' she whispered, clutching him fast by the arm, when he asked alarmedly, if she was taken ill. 'Isaac! does the woman's face remind you of nothing?'

Before he could answer, before he could look round to where Rebecca stood, astonished and angered by her reception, at the lower end of the room, his mother pointed impatiently to her writing-desk and gave him the key.

'Open it,' she said, in a quick breathless whisper.

'What does this mean? Why am I treated as if I had no business here? Does your mother want to insult me?' asked Rebecca, angrily.

'Open it, and give me the paper in the left-hand drawer. Quick! quick! for heaven's sake!' said Mrs. Scatchard, shrinking further back in terror.

Isaac gave her the paper. She looked it over eagerly for a moment – then followed Rebecca, who was now turning away haughtily to leave the room, and caught her by the shoulder – abruptly raised the long, loose sleeve of her gown – and glanced at her hand and arm. Something like fear began to steal over the angry expression of Rebecca's face, as she shook herself free from the old woman's grasp. 'Mad!' she said to herself, 'and Isaac never told me.' With those few words she left the room.

Isaac was hastening after her, when his mother turned and stopped his further progress. It wrung his heart to see the misery and terror in her face as she looked at him.

'Light grey eyes,' she said, in low, mournful, awestruck tones, pointing towards the open door: 'A droop in the left eyelid; flaxen hair, with a yellow streak in it; white arms with a down on them; little, lady's hand, with a reddish look under the finger-nails. *The Dream Woman!* Isaac, the Dream Woman!'

That faint cleaving doubt which he had never been able to shake off in Rebecca Murdoch's presence, was fatally set at rest for ever. He *had* seen her face, then, before – seven years before, on his birthday, in the bedroom of the lonely inn.

'Be warned! Oh, my son, be warned! Isaac! let her go, and do you stop with me!'

Something darkened the parlour window as those words were said. A sudden chill ran through him, and he glanced sidelong at the shadow. Rebecca Murdoch had come back. She was peering in curiously at them over the low window blind.

'I have promised to marry, mother,' he said, 'and marry I must.'

The tears came into his eyes as he spoke, and dimmed his sight; but he could just discern the fatal face outside, moving away from the window.

His mother's head sank lower.

'Are you faint?' he whispered.

'Broken-hearted, Isaac.'

He stooped down and kissed her. The shadow, as he did so, returned to the window; and the fatal face peered in curiously once more.

4

Three weeks after that day Isaac and Rebecca were man and wife. All that was hopelessly dogged and stubborn in the man's moral nature seemed to have closed round his fatal passion, and to have fixed it unassailably in his heart.

After that first interview in the cottage parlour, no consideration could induce Mrs. Scatchard to see her son's wife again, or even to talk of her when Isaac tried hard to plead her cause after their marriage.

This course of conduct was not in any degree occasioned by a discovery of the degradation in which Rebecca had lived. There was no question of that between mother and son. There was no question of anything but the fearfully exact resemblance between the living, breathing woman, and the spectre-woman of Isaac's dream.

Rebecca, on her part, neither felt nor expressed the slightest sorrow at the estrangement between herself and her mother-in-law. Isaac, for the sake of peace, had never contradicted her first idea that age and long illness had affected Mrs. Scatchard's mind. He even allowed his wife to upbraid him for not having confessed this to her at the time of their marriage engagement, rather than risk anything by hinting at the truth. The sacrifice of his integrity before his one all-mastering delusion, seemed but a small thing, and cost his conscience but little, after the sacrifices he had already made.

The time of waking from his delusion – the cruel and the rueful time – was not far off. After some quiet months of married life, as the summer was ending, and the year was getting on towards the month of his birthday, Isaac found his wife altering towards him. She grew sullen and contemptuous; she formed acquaintances of the most dangerous kind, in defiance of his objections, his entreaties, and his commands; and, worst of all, she learnt, ere long, after every fresh difference with her husband, to seek the deadly self-oblivion of drink. Little by little, after the first miserable discovery that his wife was keeping company with drunkards, the shocking certainty forced itself on Isaac that she had grown to be a drunkard herself.

He had been in a sadly desponding state for some time before the occurrence of these domestic calamities. His mother's health, as he could but too plainly discern every time he went to see her at the cottage, was failing fast; and he upbraided himself in secret as the cause of the bodily and mental suffering she endured. When to his remorse on his mother's account was added the shame and misery occasioned by the discovery of his wife's degradation, he sank under the double trial, his face began to alter fast, and he looked, what he was, a spirit-broken man.

His mother, still struggling bravely against the illness that was hurrying her to her grave, was the first to notice the sad alteration in him, and the first to hear of his last worst trouble with his wife. She could only weep bitterly, on the day when he made his humiliating confession; but on the next occasion when he went to see her, she had taken a resolution, in reference to his domestic afflictions, which astonished, and even alarmed him. He found her dressed to go out, and on asking the reason, received this answer:

'I am not long for this world, Isaac,' she said; 'and I shall not feel easy on my death-bed, unless I have done my best to the last to make my son happy. I mean to put my own fears and my own feelings out of the question, and go with you to your wife, and try what I can do to reclaim her. Give me your arm, Isaac; and let me do the last thing I can in this world to help my son, before it is too late.'

He could not disobey her; and they walked together slowly towards his miserable home.

It was only one o'clock in the afternoon when they reached the cottage where he lived. It was their dinner hour, and Rebecca was in the kitchen. He was thus able to take his mother quietly into the parlour and then prepare his wife for the interview. She had fortunately drunk but little at that early hour, and she was less sullen and capricious than usual.

He returned to his mother with his mind tolerably at ease. His wife soon followed him into the parlour, and the meeting between her and Mrs. Scatchard passed off better than he had ventured to anticipate; though he observed, with secret apprehension, that his mother, resolutely as she controlled herself in other respects, could not look his wife in the face when she spoke to her. It was a relief to him, therefore, when Rebecca began to lay the cloth.

She laid the cloth, brought in the breadtray, and cut a slice from the loaf for her husband, then returned to the kitchen. At that moment, Isaac, still anxiously watching his mother, was startled by seeing the same ghastly change pass over her face which had altered it so awfully on the morning when Rebecca and she first met. Before he could say a word, she whispered with a look of horror:

'Take me back! – home, home, again, Isaac! Come with me and never go back again!'

He was afraid to ask for an explanation; he could only sign to her to be silent, and help her quickly to the door. As they passed the bread-tray on the table, she stopped and pointed to it.

'Did you see what your wife cut your bread with?' she asked in a low whisper.

'No, mother; I was not noticing. What was it?'

'Look!'

He did look. A new clasp-knife, with a buckhorn handle, lay with the loaf in the bread-tray. He stretched out his hand, shudderingly, to possess himself of it; but at the same time there was a noise in the kitchen, and his mother caught his arm.

'The knife of the dream! Isaac, I'm faint with fear – take me away, before she comes back!'

He was hardly able to support her. The visible, tangible reality of the knife struck him with a panic, and utterly destroyed any faint doubts he might have entertained up to this time, in relation to the mysterious dream-warning of nearly eight years before. By a last desperate effort, he summoned self-possession enough to help his mother out of the house – so quietly, that the 'Dream Woman' (he thought of her by that name now) did not hear their departure.

'Don't go back, Isaac, don't go back!' implored Mrs. Scatchard, as he turned to go away, after seeing her safely seated again in her own room.

'I must get the knife,' he answered under his breath. His mother tried to stop him again; but he hurried out without another word.

On his return, he found that his wife had discovered their secret departure from the house. She had been drinking, and was in a fury of passion. The dinner in the kitchen was flung under the grate; the cloth was off the parlour table. Where was the knife?

Unwisely, he asked for it. She was only too glad of the opportunity of irritating him, which the request afforded her. 'He wanted the knife; did he? Could he give her a reason why? – No? Then he should not have it – not if he went down on his knees to ask for it.' Further recriminations elicited the fact that she had bought it as a bargain, and that she considered it as her own special property. Isaac saw the uselessness of attempting to get the knife by fair means, and determined to search for it, later in the day, in secret. The search was unsuccessful. Night came on, and he left the house to walk about the streets. He was afraid, now, to sleep in the same room with her.

Three weeks passed. Still sullenly enraged with him, she would not give up the knife; and still that fear of sleeping in the same room with her possessed him. He walked about at night, or dozed in the parlour, or sat watching by his mother's bedside. Before the expiration of the first week in the new month his mother died. It wanted then but ten days of her son's birthday. She had longed to live till that anniversary. Isaac was present at her death; and her last words in this world were addressed to him:

'Don't go back, my son – don't go back!'

He was obliged to go back, if it were only to watch his wife. Exasperated to the last degree by his distrust of her, she had revengefully sought to add a sting to his grief, during the last days of his mother's illness, by declaring that she would assert her right to attend the funeral. In spite of all that he could do or say, she held with wicked pertinacity to her word; and on the day appointed for the burial, forced herself – inflamed and shameless with drink – into her husband's presence, and declared that she would walk in the funeral procession to his mother's grave.

This last, worst outrage, accompanied by all that was most insulting in word and look, maddened him for the moment. He struck her.

The instant the blow was dealt he repented it. She crouched down, silent, in a corner of the room, and eyed him steadily; it was a look that cooled his hot blood and made him tremble. But there was no time now to think of a means of making atonement. Nothing remained but to risk the worst till the funeral was over. There was but one way of making sure of her. He locked her into her bedroom.

When he came back, some hours after, he found her sitting, very much altered in look and bearing, by the bedside, with a bundle on her lap. She rose and faced him quietly, and spoke with a strange stillness in her voice, a strange repose in her eyes, a strange composure in her manner.

'No man has ever struck me twice,' she said, 'and my husband shall have no second opportunity. Set the door open and let me go. From this day forth we see each other no more.'

Before he could answer she passed him, and left the room. He saw her walk away up the street.

Would she return?

All that night he watched and waited; but no footstep came near the house. The next night, overcome by fatigue, he lay down in bed in his clothes, with the door locked, the key on the table, and the candle burning. His slumber was not disturbed. The third night, the fourth, the fifth, the sixth passed, and nothing happened. He lay down on the seventh, still in his clothes, still with the door locked, the key on the table, and the candle burning; but easier in his mind.

Easier in his mind, and in perfect health of body, when he fell off to sleep. But his rest was disturbed. He woke twice, without any sensation of uneasiness. But the third time it was that never-to-be-forgotten shivering of the night at the lonely inn, that dreadful sinking pain in the heart, which once more aroused him in an instant.

His eyes opened towards the left-hand side of the bed, and there stood . . .

The Dream Woman again? No! His wife; the living reality, with the dream-spectre's face – in the dream-spectre's attitude; the fair arm up; the knife clasped in the delicate, white hand.

He sprang upon her almost at the instant of seeing her, and yet not quickly enough to prevent her from hiding the knife. Without a word from him, without a cry from her, he pinioned her in a chair. With one hand he felt up her sleeve; and there, where the Dream Woman had hidden the knife, his wife had hidden it – the knife with the buckhorn handle, that looked like new.

In the despair of that fearful moment his brain was steady, his heart was calm. He looked at her fixedly, with the knife in his hand, and said these last words:

'You told me we should see each other no more, and you have come back. It is my turn now to go, and to go for ever. *I* say that we shall see each other no more; and *my* word shall not be broken.'

He left her, and set forth into the night. There was a bleak wind abroad, and the smell of recent rain was in the air. The distant church clocks chimed the quarter as he walked rapidly beyond the last houses in the suburb. He asked the first policeman he met, what hour that was, of which the quarter past had just struck.

The man referred sleepily to his watch, and answered, 'Two o'clock.' Two in the morning. What day of the month was this day that had just begun? He reckoned it up from the date of his mother's funeral. The fatal parallel was complete – it was his birthday!

Had he escaped the mortal peril which his dream foretold? or had he only received a second warning?

As this ominous doubt forced itself on his mind, he stopped, reflected, and turned back again towards the city. He was still resolute to hold to his word, and never to let her see him more, but there was a thought now in his mind of having her watched and followed. The knife was in his possession; the world was before him; but a new distrust of her – a vague, unspeakable, superstitious dread – had overcome him.

'I must know where she goes, now she thinks I have left her,' he said to himself, as he stole back wearily to the precincts of his house.

It was still dark. He had left the candle burning in the bed chamber, but when he looked up to the window of the room now, there was no light in it. He crept cautiously to the house door. On going away, he remembered to have closed it; on trying it now, he found it open.

He waited outside, never losing sight of the house till daylight. Then he ventured indoors – listened, and heard nothing – looked into the kitchen, scullery, parlour; and found nothing: went up at last into the bedroom – it was empty. A picklock lay on the floor, betraying how she had gained entrance in the night, and that was the only trace of her.

Whither had she gone? No mortal tongue could tell him. The darkness had covered her flight; and when the day broke no man could say where the light found her.

Before leaving the house and the town for ever, he gave instructions to a friend and neighbour to sell his furniture for anything that it would fetch, and to apply the proceeds towards employing the police to trace her. The directions were honestly followed, and the money was all spent; but the enquiries led to nothing. The picklock on the bedroom floor remained the last useless trace of the Dream Woman.

At this part of the narrative the landlord paused; and, turning towards the window of the room in which we were sitting, looked in the direction of the stable-yard.

'So far,' he said, 'I tell you what was told to me. The little that remains to be added lies within my own experience. Between two and three months after the events

I have just been relating, Isaac Scatchard came to me, withered and old-looking before his time, just as you saw him to-day. He had his testimonials to character with him, and he asked me for employment here. Knowing that my wife and he were distantly related, I gave him a trial in consideration of that relationship, and liked him in spite of his queer habits. He is as sober, honest, and willing a man as there is in England. As for his restlessness at night, and his sleeping away his leisure time in the day, who can wonder at it after hearing his story? Besides, he never objects to being roused up, when he's wanted, so there's not much inconvenience to complain of, after all.'

'I suppose he is afraid of a return of that dreadful dream, and of waking out of it in the dark?'

'No,' returned the landlord. 'The dream comes back to him so often, that he has got to bear with it by this time resignedly enough. It's his wife keeps waking him at night, as he has often told me.'

'What! Has she never been heard of yet?'

'Never. Isaac himself has the one perpetual thought, that she is alive and looking for him. I believe he wouldn't let himself drop off to sleep towards two in the morning for a king's ransom. Two in the morning he says, is the time she will find him, one of these days. Two in the morning is the time, all the year round, when he likes to be most certain that he has got the clasp-knife safe about him. He does not mind being alone, as long as he is awake, except on the night before his birthday, when he firmly believes himself to be in peril of his life. The birthday has only come round once since he has been here, and then he sat up along with the night-porter. "She's looking for me," is all he says, when anybody speaks to him about the one anxiety of his life; "she's looking for me." He may be right. She *may* be looking for him. Who can tell?'

'Who can tell?' said I.

THE TAPESTRIED CHAMBER

Sir Walter Scott

About the end of the American War, when the officers of Lord Cornwallis's army which surrendered at Yorktown, and others, who had been made prisoners during the impolitic and ill-fated controversy, were returning to their own country, to relate their adventures and repose themselves after their fatigues, there was amongst them a general officer of the name of Browne. He was an officer of merit, as well as a gentleman of high consideration for family and attainments.

Some business had carried General Browne upon a tour through the western counties, when, in the conclusion of a morning stage, he found himself in the vicinity of a small country town, which presented a scene of uncommon beauty and of a character peculiarly English.

The little town, with its stately old church whose tower bore testimony to the devotion of ages long past, lay amidst pasture and corn-fields of small extent, but bounded and divided with hedge-row timber of great age and size. There were few marks of modern improvement. The environs of the place intimated neither the solitude of decay, nor the bustle of novelty; the houses were old, but in good repair; and the beautiful little river murmured freely on its way to the left of the town, neither restrained by a dam, nor bordered by a towing-path.

Upon a gentle eminence, nearly a mile to the southward of the town, were seen amongst many venerable oaks and tangled thickets the turrets of a castle, as old as the wars of York and Lancaster, but which seemed to have received important alterations during the age of Elizabeth and her successors. It had not been a place of great size; but whatever accommodation it formerly afforded, was, it must be supposed, still to be obtained within its walls; at least, such was the inference which General Browne drew from observing the smoke arise merrily from several of the ancient wreathed and carved chimney-stalks. The wall of the park ran alongside of the highway for two or three hundred yards; and through the different points by which the eye found glimpses into the woodland scenery, it seemed to be well stocked. Other points of view opened in succession; now a full one, of the front of the old castle, and now a side glimpse at its particular towers; the former rich in all the bizarrerie of the Elizabethian school, while the simple and solid strength of other parts of the building seemed to show that they had been raised more for defence than ostentation.

Delighted with the partial glimpses which he obtained of the castle through the woods and glades by which this ancient feudal fortress was surrounded, our military traveller was determined to inquire whether it might not deserve a nearer view, and whether it contained family pictures or other objects of curiosity worthy of a stranger's visit; when, leaving the vicinity of the park, he rolled through a clean and well-paved street, and stopped at the door of a well-frequented inn.

Before ordering horses to proceed on his journey. General Browne made inquiries concerning the proprietor of the château which had so attracted his admiration, and was equally surprised and pleased at hearing in reply a nobleman named whom we shall call Lord Woodville. How fortunate! Much of Browne's early recollections, both at school and at college, had been connected with young Woodville, whom, by a few questions, he now ascertained to be the same with the owner of this fair domain. He had been raised to the peerage by the decease of his father a few months before, and as the general learned from the landlord, the term of mourning being ended, was now taking possession of his paternal estate in the jovial season of merry autumn, accompanied by a select party of friends to enjoy the sports of a country famous for game.

This was delightful news to our traveller. Frank Woodville had been Richard Browne's fag at Eton, and his chosen intimate at Christ Church; their pleasures and their tasks had been the same; and the honest soldier's heart warmed to find his early friend in possession of so delightful a residence, and of an estate, as the landlord assured him with a nod and a wink, fully adequate to maintain and add to his dignity. Nothing was more natural than that the traveller should suspend a journey, which there was nothing to render hurried, to pay a visit to an old friend under such agreeable circumstances.

The fresh horses, therefore, had only the brief task of conveying the general's travelling carriage to Woodville Castle. A porter admitted them at a modern Gothic Lodge, built in that style to correspond with the castle itself, and at the same time rang a bell to give warning of the approach of visitors. Apparently the sound of the bell had suspended the separation of the company, bent on the various amusements of the morning; for, on entering the court of the château, several young men were lounging about in their sporting dresses, looking at, and criticising, the dogs which the keepers held in readiness to attend their pastime. As General Browne alighted, the young lord came to the gate of the hall, and for an instant gazed, as at a stranger, upon the countenance of his friend, on which war, with its fatigues and its wounds, had made a great alteration. But the uncertainty lasted no longer than till the visitor had spoken, and the hearty greeting which followed was such as can only be exchanged betwixt those who have passed together merry days of careless boyhood or early youth.

'If I could have formed a wish, my dear Browne,' said Lord Woodville, 'it would have been to have you here, of all men, upon this occasion, which my friends are good enough to hold as a sort of holiday. Do not think that you have been unwatched during the years you have been absent from us. I have traced you through your dangers, your triumphs, your misfortunes, and was delighted to see that, whether in victory or defeat, the name of my old friend was always distinguished with applause.'

The general made a suitable reply, and congratulated his friend on his new dignities, and the possession of a place and domain so beautiful.

'Nay, you have seen nothing of it as yet,' said Lord Woodville, 'and I trust you do not mean to leave us till you are better acquainted with it. It is true, I confess, that my present part is pretty large, and the old house, like other places of the kind, does not possess so much accommodation as the extent of the outward walls appears to promise. But we can give you a comfortable, old-fashioned room; and I venture to suppose that your campaigns have taught you to be glad of worse quarters.'

The general shrugged his shoulders and laughed. 'I presume,' he said, 'the worst apartment in your château is considerably superior to the old tobacco-cask, in which I was fain to take up my night's lodgings when I was in the bush, as the Virginians call it, with the light corps. There I lay, like Diogenes himself, so delighted with my covering from the elements, that I made a vain attempt to have it rolled on to my next quarters; but my commander, for the time, would give way to no such luxurious provision, and I took farewell of my beloved cask with tears in my eyes.'

'Well, then, since you do not fear your quarters,' said Lord Woodville, 'you will stay with me a week at least. Of guns, dogs, fishing-rods, flies, and means of sport by sea and land, we have enough and to spare: you cannot pitch on an amusement, but you will pitch on the means of pursuing it. But if you prefer the gun and pointers, I will go with you myself and see whether you have mended your shooting since you have been amongst the Indians of the back settlements.'

The general gladly accepted his friendly host's proposal in all its points. After a morning of manly exercise, the company met at dinner, where it was the delight of Lord Woodville to conduce to the display of the high properties of his recovered friend, so as to recommend him to his guests, most of whom were persons of distinction. He led General Browne to speak of the scenes he had witnessed; and as every word marked alike the brave officer and the sensible man, who retained possession of his cool judgment under the most imminent dangers, the company looked upon the soldier with general respect, as on one who had proved himself possessed of an uncommon portion of personal courage – that attribute, of all others, of which everybody desires to be thought possessed.

The day at Woodville Castle ended as usual in such mansions. The hospitality stopped within the limits of good order; music, in which the young lord was a proficient, succeeded to the circulation of the bottle: cards and billiards, for those who preferred such amusements, were in readiness: but the exercise of the morning required early hours, and not long after eleven o'clock the guests began to retire to their several apartments.

The young lord himself conducted his friend, General Browne, to the chamber destined for him, which answered the description he had given of it, being comfortable, but old-fashioned. The bed was of the massive form used in the end of the seventeenth century, and the curtains of faded silk heavily trimmed with tarnished gold. But then the sheets, pillows, and blankets looked delightful to the campaigner, when he thought of his mansion: the cask. There was an air of gloom in the tapestry hangings, which, with their worn-out graces, curtained the walls of the little chamber, and gently undulated as the autumnal breeze found its way through the ancient lattice window, which pattered and whistled as the air gained entrance. The toilet, too, with its mirror, turbaned, after the manner of the beginning of the century, with a coiffure of murrey-coloured silk, and its hundred strange-shaped boxes, providing for arrangements which had been obsolete for more than fifty years, had an antique and in so far a melancholy aspect. But nothing could blaze more brightly and cheerfully than the two large wax candles; or if aught could rival them, it was the flaming, bickering faggots in the chimney, that sent at once their gleam and their warmth through the snug apartment; which, notwithstanding the general antiquity of its appearance, was not wanting in the least convenience that modern habits rendered either necessary or desirable.

'This is an old-fashioned sleeping-apartment, General,' said the young lord; 'but I hope you will find nothing that makes you envy your old tobacco-cask.'

'I am not particular respecting my lodgings,' replied the general; 'yet were I to make any choice, I would prefer this chamber, by many degrees, to the gayer and more modern rooms of your family mansion. Believe me that when I unite its modern air of comfort with its venerable antiquity, and recollect that it is your lordship's property, I shall feel in better quarters here than if I were in the best hotel London could afford.'

'I trust – I have no doubt – that you will find yourself as comfortable as I wish you, my dear General,' said the young nobleman; and once more bidding his guest good night, he shook him by the hand and withdrew.

The general again looked round him, and internally congratulating himself on his return to peaceful life, the comforts of which were endeared by the recollection of the hardships and dangers he had lately sustained, undressed himself, and prepared himself for a luxurious night's rest.

Here, contrary to the custom of this species of tale, we leave the general in possession of his apartment until the next morning.

The company assembled for breakfast at an early hour, but without the appearance of General Browne, who seemed the guest that Lord Woodville was desirous of honouring above all whom his hospitality had assembled around him. He more than once expressed surprise at the general's absence, and at length sent a servant to make inquiry after him. The man brought back information that General Browne had been walking abroad since an early hour of the morning, in defiance of the weather, which was misty and ungenial.

'The custom of a soldier,' said the young nobleman to his friends. 'Many of them acquire habitual vigilance, and cannot sleep after the early hour at which their duty usually commands them to be alert.'

Yet the explanation which Lord Woodville thus offered to the company seemed hardly satisfactory to his own mind, and it was in a fit of silence and abstraction that he awaited the return of the general. It took place near an hour after the breakfast bell had rung. He looked fatigued and feverish. His hair – the powdering and arrangement of which was at this time one of the most important occupations of a man's whole day, and marked his fashion as much as, in the present time, the tying of a cravat or the want of one – was dishevelled, uncurled, void of powder, and dank with dew. His clothes were huddled on with a careless negligence, remarkable in a military man, whose real or supposed duties are usually held to include some attention to the toilet; and his looks were haggard and ghastly in a peculiar degree.

'So you have stolen a march upon us this morning, my dear General,' said Lord Woodville; 'or you have not found your bed so much to your mind as I had hoped and you seemed to expect. How did you rest last night?'

'Oh, excellently well! remarkably well! Never better in my life,' said General Browne rapidly, and yet with an air of embarrassment which was obvious to his friend.

He then hastily swallowed a cup of tea, and neglecting or refusing whatever else was offered, seemed to fall into a fit of abstraction.

'You will take the gun today, General,' said his friend and host, but had to repeat the question twice ere he received the abrupt answer: 'No, my lord; I cannot have the honour of spending another day with your lordship; my post-horses are ordered, and will be here directly.'

All who were present showed surprise, and Lord Woodville immediately replied, 'Post-horses, my good friend! what can you possibly want with them when you promised to stay with me quietly for at least a week?'

'I believe,' said the general, obviously much embarrassed, 'that I might, in the pleasure of my first meeting with your lordship, have said something about stopping here a few days; but I have since found it altogether impossible.'

'That is very extraordinary,' answered the young nobleman. 'You seemed quite disengaged yesterday, and you cannot have had a summons today; for our post has not come up from the town, and therefore you cannot have received any letters.'

General Browne, without giving any further explanation, muttered something of indispensable business, and insisted on the absolute necessity of his departure in a manner which silenced all opposition on the part of his host – who saw that his resolution was taken, and forebore further importunity.

'At least, however,' he said, 'permit me, my dear Browne, since go you will, or must, to show you the view from the terrace, which the mist that is now rising will soon display.'

He threw open a sash window, and stepped down upon the terrace as he spoke. The general followed him mechanically, but seemed little to attend to what his host was saying, as, looking across an extended and rich prospect, he pointed out the different objects worthy of observation. Thus they moved on till Lord Woodville had attained his purpose of drawing his guest entirely apart from the rest of the company, when, turning round upon him with an air of great solemnity, he addressed him thus:

'Richard Browne, my old and very dear friend, we are now alone. Let me conjure you to answer me upon the word of a friend, and the honour of a soldier. How did you in reality rest during the night?'

'Most wretchedly indeed, my lord,' answered the general, in the same tone of solemnity; 'so miserably that I would not run the risk of such a second night, not only for all the lands belonging to this castle, but for all the country which I see from this elevated point of view.'

'This is most extraordinary,' said the young lord, as if speaking to himself, 'then there must be something in the reports concerning that apartment.' Again turning to the general, he said, 'For God's sake, my dear friend, be candid with me, and let me know the disagreeable particulars which have befallen you under a roof where, with consent of the owner, you should have met nothing save comfort.'

The general seemed distressed by this appeal, and paused a moment before he replied. 'My dear lord,' he at length said, 'what happened to me last night is of a nature so peculiar and so unpleasant, that I could hardly bring myself to detail it even to your lordship, were it not that, independent of my wish to gratify any request of yours, I think that sincerity on my part may lead to some explanation about a circumstance equally painful and mysterious. To others, the communications I am about to make, might place me in the light of a weak-minded, superstitious fool who suffered his own imagination to delude and bewilder him; but you have known me in childhood and youth, and will not suspect me of having adopted in manhood the feelings and frailties from which my early years were free.' Here he paused, and his friend replied:

'Do not doubt my perfect confidence in the truth of your communication, however strange it may be,' replied Lord Woodville, 'I know your firmness of disposition too well to suspect you could be made the object of imposition, and am aware that your honour and your friendship will equally deter you from exaggerating whatever you may have witnessed.

'Well then,' said the general, 'I will proceed with my story as well as I can, relying upon your candour; and yet distinctly feeling that I would rather face a battery than recall to my mind the odious recollections of last night.'

He paused a second time, and then, perceiving that Lord Woodville remained silent and in an attitude of attention, he commenced, though not without obvious reluctance, the history of his night's adventures in the Tapestried Chamber.

'I undressed and went to bed as soon as your lordship left me yesterday evening; but the wood in the chimney, which nearly fronted my bed, blazed brightly and cheerfully, and, aided by a hundred exciting recollections of my childhood and youth which had been recalled by the unexpected pleasure of meeting your lordship, prevented me from falling immediately asleep. I ought, however, to say that these reflections were all of a pleasant and agreeable kind, grounded on a sense of having for a time exchanged the labour, fatigues, and dangers of my profession, for the enjoyments of a peaceful life, and the reunion of those friendly and affectionate ties which I had torn asunder at the rude summons of war.

'While such pleasing reflections were stealing over my mind, and gradually lulling me to slumber, I was suddenly aroused by a sound like that of the rustling of a silken gown and the tapping of a pair of high-heeled shoes, as if a woman were walking in the apartment. Ere I could draw the curtain to see what the matter was, the figure of a little woman passed between the bed and the fire. The back of this form was turned to me, and I could observe, from the shoulders and the neck, it was that of an old woman whose dress was an old-fashioned gown which, I think, ladies call a sacque; that is, a sort of robe, completely loose in the body, but gathered into small plaits upon the neck and shoulders, which fall down to the ground and terminate in a species of train.

'I thought the intrusion singular enough, but never harboured for a moment the idea that what I saw was anything more than the mortal form of some old woman about the establishment who had a fancy to dress like her grandmother, and who, having perhaps (as your lordship mentioned that you were rather straitened for room) been dislodged from her chamber for my accommodation, had forgotten the circumstance, and returned by twelve to her old haunt. Under this persuasion I moved myself in bed and coughed a little to make the intruder sensible of my being in possession of the premises. She turned slowly round, but gracious Heaven! my lord, what a countenance did she display to me! There was no longer any question what she was, or any thought of her being a living being. Upon a face which wore the fixed features of a corpse, were imprinted the vilest and most hideous passions which had animated her while she lived. The body of some atrocious criminal seemed to have been given up from the grave, and the soul restored from the penal fire, in order to form, for a space, a union with the ancient accomplice of its guilt. I started up in bed, and sat upright, supporting myself on my palms, as I gazed at this horrible spectre. The hag made, as it seemed, a single and swift stride to the bed where I lay, and squatted herself down upon it, in precisely the same attitude which I had assumed in the extremity of horror, advancing her diabolical countenance within half a yard of mine, with a grin which seemed to intimate the malice and the derision of an incarnate fiend.'

Here General Browne stopped and wiped from his brow the cold perspiration with which the recollection of his horrible vision had covered it.

'My lord,' he said, 'I am no coward. I have been in all the mortal dangers incidental to my profession, and I may truly boast that no man ever knew Richard Browne dishonour the sword he wears; but in these horrible circumstances, under the eyes, and, it seemed, almost in the grasp of an incarnation of an evil spirit, all firmness forsook me, all manhood melted from me like wax in the furnace, and I felt my hair individually bristle. The current of my life-blood ceased to flow, and I sank back in a swoon, as very a victim to panic terror as ever was a village girl or a child of ten years old. How long I lay in this condition I cannot pretend to guess.

'But I was roused by the castle clock striking one, so loud that it seemed as if it were in the very room. It was some time before I dared open my eyes lest they should again encounter the horrible spectacle. When, however, I summoned courage to look up, she was no longer visible. My first idea was to pull my bell, wake the servants, and remove to a garret or a hay-loft, to be ensured against a second visitation. Nay, I will confess the truth, that my resolution was altered, not by the shame of exposing myself, but by the very fear that, as the bell-cord hung by the chimney, I might, in making my way to it, be again crossed by the fiendish hag, who, I figured to myself, might be still lurking about some corner of the apartment.

'I will not pretend to describe what hot and cold fever fits tormented me for the rest of the night, through broken sleep, weary vigils, and that dubious state which forms the neutral ground between them. A hundred terrible objects appeared to haunt me; but there was the great difference betwixt the vision which I have described and those which followed, that I knew the last to be deceptions of my own fancy and over-excited nerves.

'Day at last appeared, and I rose from my bed ill in health, and humiliated in mind. I was ashamed of myself as a man and a soldier, and still more so at feeling my own extreme desire to escape from the haunted apartment, which, however, conquered all other considerations; so that, huddling on my clothes with the most careless haste, I made my escape from your lordship's mansion, to seek in the open air some relief to my nervous system, shaken as it was by this horrible encounter with a visitant, for such I must believe her, from the other world. Your lordship has now heard the cause of my discomposure, and of my sudden desire to leave your hospitable castle. In other places I trust we may often meet; but God protect me from spending a second night under that roof!'

Strange as the general's tale was, he spoke with such a deep air of conviction that it cut short all the usual commentaries which are made on such stories. Lord Woodville never once asked him if he was sure he did not dream of the apparition, or suggested any of the possibilities by which it is fashionable to explain supernatural appearances as wild vagaries of the fancy or deceptions of the optic nerves. On the contrary he seemed deeply impressed with the truth and reality of what he had heard; and, after a considerable pause, regretted, with much appearance of sincerity, that his early friend should in his house have suffered so severely.

'I am the more sorry for your pain, my dear Browne,' he continued, 'that it is the unhappy, though most unexpected, result of an experiment of my own! You must know, that for my father and grandfather's time, at least, the apartment which was assigned to you last night had been shut on account of reports that it was disturbed by supernatural sights and noises. When I came, a few weeks since, into possession of the estate, I thought the accommodation which the castle afforded for my friends was not extensive enough to permit the inhabitants of the invisible world to retain possession of a comfortable sleeping-apartment. I therefore caused the Tapestried Chamber, as we call it, to be opened; and without destroying its air of antiquity, I had such new articles of furniture placed in it as became the modern times. Yet as the opinion that the room was haunted very strongly prevailed among the domestics, and was also known in the neighbourhood and to many of my friends, I feared some prejudice might be entertained by the first occupant of the Tapestried Chamber, which might tend to revive the evil report which it had laboured under, and so disappoint my purpose of rendering it a useful part of the house. I must confess, my dear Browne, that your arrival yesterday, agreeable to me for a thousand reasons besides, seemed the most favourable opportunity of removing the unpleasant rumours which attached to the room, since your courage was indubitable and your mind free of any preoccupation on the subject. I could not, therefore, have chosen a more fitting subject for my experiment.'

'Upon my life!' said General Browne, somewhat hastily, 'I am infinitely obliged to your lordship – very particularly indebted indeed. I am likely to remember for some time the consequences of the experiment, as your lordship is pleased to call it.'

'Nay, now you are unjust, my dear friend,' said Lord Woodville. 'You have only to reflect for a single moment in order to be convinced that I could not augur the possibility of the pain to which you have been so unhappily exposed. I was yesterday morning a complete sceptic on the subject of supernatural appearances. Nay, I am sure that had I told you what was said about your room, those very reports would have induced you, by your own choice, to select it for your accommodation. It was my misfortune, perhaps my error, but really cannot be termed my fault, that you have been afflicted so strangely.'

'Strangely indeed!' said the general, resuming his good temper, 'and I acknowledge that I have no right to be offended with your lordship for treating me like what I used to think myself – a man of some firmness and courage. But I see my post-horses have arrived, and I must not detain your lordship from your amusement.'

'Nay, my old friend,' said Lord Woodville, 'since you

cannot stay with us another day, which, indeed, I can no longer urge, give me at least half an hour more. You used to love pictures, and I have a gallery of portraits, some of them by Vandyke, representing ancestry to whom the property and castle formerly belonged. I think that several of them will strike you as possessing merit.'

General Browne accepted the invitation, though somewhat unwillingly. It was evident he was not to breathe freely or at ease until he left Woodville Castle far behind him. He could not refuse his friend's invitation, however; and the less so, that he was a little ashamed of the peevishness which he had displayed towards his well-meaning entertainer.

The general, therefore, followed Lord Woodville through several rooms, into a long gallery hung with pictures, which the latter pointed out to his guest, telling the names, and giving some account of the personages whose portraits presented themselves in progression. General Browne was but little interested in the details which these accounts conveyed to him. They were, indeed, of the kind which are usually found in the old family gallery. Here was a cavalier who had ruined the estate in the royal cause; there a fine lady who had reinstated it by contracting a match with a wealthy Roundhead. There hung a gallant who had been in danger for corresponding with the exiled Court of St. Germain's; here one who had taken arms for William at the Revolution; and there a third that had thrown his weight alternately into the scale of Whig and Tory.

While Lord Woodville was cramming these words into his guest's ear, 'against the stomach of his sense,' they gained the middle of the gallery, when he beheld General Browne suddenly start, and assume an attitude of the utmost surprise, not unmixed with fear, as his eyes were caught and suddenly riveted by a portrait of an old lady in a sacque, the fashionable dress of the end of the seventeenth century.

'There she is!' he exclaimed. 'There she is, in form and features, though inferior in demoniac expression to the accursed hag who visited me last night!'

'If that be the case,' said the young nobleman, 'there can remain no longer any doubt of the horrible reality of your apparition. That is the picture of a wretched ancestress of

119

mine, of whose crimes a black and fearful catalogue is recorded in a family history in my charter-chest. The recital of them would be too horrible; it is enough to say, that in yon fatal apartment incest and unnatural murder were committed. I will restore it to the solitude to which the better judgment of those who preceded me had consigned it; and never shall anyone, so long as I can prevent it, be exposed to a repetition of the supernatural horrors which could shake such courage as yours.'

Thus the friends, who had met with such glee, parted in a very different mood; Lord Woodville to command the Tapestried Chamber to be unmantled and the door built up; and General Browne to seek in some less beautiful country, and with some less dignified friend, forgetfulness of the painful night which he had passed in Woodville Castle.

THE OPEN DOOR

Mrs. Oliphant

I took the house of Brentwood on my return from India in 18—, for the temporary accommodation of my family, until I could find a permanent home for them. It had many advantages which made it peculiarly appropriate. It was within reach of Edinburgh, and my boy Roland, whose education had been considerably neglected, could go in and out of school, which was thought to be better for him than either leaving home altogether or staying there always with a tutor. The first of these expedients would have seemed preferable to me, the second commended itself to his mother. The doctor, like a judicious man, took the midway between. 'Put him on his pony, and let him ride into the High School every morning; it will do him all the good in the world,' Dr. Simson said; 'and when it is bad weather there is the train.' His mother accepted this solution of the difficulty more easily than I could have hoped; and our pale-faced boy, who had never known anything more invigorating than Simla, began to encounter the brisk breezes of the North in the subdued severity of the month of May. Before the time of the vacation in July we had the satisfaction of seeing him begin to acquire something of the brown and ruddy complexion of his schoolfellows. The English system did not commend itself to Scotland in these days. There was no little Eton at Fettes; nor do I think, if there had been, that a genteel exotic of that class would have tempted either my wife or me. The lad was doubly precious to us, being the only one left us of many; and he was fragile in body, we believed, and deeply sensitive in mind. To keep him at home, and yet to send him to school – to combine the advantages of the two systems – seemed to be everything that could be desired. The two girls also found at Brentwood everything they wanted. They were near enough to Edinburgh to have masters and lessons as many as they required for completing that never-ending education which the young people seem to require nowadays. Their mother married me when she was younger than Agatha, and I should like to see them improve upon their mother! I myself was then no more than twenty-five – an age at which I see the young fellows now groping about them, with no notion what they are going to do with their lives. However, I suppose every generation has a conceit of itself which elevates it, in its own opinion, above that which comes after it.

Brentwood stands on that fine and wealthy slope of country, one of the richest in Scotland, which lies between the Pentland Hills and the Firth. In clear weather you could see the blue gleam – like a bent bow, embracing the wealthy fields and scattered houses – of the great estuary on one side of you; and on the other the blue heights, not gigantic like those we had been used to, but just high enough for all the glories of the atmosphere, the play of clouds, and sweet reflections which give to a hilly country an interest and a charm which nothing else can emulate. Edinburgh, with its two lesser heights – the Castle and the Calton Hill – its spires and towers piercing through the smoke, and Arthur's Seat lying crouched behind, like a guardian no longer very needful, taking his repose beside the well-loved charge, which is now, so to speak, able to take care of itself without him – lay at our right hand. From the lawn and the drawing-room windows we could see all these varieties of landscape. The colour was sometimes a little chilly, but sometimes, also, as animated and full of vicissitude as a drama. I was never tired of it. Its colour and freshness revived the eyes which had grown weary of arid plains and blazing skies. It was always cheery, and fresh, and full of repose.

The village of Brentwood lay almost under the house, on the other side of the deep little ravine, down which a stream – which ought to have been a lovely, wild, and frolicsome little river – flowed between its rocks and trees. The river, like so many in that district, had, however, in its earlier life been sacrificed to trade, and was grimy with paper-making. But this did not affect our pleasure in it so much as I have known it to affect other streams. Perhaps our water was more rapid – perhaps less clogged with dirt and refuse. Our side of the dell was charmingly *accidenté*, and clothed with fine trees, through which various paths wound down to the river-side and to the village bridge which crossed the stream. The village lay in the hollow, and climbed, with very prosaic houses, the other side. Village architecture does not flourish in Scotland. The blue slates and the grey stone are sworn foes to the picturesque; and though I do not, for my part, dislike the interior of an old-fashioned pewed and galleried church, with its little family settlements on all sides, the square box outside, with its bit of a spire like a handle to lift it by, is not an improvement to the landscape. Still, a cluster of houses on different elevations – with scraps of garden coming in between, a hedgerow with clothes laid out to dry, the opening of a street with its rural sociability, the women at their doors, the slow wagon lumbering along – gives a centre to the landscape. It was cheerful to look at, and convenient in a hundred ways. Within ourselves we had walks in plenty, the glen being always beautiful in all its phases, whether the woods were green in the spring or ruddy in the autumn. In the park which surrounded the house were the ruins of the former mansion of Brentwood, a much smaller and less important house than the solid Georgian edifice which we inhabited. The ruins were picturesque, however, and gave importance to the place. Even we, who were but temporary tenants, felt a vague pride in them, as if they somehow reflected a certain consequence upon ourselves. The old building had the remains of a tower, an indistinguishable mass of masonwork, overgrown with ivy, and the shells of walls attached to this were half filled up with soil. I had never examined it closely, I am ashamed to say. There was a large room, or what had been a large room, with the lower part of the windows still existing, on the principal floor, and underneath other windows, which were perfect, though half filled up with fallen soil, and waving with a wild growth of brambles and chance growths of all kinds. This was the oldest part of all. At a little distance were some very commonplace and disjointed fragments of the building, one of them suggesting a certain pathos by its very commonness and the complete wreck which it showed. This was the end of a low gable, a bit of grey wall, all encrusted with lichens, in which was a common doorway. Probably it had been a servants' entrance, a back door, or opening into what are called 'the offices' in Scotland. No offices remained to be entered – pantry and kitchen had all been swept out of being; but there stood the doorway open and vacant, free to all the winds, to the rabbits, and every wild creature. It struck my eye, the first time I went to Brentwood, like a melancholy comment upon a life that was over. A door that led to nothing – closed once perhaps with anxious care, bolted and guarded, now void of any meaning. It impressed me, I remember, from the first; so perhaps it may be said that my mind was prepared to attach to it an importance which nothing justified.

The summer was a very happy period of repose for us all. The warmth of Indian suns was still in our veins. It seemed to us that we could never have enough of the greenness, the dewiness, the freshness of the northern landscape. Even its mists were pleasant to us, taking all the fever out of us, and pouring in vigour and refreshment. In autumn we followed the fashion of the time, and went away for change which we did not in the least require. It was when the family had settled down for the winter, when the days were short and dark, and the rigorous reign of frost upon us, that the incidents occurred which alone could justify me in intruding upon the world my private affairs. These incidents were, however, of so curious a character, that I hope my inevitable references to my own family and pressing personal interests will meet with a general pardon.

I was absent in London when these events began. In London an old Indian plunges back into the interests with which all his previous life has been associated, and meets old friends at every step. I had been circulating among some half-dozen of these – enjoying the return to my former life in shadow, though I had been so thankful in substance to throw it aside – and had missed some of my home letters, what with going down from Friday to Monday to old Benbow's place in the country, and stopping on the way back to dine and sleep at Sellar's and to take a look into Cross's stables, which occupied another day. It is never safe to miss one's letters. In this transitory life, as the Prayer-book says, how can one ever be certain what is going to happen? All was well at home. I knew exactly (I thought) what they would have to say to me: 'The weather has been so fine, that Roland has not once gone by train, and he enjoys the ride beyond anything.' 'Dear papa, be sure that you don't forget anything, but bring us so-and-so, and so-and-so' – a list as long as my arm. Dear girls and dearer mother! I would not for the world have forgotten their commissions, or lost their little letters, for all the Benbows and Crosses in the world.

But I was confident in my home-comfort and peacefulness. When I got back to my club, however, three or four letters were lying for me, upon some of which I noticed the 'immediate,' 'urgent,' which old-fashioned people and anxious people still believe will influence the post-office and quicken the speed of the mails. I was about to open one of these, when the club porter brought me two telegrams, one of which, he said, had arrived the night before. I opened, as was to be expected, the last first, and this was what I read: 'Why don't you come or answer? For God's sake, come. He is much worse.' This was a thunderbolt to fall upon a man's head who had one only son, and he the light of his eyes! The other telegram, which I opened with hands trembling so much that I lost time by my haste, was to much the same purport: 'No better; doctor afraid of brain-fever. Calls for you day and night. Let nothing detain you.' The first thing I did was to look up the time-tables to see if there was any way of getting off sooner than by the night-train, though I knew well enough there was not; and then I read the letters, which furnished, alas! too clearly, all the details. They told me that the boy had been pale for some time, with a scared look. His mother had noticed it before I left home, but would not say anything to alarm me. This look had increased day by day; and soon it was observed that Roland came home at a wild gallop through the park, his pony panting and in foam, himself 'as white as a sheet,' but with the perspiration streaming from his forehead. For a long time he had resisted all questioning, but at length had developed such strange changes of mood, showing a reluctance to go to school, a desire to be fetched in the carriage at night – which was a ridiculous piece of luxury – an unwillingness to go out into the grounds, and nervous starts at every sound, that his mother had insisted upon an explanation. When the boy – our boy Roland, who had never known what fear was – began to talk to her of voices he had heard in the park, and shadows that had appeared to him among the ruins, my wife promptly put him to bed and sent for Dr. Simson – which, of course, was the only thing to do.

I hurried off that evening, as may be supposed, with an anxious heart. How I got through the hours before the starting of the train, I cannot tell. We must be thankful for the quickness of the railway when in anxiety; but to have thrown myself into a post-chaise as soon as horses could be put to, would have been a relief. I got to Edinburgh very early in the blackness of the winter morning, and scarcely dared look the man in the face at whom I gasped, 'What news?' My wife had sent the brougham for me, which I concluded, before the man spoke, was a bad sign. His answer was that stereotyped answer which leaves the imagination so wildly free – 'Just the same.' Just the same! What might that mean? The horses seemed to me to creep along the long, dark country road. As we dashed through the park, I thought I heard someone moaning among the trees, and clenched my fist at him(whoever he might be) with fury. Why had the fool of a woman at the gate allowed anyone to come in to disturb the quiet of the place? If I had not been in such hot haste to get home, I think I should have stopped the carriage and got out to see what tramp it was that had made an entrance, and chosen my grounds, of all places in the world – when my boy was ill! – to grumble and groan in. But I had no reason to complain of our slow pace here. The horses flew like lightning along the intervening path, and drew up at the door all panting, as if they had run a race. My wife stood waiting to receive me with a pale face, and a candle in her hand, which made her look paler still as the wind blew the flame about. 'He is sleeping,' she said in a whisper, as if her voice might wake him. And I replied, when I could find my voice, also in a whisper, as though the jingling of the horses' furniture and the sound of their hoofs must not have been more dangerous. I stood on the steps with her a moment, almost afraid to go in, now that I was here; and it seemed to me that I saw without observing, if I may say so, that the horses were unwilling to turn round, though their stables lay that way, or that the men were unwilling. These things occurred to me afterwards, though at the moment I was not capable of anything but to ask questions and to hear the condition of the boy.

I looked at him from the door of his room, for we were afraid to go near, lest we should disturb that blessed sleep. It looked like actual sleep – not the lethargy into which my wife told me he would sometimes fall. She told me everything in the next room, which communicated with his, rising now and then and going to the door of communication; and in this there was much that was very startling and confusing to the mind. It appeared that ever since the winter began, since it was early dark and night had fallen before his return from school, he had been hearing voices among the ruins – at first only a groaning, he said, at which his pony was as much alarmed as he was, but by degrees a voice. The tears ran down my wife's cheeks as she described to me how he would start up in the night and cry out, 'Oh, mother, let me in! oh, mother, let me in!' with a pathos which rent her heart. And she sitting there all the time, only longing to do everything his heart could desire! But though she would try to soothe him, crying, 'You are at home, my darling. I am here. Don't you know me? Your mother is here,' he would only stare at her, and after a while spring up again with the same cry. At other times he would be quite reasonable, she said, asking eagerly when I was coming, but declaring that he must go with me as soon as I did, 'to let them in.' 'The doctor thinks his nervous system must have received a shock,' my wife said. 'Oh, Henry, can it be that we have pushed him on too much with his work – a delicate boy like Roland? – and what is his work in comparison with his health? Even you would think little of honours or prizes if it hurt the boy's health.' Even I! as if I were an inhuman father sacrificing my child to my ambition. But I would not increase her trouble by taking any notice. After a while they persuaded me to lie down, to rest, and to eat – none of which things had been possible since I received their letters. The mere fact of being on the spot, of course, in itself was a great thing; and when I knew that I could be called in a moment, as soon as he was awake and wanted me, I felt capable, even in the dark, chill morning twilight, to snatch an hour or two's sleep. As it happened, I was so worn out with the strain of anxiety and he so quieted and consoled by knowing I had come, that I was not disturbed till the afternoon, when the twilight had again settled down. There was just daylight enough to see his face when I went to him: and what a change in a fortnight! He was paler and more worn, I thought, than ever in those dreadful days in the plains before we left India. His hair seemed to me to have grown long and lank; his eyes were like blazing lights projecting out of his white face. He got hold of my hand in a cold and tremendous clutch, and waved to everybody to go away. 'Go away – even mother,' he said, 'go away.' This went to her heart, for she did not like that even I should have more of the boy's confidence than herself; but my wife has never been a woman to think of herself, and she left us alone. 'Are they all gone?' he said, eagerly. 'They would not let me speak. The doctor treated me as if I were a fool. You know I am not a fool, papa.'

'Yes, yes, my boy, I know; but you are ill, and quiet is so necessary. You are not only not a fool, Roland, but you are reasonable and understand. When you are ill you must deny yourself; you must not do everything that you might do being well.'

He waved his thin hand with a sort of indignation. 'Then, father, I am not ill,' he cried. 'Oh, I thought when you came you would not stop me – you would see the sense of it! What do you think is the matter with me? Simson is well enough, but he is only a doctor. What do you think is the matter with me? I am no more ill than you are. A doctor, of course, he thinks you are ill the moment he looks at you – that's what he's there for – and claps you into bed.'

'Which is the best place for you at present, my dear boy.'

'I made up my mind,' cried the little fellow, 'that I would stand it till you came home. I said to myself, I won't frighten mother and the girls. But now, father,' he cried, half jumping out of bed, 'it's not illness – it's a secret.'

His eyes shone so wildly, his face was so swept with strong feeling, that my heart sank within me. It could be nothing but fever that did it, and fever had been so fatal. I got him into my arms to put him back into bed. 'Roland,' I said, humouring the poor child, which I knew was the only way, 'if you are going to tell me this secret to do any good, you know you must be quite quiet, and not excite yourself. If you excite yourself, I must not let you speak.'

'Yes, father,' said the boy. He was quiet directly, like a man, as if he quite understood. When I had lain him back on his pillow, he looked up at me with that grateful sweet look with which children, when they are ill, break one's heart, the water coming into his eyes in his weakness. 'I was sure as soon as you were here you would know what to do,' he said.

'To be sure, my boy. Now keep quiet, and tell it all out like a man.' To think I was telling lies to my own child! for I did it only to humour him, thinking, poor little fellow, his brain was wrong.

'Yes, father. Father, there is someone in the park — someone that has been badly used.'

'Hush, my dear; you remember, there is to be no excitement. Well, who is this somebody, and who has been ill-using him? We will soon put a stop to that.'

'Ah,' cried Roland, 'but it is not so easy as you think. I don't know who it is. It is just a cry. Oh, if you could hear it! It gets into my head in my sleep. I heard it as clear — as clear; and they think that I am dreaming — or raving perhaps,' the boy said, with a sort of disdainful smile.

This look of his perplexed me; it was less like fever than I thought. 'Are you quite sure you have not dreamt it, Roland?' I said.

'Dreamt? — that!' He was springing up again when he suddenly bethought himself, and lay down with the same sort of smile on his face. 'The pony heard it too,' he said. 'She jumped as if she had been shot. If I had not grasped at the reins — for I was frightened, father —'

'No shame to you, my boy,' said I, though I scarcely knew how.

'If I hadn't held to her like a leech, she'd have pitched me over her head, and she never drew breath till we were at the door. Did the pony dream it?' he said. with a soft disdain, yet indulgence for my foolishness. Then he added slowly: 'It was only a cry the first time, and all the time before you went away. I wouldn't tell you, for it was so wretched to be frightened. I thought it might be a hare or a rabbit snared, and I went in the morning and looked, but there was nothing. It was after you went I heard it really first, and this is what he says.' He raised himself on his elbow close to me, and looked me in the face. ' "Oh, mother, let me in! oh, mother, let me in!"' As he said the words a mist came over his face, the mouth quivered, the soft features all melted and changed, and when he had ended these pitiful words, dissolved in a shower of heavy tears.

Was it an hallucination? Was it the fever of the brain? Was it the disordered fancy caused by great bodily weakness? How could I tell? I thought it wisest to accept it as if it were all true.

'This is very touching, Roland,' I said.

'Oh, if you had just heard it, father! I said to myself, if father heard it he would do something; but, mamma, you know, she's given over to Simson, and that fellow's a doctor, and never thinks of anything but clapping you into bed.'

'We must not blame Simson for being a doctor, Roland.'

'No, no,' said my boy, with delightful toleration and indulgence; 'oh, no; that's the good of him – that's what he's for; I know that. But you – you are different; you are just, father: and you'll do something – directly, papa, directly – this very night.'

'Surely,' I said. 'No doubt it is some little lost child.'

He gave me a sudden, swift look, investigating my face as though to see whether, after all, this was everything my eminence as 'father' came to – no more than that? Then he got hold of my shoulder, clutching it with his thin hand: 'Look here,' he said, with a quiver in his voice; 'suppose it wasn't – living at all!'

'My dear boy, how then could you have heard it?' I said.

He turned away from me with a pettish exclamation – 'As if you didn't know better than that!'

'Do you want to tell me it is a ghost?' I said.

Roland withdrew his hand; his countenance assumed an aspect of great dignity and gravity; a slight quiver remained about his lips. 'Whatever it was – you always said we were not to call names. It was something – in trouble. Oh, father, in terrible trouble!'

'But, my boy,' I said – I was at my wits' end – 'if it was a child that was lost, or any poor human creature – but, Roland, what do you want me to do?'

'I should know if I was you,' said the child, eagerly. 'That is what I always said to myself – Father will know.

Oh, papa. papa, to have to face it night after night, in such terrible, terrible trouble! and never to be able to do it any good. I don't want to cry; it's like a baby, I know; but what can I do else? – out there all by itself in the ruin, and nobody to help it. I can't bear it, I can't bear it!' cried my generous boy. And in his weakness he burst out, after many attempts to restrain it, into a great childish fit of sobbing and tears.

I do not know that I ever was in a greater perplexity in my life; and afterwards, when I thought of it, there was something comic in it too. It is bad enough to find your child's mind possessed with the conviction that he has seen – or heard – a ghost. But that he should require you to go instantly and help that ghost, was the most bewildering experience that had ever come my way. I was a sober man myself, and not superstitious – at least any more than everybody is superstitious. Of course I do not believe in ghosts; but I don't deny, any more than other people, that there are stories that I cannot pretend to understand. My blood got a sort of chill in my veins at the idea that Roland should be a ghost-seer; for that generally means an hysterical temperament and weak health, and all that men most hate and fear for their children. But that I should take up his ghost and right its wrongs, and save it from its trouble, was such a mission as was enough to confuse any man. I did my best to console my boy without giving any promise of this astonishing kind; but he was too sharp for me. He would have none of my caresses. With sobs breaking in at intervals upon his voice, and the rain-drops hanging on his eyelids, he yet returned to the charge.

'It will be there now – it will be there all the night. Oh, think, papa, think of it as me! I can't rest for thinking of it. Don't!' he cried, putting away my hand – 'don't! You go and help it, and mother can take care of me.'

'But, Roland, what can I do?'

My boy opened his eyes, which were large with weakness and fever, and gave me a smile such, I think, as sick children only know the secret of. 'I was sure you would know as soon as you came. I always said – Father will know: and mother,' he cried, with a softening of repose upon his face, his limbs relaxing, his form sinking with a luxurious ease in his bed – 'mother can come and take care of me.'

I called her, and saw him turn to her with the complete dependence of a child, and then I went away and left them, as perplexed a man as any in Scotland. I must say, however, I had this consolation, that my mind was greatly eased about Roland. He might be under an hallucination, but his head was clear enough, and I did not think him so ill as everybody else did. The girls were astonished even at the ease with which I took it. 'How do you think he is?' they said in a breath, coming round me, laying hold of me. 'Not half as ill as I expected,' I said; 'not very bad at all.' 'Oh, papa, you are a darling,' cried Agatha, kissing me, and crying upon my shoulder; while little Jeanie, who was as pale as Roland, clasped both her arms round mine, and could not speak at all. I knew nothing about it, not half so much as Simson: but they believed in me; they had a feeling that all would go right now. God is very good to you when your children look to you like that. It makes one humble, not proud. I was not worthy of it; and then I recollected that I had to act the part of a father to Roland's ghost which made me almost laugh, though I might just as well have cried. It was the strangest mission that ever was entrusted to mortal man.

It was then I remembered suddenly the look of the men when they turned to take the brougham to the stables in the dark that morning: they had not liked it, and the horses had not liked it. I remembered that even in my anxiety about Roland I had heard them tearing along the avenue back to the stables, and had made a memorandum mentally that I must speak of it. It seemed to me that the best thing I could do was to go to the stables now and make a few inquiries. It is impossible to fathom the minds of rustics; there might be some devilry of practical joking, for anything I knew; or they might have some interest in getting up a bad reputation for the Brentwood avenue. It was getting dark by the time I went out, and nobody who knows the country will need to be told how black is the darkness of a November night under high laurel-bushes and yew-trees. I walked into the heart of the shrubberies two or three times, not seeing a step before me, till I came out upon the broader carriage road, where the trees opened a little, and there was a faint grey glimmer of sky visible, under which the great limes and elms stood darkling like ghosts; but it grew black again as I approached the corner where the ruins lay. Both eyes and ears were on the alert, as may be supposed; but I could see nothing in the absolute gloom, and, so far as I can recollect, I heard nothing. Nevertheless there came a strong impression upon me that somebody was there. It is a sensation that most people have felt. I have seen when it has been strong enough to awake me out of sleep, the sense of someone looking at me. I suppose my imagination had been affected by Roland's story; and the mystery of the darkness is always full of suggestions. I stamped my feet violently on the gravel to rouse myself, and called out sharply, 'Who's there?' Nobody answered, nor did I expect anyone to answer, but the impression had been made. I was so foolish that I did not like to look back, but went sideways, keeping an eye on the gloom behind. It was with great relief that I spied the light in the stables, making a sort of oasis in the darkness. I walked very quickly into the midst of that lighted and cheerful place, and thought the clank of the groom's pail one of the pleasantest sounds I had ever heard. The coachman was the head of this little colony, and it was to his house I went to pursue my investigations. He was a native of the district, and had taken care of the place in the absence of the family for years; it was impossible but that he must know everything that was going on, and all the traditions of the place. The men, I could see, eyed me anxiously when I thus appeared at such an hour among them, and followed me with their eyes to Jarvis's house, where he lived alone with his old wife, their children being all married and out in the world. Mrs. Jarvis met me with anxious questions. How was the poor young gentleman? but the others knew, I could see by their faces, that not even this was the foremost thing in my mind.

'Noises? – ou ay, there'll be noises – the wind in the trees, and the water soughing down the glen. As for tramps, Cornel, no, there's little o' that kind o' cattle about here; and Merran at the gate's a careful body.' Jarvis moved about with some embarrassment from one leg to another as he spoke. He kept in the shade, and did not look at me more than he could help. Evidently his mind was perturbed, and he had reasons for keeping his own counsel. His wife sat by, giving him a quick look now and then, but saying nothing. The kitchen was very snug and warm and bright – as different as could be from the chill and mystery of the night outside.

'I think you are trifling with me, Jarvis,' I said.

'Triflin', Cornel? no me. What would I trifle for? If the deevil himself was in the auld hoose, I have no interest in't one way or another—'

'Sandy, hold your peace!' cried his wife, imperatively.

'And what am I to hold my peace for, wi' the Cornel standing there asking a' thae questions? I'm saying, if the deevil himself—'

'And I'm telling ye hold your peace!' cried the woman, in great excitement. 'Dark November weather and lang nichts, and us that ken a' we ken. How daur ye name – a name that shouldna be spoken?' She threw down her stocking and got up, also in great agitation. 'I tell't ye you never could keep it. It's no a thing that will hide; and the haill toun kens as well as you or me. Tell the Cornel straight out – or see, I'll do it. I dinna hold wi' your secrets: and a secret that the haill toun kens!' She snapped her fingers with an air of large disdain. As for Jarvis, ruddy and big as he was, he shrank to nothing before this decided woman. He repeated to her two or three times her own adjuration, 'Hold your peace!' then, suddenly changing his tone, cried out, 'Tell him then, confound ye! I'll wash my hands o't. If a' the ghosts in Scotland were in the auld hoose, is that ony concern o' mine?'

After this I elicited without much difficulty the whole story. In the opinion of the Jarvises, and of everybody about, the certainty that the place was haunted was beyond all doubt. As Sandy and his wife warmed to the tale, one tripping up another in their eagerness to tell everything, it gradually developed as distinct a superstition as I ever heard, and not without poetry and pathos. How long it was since the voice had been heard first, nobody could tell with certainty. Jarvis's opinion was that his father, who had been coachman at Brentwood before him, had never heard any thing about it, and that the whole thing had arisen within the last ten years, since the complete dismantling of the old house: which was a wonderfully modern date for a tale so well authenticated. According to these witnesses, and to several whom I questioned afterwards, and who were all in perfect agreement, it was only in the months of November and December that 'the visitation' occurred. During these months, the darkness of the year, scarcely a night passed without the recurrence of these inexplicable cries. Nothing, it was said, had ever been seen – at least nothing that could be identified. Some people, bolder or more imaginative than the others, had seen the darkness moving, Mrs. Jarvis said, with unconscious poetry. It began when night fell and continued, at intervals, till day broke. Very often it was only an inarticulate cry and moaning, but sometimes the words which had taken possession of my poor boy's fancy had been distinctly audible – 'Oh, mother, let me in!' The Jarvises were not aware that there had ever been any investigation into it. The estate of Brentwood had lapsed into the hands of a distant branch of the family, who had lived but little there; and of the many people who had taken it, as I had done, few had remained through two Decembers. And nobody had taken the trouble to make a very close examination into the facts. 'No, no,' Jarvis said, shaking his head, 'No, no, Cornel. Wha wad set themsels up for a laughin'-stock to a' the country-side, making a wark about a ghost? Naebody believes in ghosts. It bid to be the wind in the trees, the last gentleman said, or some effec' o' the water wrastlin' among the rocks. He said it was a' quite easy explained: but he gave up the hoose. And when you cam, Cornel, we were awful anxious you should never hear. What for should I have spoiled the bargain and hairmed the property for nothing?'

'Do you call my child's life nothing?' I said in the trouble of the moment, unable to restrain myself. 'And instead of telling this all to me, you have told it to him – to a delicate boy, a child unable to sift evidence, or judge for himself, a tender-hearted young creature—'

I was walking about the room with an anger all the hotter that I felt it to be most likely quite unjust. My heart was full of bitterness against the solid retainers of a family who were content to risk other people's children and comfort rather than let the house lie empty. If I had been warned I might have taken precautions, or left the place, or sent Roland away, a hundred things which now I could not do; and here I was with my boy in a brain-fever, and his life, the most precious life on earth, hanging in the balance, dependent on whether or not I could get to the reason of a common-place ghost story! I paced about in high wrath, not seeing what I was to do; for, to take Roland away, even if he were able to travel, would not settle his agitated mind; and I feared even that a scientific explanation of refracted sound, or reverberation, or any other of the easy certainties with which we elder men are silenced, would have very little effect upon the boy.

'Cornel,' said Jarvis, solemnly, 'and *she'll* bear me witness – the young gentleman never heard a word from me – no, nor from either groom or gardener; I'll gie my word for that. In the first place, he's no a lad that invites ye to talk. There are some that are, and some that arena. Some will draw ye on, till ye've tellt them a' the clatter of the toun, and a' ye ken, and while mair. But Maister Roland, his mind's fu' of his books. He's aye civil and kind, and a fine lad; but no that sort. And ye see it's for a' our interest, Cornel, that you should stay at Brentwood. I took it upon me mysel to pass the word – 'No a syllable to Maister Roland, nor to the young leddies – no a syllable.' The women-servants, that have little reason to be out at night, ken little or nothing about it. And some think it grand to have a ghost so long as they're no in the way of coming across it. If you had been tellt the story to begin with, maybe ye would have thought so yourself.'

This was true enough, though it did not throw any light upon my perplexity. If we had heard of it to start with, it is possible that all the family would have considered the possession of a ghost a distinct advantage. It is the fashion of the times. We never think what a risk it is to play with young imaginations, but cry out, in the fashionable jargon, 'A ghost! – nothing else was wanted to make it perfect,' I should not have been above this myself. I should have smiled, of course, at the idea of the ghost at all, but then to feel that it was mine would have pleased my vanity. Oh, yes, I claim no exemption. The girls would have been delighted. I could fancy their eagerness, their interest, and excitement. No; if we had been told, it would have done no good – we should have made the bargain all the more eagerly, the fools that we are. 'And there has been no attempt to investigate it,' I said, 'to see what it really is?'

'Eh, Cornel,' said the coachman's wife, 'wha would investigate, as ye call it, a thing that nobody believes in? Ye would be the laughing-stock of a' the country-side, as my man says.'

'But you believe in it,' I said, turning upon her hastily. The woman was taken by surprise. She made a step backward out of my way.

'Lord, Cornel, how ye frichten a body! Me! – there's awful strange things in this world. An unlearned person doesna ken what to think. But the minister and the gentry they just laugh in your face. Inquire into the thing that is not! Na, na, we just let it be.'

'Come with me, Jarvis,' I said hastily, 'and we'll make an attempt at least. Say nothing to the men or to anybody. I'll come back after dinner, and we'll make a serious attempt to see what it is, if it is anything. If I hear it – which I doubt – you may be sure I shall never rest till I make it out. Be ready for me about ten o'clock.'

'Me, Cornel!' Jarvis said, in a faint voice. I had not been looking at him in my own preoccupation, but when I did so, I found that the greatest change had come over the fat and ruddy coachman. 'Me, Cornel!' he repeated, wiping the perspiration from his brow. His ruddy face hung in flabby folds, his knees knocked together, his voice seemed half extinguished in his throat. Then he began to rub his hands and smile upon me in a deprecating, imbecile way. 'There's nothing I wouldna do to pleasure ye, Cornel,' taking a step farther back. 'I'm sure *she* kens I've aye said I never had to do with a mair fair, weelspoken gentleman—' Here Jarvis came to a pause, again looking at me, rubbing his hands.

'Well?' I said.

'But eh, sir!' he went on, with the same imbecile yet insinuating smile, 'if ye'll reflect that I am no used to my feet. With a horse atween my legs, or the reins in my hand, I'm maybe nae worse than other men; but on fit, Cornel – It's no the – bogles; – but I've been cavalry, ye see,' with a little hoarse laugh, 'a' my life. To face a thing ye didna understan' – on your feet, Cornel.'

'Well, sir if *I* do it,' said I tartly, 'why shouldn't you?'

'Eh, Cornel, there's an awfu' difference. In the first place, ye tramp about the haill country-side, and think naething of it; but a walk tires me mair than a hunard miles' drive: and then ye'e a gentleman, and do your ain pleasure; and you're no so ould as me; and it's for your ain bairn, ye see, Cornel; and then—'

'He believes in it, Cornel, and you dinna believe in it,' the woman said.

'Will you come with me?' I said, turning to her.

She jumped back, upsetting her chair in her bewilderment. 'Me!' with a scream, and then fell into a sort of hysterical laugh. 'I wouldna say but what I would go; but what would the folk say to hear of Cornel Mortimer with an auld silly woman at his heels?'

The suggestion made me laugh too, though I had little inclination for it. 'I'm sorry you have so little spirit, Jarvis,' I said. 'I must find someone else, I suppose.'

Jarvis, touched by this, began to remonstrate, but I cut him short. My butler was a soldier who had been with me in India, and was not supposed to fear anything – man or devil – certainly not the former; and I felt that I was losing time. The Jarvises were too thankful to get rid of me. They attended me to the door with the most anxious courtesies. Outside the two grooms stood close by, a little confused by my sudden exit. I don't know if perhaps, they had been listening – at least standing as near as possible, to catch any scrap of the conversation. I waved my hand to them as I went past in answer to their salutations, and it was very apparent to me that they also were glad to see me go.

And it will be thought very strange, but it would be weak not to add, that I myself, though bent on the investigation I have spoken of, pledged to Roland to carry it out, and feeling that my boy's health, perhaps his life, depended on the result of my inquiry – I felt the most unaccountable reluctance to pass these ruins on my way home. My curiosity was intense; and yet it was all my mind could do to pull my body along. I dare say the scientific people would describe it the other way, and attribute my cowardice to the state of my stomach. I went on; but if I had followed my impulse, I should have turned and bolted. Everything in me seemed to cry out against it; my heart thumped, my pulses all began, like sledgehammers, beating against my ears and every sensitive part. It was very dark, as I have said; the old house, with its shapeless tower, loomed a heavy mass through the darkness, which was only not entirely so solid as itself. On the other hand, the great dark cedars of which we were so proud seemed to fill up the night. My foot strayed out of the path in my confusion and the gloom together, and I brought myself up with a cry as I felt myself knock against something solid. What was it? The contact with hard stone and lime, and prickly bramblebushes restored me a little to myself. 'Oh, it's only the old gable,' I said aloud, with a little laugh to reassure myself. The rough feeling of the stones recoiled me. As I groped about thus, I shook off my visionary folly. What so easily explained as that I should have strayed from the path in the darkness? This brought me back to common existence, as if I had been shaken by a wise hand out of all the silliness of superstition. How silly it was, after all! What did it matter which path I took? I laughed again, this time with better heart – when suddenly, in a moment, the blood was chilled in my veins, a shiver stole along my spine, my faculties seemed to forsake me. Close by me at my side, at my feet, there was a sigh. No, not a groan, not a moaning, not anything so tangible – a perfectly soft, faint, inarticulate sigh. I sprang back, and my heart stopped beating. Mistaken! no, mistake was impossible. I heard it as clearly as I hear myself speak; a long, soft, weary sigh, as if drawn to the utmost, and emptying out a load of sadness that filled the breast. To hear this in the solitude, in the dark, in the night (though it was still early), had an effect which I cannot describe. I feel it now – something cold creeping over me, up into my hair, and down to my feet, which refused to move. I cried out, with a trembling voice, 'Who is there?' as I had done before – but there was no reply.

I got home I don't quite know how; but in my mind there was no longer any indifference as to the thing, whatever it was, that haunted these ruins. My scepticism disappeared like a mist. I was as firmly determined that there was something as Roland was. I did not for a moment pretend to myself that it was possible I could be deceived; there were movements and noises which I understood all about, cracklings of small branches in the frost, and little rolls of gravel on the path, such as have a very eerie sound sometimes, and perplex you with wonder as to who has done it, *when there is no real mystery;* but I assure you all these little movements of Nature don't affect you one bit *when there is something*. I understood *them*. I did not understand the sigh. That was not simple Nature; there was meaning in it – feeling, the soul of a creature invisible. This is the thing that human nature trembles at – a creature invisible, yet with sensations, feelings, a power somehow of expressing itself. I had not the same sense of unwillingness to turn my back upon the scene of the mystery which I had experienced in going by the stables; but I almost ran home, impelled by eagerness to get everything done that had to be done in order to apply myself to finding it out. Bagley was in the hall as usual when I went in. He was always there in the afternoon, always with the appearance of perfect occupation, yet, as far as I knew, never doing anything. The door was open, so that I hurried in without any pause, breathless; but the sight of his calm regard, as he came to help me off with my overcoat, subdued me in a moment. Anything out of the way, anything incomprehensible, fades to nothing in the presence of Bagley. You saw and wondered how he was made; the parting of his hair, the tie of his white neckcloth, the fit of his trousers, all perfect as works of art; but you could see how they were done, which makes all the difference. I flung myself upon him, so to speak, without waiting to note the extreme unlikeness of the man to anything of the kind I meant. 'Bagley,' I said, 'I want you to come out with me to-night to watch for—'

'Poachers, Colonel,' he said, a gleam of pleasure running all over him.

'No, Bagley; a great deal worse,' I cried.

'Yes, Colonel; at what hour, sir?' the man said; but then I had not told him what it was.

It was ten o'clock when we set out. All was perfectly quiet indoors. My wife was with Roland, who had been quite calm, she said, and who (though, no doubt, the fever must run its course) had been better since I came. I told Bagley to put on a thick greatcoat over his evening coat, and did the same myself – with strong boots; for the soil was like a sponge, or worse. Talking to him, I almost forgot what we were going to do. It was darker even than it had been before, and Bagley kept very close to me as we went along. I had a small lantern in my hand, which gave us a partial guidance. We had come to the corner where the path turns. On one side was the bowling-green, which the girls had taken possession of for their croquet ground – a wonderful enclosure surrounded by high hedges of holly, three hundred years old and more; on the other the ruins. Both were black as night; but before we got so far, there was a little opening in which we could just discern the trees and the lighter line of the road. I thought it best to pause there and take breath. 'Bagley,' I said, 'there is something about these ruins I don't understand. It is there I am going. Keep your eyes open and your wits about you. Be ready to pounce upon any stranger you see – anything, man or woman. Don't hurt, but seize – anything you see.' 'Colonel,' said Bagley, with a little tremor in his breath, 'they do say there's things there – as is neither man nor woman.' There was no time for words. 'Are you game to follow me, my man? that's the question,' I said. Bagley fell in without a word, and saluted. I knew then I had nothing to fear.

We went, so far as I could guess, exactly as I had come when I heard that sigh. The darkness, however, was so complete that all marks, as of trees or paths, disappeared. One moment we felt our feet on the gravel, another sinking noiselessly into the slippery grass, that was all. I had shut up my lantern, not wishing to scare anyone, whoever it might be. Bagley followed, it seemed to me exactly in my footsteps as I made my way, as I supposed, towards the mass of the ruined house. We seemed to take a long time groping along seeking this; the squash of the wet soil under our feet was the only thing that marked our progress. After a while I stood still to see, or rather feel, where we were. The darkness was very still, but no stiller than is usual in a winter's night. The sounds I have mentioned – the crackling of twigs, the roll of a pebble, the sound of some rustle in the dead leaves, or creeping creatures on the grass – were audible when you listened, all mysterious enough when your mind is disengaged, but to me cheering now as signs of the livingness of Nature, even in the death of the frost. As we stood still there came up from the trees in the glen the prolonged hoot of an owl. Bagley started with alarm, being in a state of general nervousness, and not knowing what he was afraid of. But to me the sound was encouraging and pleasant, being so comprehensible. 'An owl,' I said, under my breath. 'Y—es, Colonel,' said Bagley, his teeth chattering. We stood still about five minutes, while it broke into the still brooding of the air, the sound widening out in circles, dying upon the darkness. This sound, which is not a cheerful one, made me almost gay. It was natural, and relieved the tension of the mind. I moved on with new courage, my nervous excitement calming down.

When all at once, quite suddenly, close to us, at our feet, there broke out a cry. I made a spring backwards in the first moment of surprise and horror, and in doing so came sharply against the same rough masonry and brambles that had struck me before. This new sound came upwards from the ground – a low, moaning, wailing voice, full of suffering and pain. The contrast between it and the hoot of the owl was indescribable; the one with a wholesome wildness and naturalness that hurt nobody – the other, a sound that made one's blood curdle, full of human misery. With a great deal of fumbling – for in spite of everything I could do to keep up my courage my hands shook – I managed to remove the slide of my lantern. The light leaped out like something living, and made the place visible in a moment. We were what would have been inside the ruined building had anything remained by the gable-wall, which I have described. It was close to us, the vacant door-way in it going out straight into the blackness outside. The light showed the bit of wall, the ivy glistening upon it in clouds of dark green, the bramble-branches waving, and below, the open door – a door that led to nothing. It was from this the voice came which died out just as the light flashed upon this strange scene. There was a moment's silence, and then it broke forth again. The sound was so near, so penetrating, so pitiful, that, on the nervous start I gave, the light fell out of my hand. As I groped for it in the dark my hand was clutched by Bagley, who I think must have dropped upon his knees; but I was too much perturbed myself to think much of this. He clutched at me in the confusion of his terror, forgetting all his usual decorum. 'For God's sake, what is it, sir?' he gasped. If I yielded, there was evidently an end to both of us. 'I can't tell,' I said, 'any more than you; that's what we've got to find out : up, man, up!' I pulled him to his feet. 'Will you go round and examine the other side, or will you stay here with the lantern?' Bagley gasped at me with a face of horror. 'Can't we stay together, Colonel?'

he said – his knees were trembling under him. I pushed him against the corner of the wall, and put the light into his hands. 'Stand fast till I come back; shake yourself together, man; let nothing pass you,' I said. The voice was within two or three feet of us, of that there could be no doubt.

I went myself to the other side of the wall, keeping close to it. The light shook in Bagley's hand, but, tremulous though it was, shone out through the vacant door, one oblong block of light marking all the crumbling corners and hanging masses of foliage. Was there something dark huddled in a heap by the side of it? I pushed forward across the light in the doorway, and fell upon it with my hands; but it was only a juniper-bush growing close against the wall. Meanwhile, the sight of my figure crossing the doorway had brought Bagley's nervous excitement to a height: he flew at me, gripping my shoulder. 'I've got him, Colonel! I've got him!' he cried, with a voice of sudden exultation. He thought it was a man, and was at once relieved. But at that moment the voice broke forth again between us, at our feet – more close to us than any separate being could be. He dropped off from me, and fell against the wall, his jaw dropping as if he were dying. I suppose, at the same moment, he saw that it was me whom he had clutched. I, for my part, had scarcely more command of myself. I snatched the light out of his hand, and flashed it all about me wildly. Nothing – the juniper-bush which I thought I had never seen before, the heavy growth of the glistening ivy, the brambles waving. It was close to my ears now, crying, crying, pleading as if for life. Either I heard the same words Roland had heard, or else, in my excitement, his imagination got possession of mine. The voice went on, growing into distinct articulation, but wavering about, now from one point, now from another, as if the owner of it were moving slowly back and forward – 'Mother! mother!' and then an outburst of wailing. As my mind steadied, getting accustomed (as one's mind gets accustomed to anything), it seemed to me as if some uneasy, miserable creature was pacing up and down before a closed door. Sometimes – but that must have been excitement – I thought I heard a sound like knocking, and then another burst, 'Oh, mother! mother!' All this close, close to the space where I was standing with my lantern

– now before me, now behind me: a creature restless, unhappy, moaning, crying, before the vacant doorway, which no one could either shut or open more.

'Do you hear it, Bagley? Do you hear what it is saying?' I cried, stepping in through the doorway. He was lying against the wall – his eyes glazed, half dead with terror. He made a motion of his lips as if to answer me, but no sounds came; then lifted his hand with a curious imperative movement as if ordering me to be silent and listen. And how long I did so I cannot tell. It began to have an interest, an exciting hold upon me, which I could not describe. It seemed to call up visibly a scene anyone could understand – a something shut out, restlessly wandering to and fro; sometimes the voice dropped, as if throwing itself down – sometimes wandered off a few paces, growing sharp and clear. 'Oh, mother, let me in! oh, mother, mother, let me in! oh, let me in!' every word was clear to me. No wonder the boy had gone wild with pity. I tried to steady my mind upon Roland, upon his conviction that I could do something, but my head swam with the excitement, even when I partially overcame the terror. At last the words died away, and there was a sound of sobs and moaning. I cried out, 'In the name of God who are you?' with a kind of feeling in my mind that to use the name of God was profane, seeing that I did not believe in ghosts or anything supernatural; but I did it all the same, and waited, my heart giving a leap of terror lest there should be a reply. Why this should have been I cannot tell, but I had a feeling that if there was an answer it would be more than I could bear. But there was no answer; the moaning went on, and then, as if it had been real, the voice rose, a little higher again, the words recommenced, 'Oh, mother, let me in! oh, mother, let me in!' with an expression that was heart-breaking to hear.

As if it had been real! What do I mean by that? I suppose I got less alarmed as the thing went on. I began to recover the use of my senses – I seemed to explain it all to myself by saying that this had once happened, that it was a recollection of a real scene. Why there should have seemed something quite satisfactory and composing in this explanation I cannot tell, but so it was. I began to listen almost as if it had been a play, forgetting Bagley, who, I almost think, had fainted, leaning against the wall. I was startled out of this strange spectatorship that had fallen upon me by the sudden rush of something which made my heart jump once more, a large black figure in the doorway waving its arms. 'Come in! come in! come in!' it shouted out hoarsely at the top of a deep bass voice, and then poor Bagley fell down senseless across the threshold. He was less sophisticated than I – he had not been able to bear it any longer. I took him for something supernatural, as he took me, and it was some time before I awoke to the necessities of the moment. I remembered only after, that from the time I began to give my attention to the man, I heard the other voice no more. It was some time before I brought him to. It must have been a strange scene; the lantern making a luminous spot in the darkness, the man's white face lying on the black earth, I over him, doing what I could for him. Probably I should have been thought to be murdering him had anyone seen us. When at last I succeeded in pouring a little brandy down his throat he sat up and looked about him wildly. 'What's up?' he said; then recognising me, tried to struggle to his feet with a faint 'Beg your pardon, Colonel.' I got him home as best I could, making him lean upon my arm. The great fellow was a weak as a child. Fortunately he did not for some time remember what had happened. From the time Bagley fell the voice had stopped, and all was still.

'You've got an epidemic in your house, Colonel,' Simson said to me next morning. 'What's the meaning of it all? Here's your butler raving about a voice. This will never do, you know; and so far as I can make out you are in it too.'

'Yes, I am in it, doctor. I thought I had better speak to you. Of course you are treating Roland all right – but the boy is not raving, he is as sane as you or me. It's all true.'

'As sane as – I – or you. I never thought the boy insane. He's got cerebral excitement, fever. I don't know what you've got. There's something very queer about the look of your eyes.'

'Come,' said I, 'you can't put us all to bed, you know. You had better listen and hear the symptoms in full.'

The doctor shrugged his shoulders, but he listened to me patiently. He did not believe a word of the story, that was clear; but he heard it all from beginning to end. 'My dear fellow,' he said, 'the boy told me just the same. It's an epidemic. When one person falls a victim to this sort of thing, it's as safe as can be – there's always two or three.'

'Then how do you account for it?' I said.

'Oh, account for it! – that's a different matter; there's no accounting for the freaks our brains are subject to. If it's delusion; if it's some trick of the echoes or the winds – some phonetic disturbance or other—'

'Come with me to-night, and judge for yourself,' I said.

Upon this he laughed aloud, then said, 'That's not such a bad idea; but it would ruin me for ever if it were known that John Simson was ghost-hunting.'

'There it is,' said I; 'you dart down on us who are unlearned with your phonetic disturbances but you daren't examine what the thing really is for fear of being laughed at. That's science!'

'It's not science – it's common sense,' said the doctor. 'The thing has delusion on the front of it. It is encouraging an unwholesome tendency even to examine. What good could come of it? Even if I am convinced. I shouldn't believe.'

'I should have said so yesterday; and I don't want you to be convinced or to believe,' said I. 'If you prove it to be a delusion, I shall be very much obliged to you for one. Come; somebody must go with me.'

'You are cool,' said the doctor. 'You've disabled this poor fellow of yours, and made him – on that point – a lunatic for life; and now you want to disable me. But for once, I'll do it. To save appearance, if you'll give me a bed, I'll come over after my last rounds.'

It was agreed that I should meet him at the gate, and that we should visit the scene of last night's occurrences before we came to the house, so that nobody might be the wiser. It was scarcely possible to hope that the cause of Bagley's sudden illness should not somehow steal into the knowledge of the servants at least, and it was better that all should be done as quietly as possible. The day seemed to be a very long one. I had to spend a certain part of it with Roland, which was a terrible ordeal for me – for what could I say to the boy? The improvement continued, but he was still in a very precarious state, and the trembling violence with which he turned to me when his mother left the room filled me with alarm. 'Father!' he said, quietly. 'Yes, my boy; I am giving my best attention to it – all is being done that I can do. I have not come to any conclusion – yet. I am neglecting nothing you said,' I cried. What I could not do was to give his active mind any encouragement to dwell upon the mystery. It was a hard predicament, for some satisfaction had to be given him. He looked at me very wistfully, with the great blue eyes which shone so large and brilliant out of his white and worn face. 'You must trust me,' I said. 'Yes, father. Father understands,' he said to himself, as if to soothe some inward doubt. I left him as soon as I could. He was about the most precious thing I had on earth, and his health was my first thought, but yet somehow, in the excitement of this other subject, I put that aside, and preferred not to dwell upon Roland, which was the most curious part of it all.

That night at eleven I met Simson at the gate. He had come by train, and I let him in gently myself. I had been so much absorbed in the coming experiment that I passed the ruins in going to meet him, almost without thought, if you can understand that. I had my lantern; and he showed me a coil of taper which he had ready for use. 'There is nothing like light,' he said, in his scoffing tone. It was a very still night, scarcely a sound, but not dark. We would keep the path without difficulty as we went along. As we approached the spot we could hear a low moaning, broken occasionally by a bitter cry. 'Perhaps that is your voice,' said the doctor; 'I thought it must be something of the kind. That's a poor brute caught in some of these infernal traps of yours; you'll find it among the bushes somewhere.' I said nothing. I felt no particular fear, but a triumphant satisfaction in what was to follow. I led him to the spot where Bagley and I had stood on the previous night. All was silent as a winter night could be – so silent that we heard far off the sound of the horses in the stables, the shutting of a window in the house. Simson lighted his taper and went peering about, poking into all the corners. We looked like two conspirators lying in wait for some unfortunate traveller; but not a sound broke the quiet. The moaning had stopped before we came up; a star or two shone over us in the sky looking down as if surprised at our strange proceedings. Dr. Simson did nothing but utter subdued laughs under his breath. 'I thought as much,' he said. 'It is just the same with tables and all other kinds of ghostly apparatus; a sceptic's presence stops everything. When I am present nothing ever comes off. How long do you think it will be necessary to stay here? Oh, I don't complain; only, when *you* are satisfied, *I* am – quite.'

I will not deny that I was disappointed beyond measure by this result. It made me look like a credulous fool. It gave the doctor such a pull over me as nothing else could. I should point all his morals for years to come, and his materialism, his scepticism, would be increased beyond endurance. 'It seems, indeed,' I said, 'that there is to be no—' 'Manifestation,' he said, laughing; 'that is what all the mediums say. No manifestations, in consequence of the presence of an unbeliever.' His laugh sounded very uncomfortable to me in the silence; and it was now near midnight. But that laugh seemed the signal; before it died away the moaning we had heard before was resumed. It started from some distance off, and came towards us, nearer and nearer, like some one walking along and moaning to himself. There could be no idea now that it was a hare caught in a trap. The approach was slow, like that of a weak person with little halts and pauses. We heard it coming along the grass, straight towards the vacant doorway. Simson had been a little startled by the first sound. He said hastily, 'That child has no business to be out so late.' But he felt, as well as I, that this was no child's voice. As it came nearer, he grew silent, and, going to the doorway with his taper, stood looking out towards the sound. The taper being unprotected blew about in the night air, though there was scarcely any wind. I threw the light of my lantern steady and white across the same space. It was a blaze of light in the midst of the blackness. A little icy thrill had gone over me at the first sound, but as it came close, I confess that my only feeling was satisfaction. The scoffer would scoff no more. The light touched his own face, and showed a very perplexed countenance. If he was afraid, he concealed it with great success, but he was perplexed. And then all that had happened on the previous night was enacted once more. It fell strangely upon me with a sense of repetition. Every cry, every sob, seemed the same as before. I listened almost without any emotion at all in my own person, thinking of its effect upon Simson. He maintained a very bold front on the whole. All that coming and going of the voice was, if our ears could be trusted, exactly in front of the vacant, blank doorway, blazing full of light, which caught and shone in the glistening leaves of the great hollies at a little distance. Not a rabbit could have crossed the turf without being seen – but there was nothing. After a time, Simson, with a certain caution and bodily reluctance, as it seemed to me, went out with his roll of taper into this space. His figure showed against the holly in full outline. Just at this moment the voice sank, as was its custom, and seemed to fling itself down at the door. Simson recoiled violently, as if someone had come up against him, then turned, and held his taper low as if examining something. 'Do you see anybody?' I cried in a whisper, feeling the chill of a nervous panic steal over me at this action. 'It's nothing but a – confounded juniper-bush,' he said. This I knew very well to be nonsense, for the juniper-bush was on the other side. He went about after this round and round, poking his taper everywhere, then returned to me on the inner side of the wall. He scoffed no longer; his face was contracted and pale. 'How long does this go on?' he whispered to me, like a man who does not wish to interrupt someone who is speaking. I had become too much perturbed myself to remark whether the successions and changes of the voice were the same as last night. It suddenly went out in the air almost as he was speaking, with a soft reiterated sob dying away. If there had been anything to be seen, I should have said that the person was at that moment crouching on the ground close to the door.

We walked home very silent afterwards. It was only when we were in sight of the house that I said, 'What do you think of it?' 'I can't tell what to think of it,' he said, quickly. He took – though he was a very temperate man – not the claret I was going to offer him, but some brandy from the tray, and swallowed it almost undiluted. 'Mind you, I don't believe a word of it,' he said, when he had lighted his candle; 'but I can't tell what to think,' he turned round to add, when he was half-way upstairs.

All of this, however, did me no good with the solution

of my problem. I was to help this weeping, sobbing thing, which was already to me as distinct a personality as any thing I knew – or what should I say to Roland? It was on my heart that my boy would die if I could not find some way of helping this creature. You may be surprised that I should speak of it this way. I did not know if it was man or woman; but I no more doubted that it was a soul in pain than I doubted my own being; and it was my business to soothe this pain – to deliver it, if that was possible. Was ever such a task given to an anxious father trembling for his only boy? I felt in my heart, fantastic as it may appear, that I must fulfil this somehow, or part with my child; and you may conceive that rather than do that I was ready to die. But even my dying would not have advanced me – unless by bringing me into the same world with the seeker at the door.

Next morning Simson was out before breakfast, and came in with evident signs of the damp grass on his boots, and a look of worry and weariness, which did not say much for the night he had passed. He improved a little after breakfast, and visited his two patients, for Bagley was still an invalid. I went out with him on his way to the train, to hear what he had to say about the boy. 'He is going on very well,' he said; 'there are no complications as yet. But mind you, that's not a boy to be trifled with, Mortimer. Not a word to him about last night.' I had to tell him then of my last interview with Roland, and of the impossible demand he had made upon me – by which, though he tried to laugh, he was much discomposed, as I could see. 'We must just perjure ourselves all round,' he said, 'and swear you exorcised it'; but the man was too kind-hearted to be satisfied with that. 'It's frightfully serious for you, Mortimer. I can't laugh as I should like to. I wish I saw a way out of it, for your sake. By the way,' he added shortly 'didn't you notice that juniper-bush on the left-hand side?' 'There was one on the right hand of the door. I noticed you made that mistake last night.' 'Mistake!' he cried, with a curious low laugh, pulling up the collar of his coat as though he felt the cold, 'there's no juniper there this morning left or right. Just go and see.' As he stepped into the train a few minutes after, he looked back upon me and beckoned me for a parting word. 'I'm coming back to-night,' he said.

I don't think I had any feeling about this as I turned away from that common bustle of the railway which made my private preoccupations feel so strangely out of date. There had been a distinct satisfaction in my mind before that his scepticism had been so entirely defeated. But the more serious part of the matter pressed upon me now. I went straight from the railway to the manse, which stood on a little plateau on the side of the river opposite to the woods of Brentwood. The minister was one of a class which is not so common in Scotland as it used to be. He was a man of good family, well educated in the Scots way, strong in philosophy, not so strong in Greek, strongest of all in experience – a man who had 'come across,' in the course of his life, most people of note that had ever been in Scotland – and who was said to be very sound in doctrine, without infringing the toleration with which old men, who are good men, are generally endowed. He was old-fashioned, perhaps he did not think so much about the troublous problems of theology as many of the young men, nor ask himself any hard questions about the Confession of Faith – but he understood human nature, which is perhaps better. He received me with a cordial welcome. 'Come away, Colonel Mortimer,' he said; 'I'm all the more glad to see you, that I feel it's a good sign for the boy. He's doing well? – God be praised – and the Lord bless him and keep him. He has many a poor body's prayers – and that can do nobody harm.'

'He will need them all, Dr. Moncrieff,' I said, 'and your counsel too.' And I told him the story – more than I had told Simson. The old clergyman listened to me with many suppressed exclamations, and at the end the water stood in his eyes.

'That's just beautiful,' he said. 'I do not mind to have heard anything like it, it's as fine as Burns when he wished deliverance to one – that is prayed for in no kirk. Ay, ay! so he would have you console the poor lost spirit? God bless the boy! There's something more than common in that, Colonel Mortimer. And also the faith of him in his father! I would like to put that into a sermon.' Then the old gentleman gave me an alarmed look, and said, 'No, no, I was not meaning a sermon, but I must write it down for the *Children's Record*.' I saw the thought that passed through his mind. Either he thought, or he feared I would think, of a funeral sermon. You may believe this did not make me more cheerful.

I can scarcely say that Dr. Moncrieff gave me any advice. How could anyone advise on such a subject? But he said, 'I think I'll come too. I'm an old man; I'm less liable to be frightened than those that are further off the world unseen. It behoves me to think of my own journey there. I've no cut-and-dried beliefs on the subject. I'll come too: and maybe at the moment the Lord will put into our heads what to do.'

This gave me a little comfort – more than Simson had given me. To be clear about the cause of it was not my grand desire. It was another thing that was in my mind – my boy. As for the poor soul at the open door, I had no more doubt, as I have said, of its existence than I had of my own. It was no ghost to me. I knew the creature, and it was in trouble. That was my feeling about it, and it was Roland's. To hear it first was a great shock to my nerves, but not now, a man will get accustomed to anything. But to do something for it was the great problem, how was I to be serviceable to a being that was invisible, that was mortal no longer? 'Maybe at the moment the Lord will put it into our heads.' That is very old-fashioned phraseology, and a week before, most likely, I should have smiled (though always with kindness) at Dr. Moncrieff's credulity; but there was a great comfort, whether rational or otherwise I cannot say, in the mere sound of the words.

The road to the station and the village lay through the glen – not by the ruins; but though the sunshine and the fresh air, and the beauty of the trees, and the sound of the water were all very soothing to the spirits, my mind was so full of my own subject that I could not refrain from turning to the right as I got to the top of the glen, and going straight to the place which I may call the scene of all my thoughts. It was lying full in the sunshine, like all the rest of the world. The ruined gable looked due east, and in the present aspect of the sun the light streamed down through the doorway as our lantern had done, throwing a flood of light upon the damp grass beyond. There was a strange suggestion in the open door – so futile, a kind of emblem of vanity – all free around – so that you could go where you pleased, and yet the semblance of an enclosure – that way of entrance, unnecessary, leading to nothing. And why any creature should pray and weep to get in – to nothing, or be kept out – by nothing! You could not dwell upon it, or it made your brain go round. I remembered, however, what Simson said about the juniper, with a little smile on my own mind as to the inaccuracy of recollection, which even a scientific man will be guilty of. I could see now the light of my lantern gleaming upon the wet glistening surface of the spiky leaves at the right hand – and he ready to go to the stake for it that it was the left! I went round to make sure. And then I saw what he had said. Right or left there was no juniper at all. I was confounded by this, though it was entirely a matter of detail: nothing at all: a bush of brambles waving, the green growing up the very walls. But after all, though it gave me a shock for a moment, what did that matter? There were marks as if a number of footsteps had been up and down in front of the door, but these might have been our steps, and all was bright, and peaceful, and still. I poked about the other ruin – the larger ruins of the old house – for some time, as I had done before. There were marks upon the grass here and there, I could not call them footsteps, all about; but that told for nothing one way or another. I had examined the ruined rooms closely the first day. They were half filled up with soil and débris, withered brackens and bramble – no refuge for any one there. It vexed me that Jarvis should see me coming from that spot when he came up to me for his orders. I don't know whether my nocturnal expeditions had got wind among the servants. But there was a significant look in his face. Something in it I felt was like my own sensation when Simson in the midst of his scepticism was struck dumb. Jarvis felt satisfied that his veracity hed been put beyond question. never spoke to a servant of mine in such a peremptory tone before. I sent him away 'with a flea in his lug,' as the man described it afterwards. Interference of any kind was intolerable to me at such a moment.

But what was strangest of all was, that I could not face Roland. I did not go up to his room as I would have naturally done at once. This the girls could not understand. They saw there was some mystery in it. 'Mother has gone to lie down,' Agatha said; 'he has had such a good night.' 'But he wants you so, papa!' cried little Jeanie, always with her two arms embracing mine in a pretty way she had. I was obliged to go at last – but what could I say? I could only kiss him and tell him to keep still – that I was doing all I could. There is something mystical about the patience of a child. 'It will come all right won't it father?' he said. 'God grant it may! I hope so, Roland.' 'Oh yes, it will come all right.' Perhaps he understood that, in the midst of my anxiety, I could not stay with him as I should have done otherwise. But the girls were more surprised than it is possible to describe. They looked at me with wondering eyes. 'If I were ill, papa, and you only stayed with me a moment. I should break my heart,' said Agatha. But the boy had a sympathetic feeling. He knew that of my own will I would not have done it. I shut myself up in the library, where I could not rest, but kept pacing up and down like a caged beast. What could I do? and if I could do nothing, what would become of my boy? These were the questions that, without ceasing, pursued each other through my mind.

Simson came out to dinner, and when the house was all still, and most of the servants in bed, we went out and met Dr. Moncrieff, as we had appointed, at the head of the glen. Simson, for his part, was disposed to scoff at the divine. 'If there are to be any spells, you know, I'll cut the whole concern,' he said. I did not make him any reply. I had not invited him; he could go or come as he pleased. He was very talkative, far more than suited my humour, as we went on. 'One thing is certain, you know, there must be some human agency,' he said. 'It is all bosh about apparations. I never have investigated the laws of sound to any great extent, and there's a great deal in ventriloquism that we don't know much about.' 'If it's the same to you,' I said, 'I wish you'd keep all that to yourself, Simson. It doesn't suit my state of mind.' 'Oh, I hope I know how to respect idiosyncrasy,' he said. The very tone of his voice irritated me beyond measure. These scientific fellows, I wonder people put up with them as they do, when you have no mind for their cold-blooded confidence. Dr. Moncrieff met us about eleven o'clock, the same time as on the previous night. He was a large man, with a venerable countenance and white hair – old, but in full vigour, and thinking less of a cold night walk than many a younger man. He had his lantern as I had. We were fully provided with means of lighting the place, and we were all of us resolute men. We had a rapid consultation as we went up, and the result was that we divided to different posts. Dr. Moncrieff remained inside the wall – if you can call that inside where there was no wall but one. Simson placed himself on the side next the ruins, so as to intercept any communication with the old house, which was what his mind was fixed upon. I was posted on the other side. To say that nothing could come near without being seen was self-evident. It had been so also on the previous night. Now, with our three lights in the midst of the darkness the whole place seemed illuminated. Dr. Moncrieff's lantern, which was a large one, without any means of shutting up – an old-fashioned lantern with a pierced and ornamental top – shone steadily, the rays shooting out of it upward into the gloom. He placed it on the grass, where the middle of the room would have been. The usual effect of the light streaming out of the doorway was prevented by the illumination which Simson and I on either side supplied. With these differences, everything seemed as on the previous night.

And what occurred was exactly the same, with the same air of repetition, point for point, as I had formerly remarked. I declare that it seemed to me as if I were pushed against, put aside, by the owner of the voice as he paced up and down in his trouble – though these are perfectly futile words, seeing that the stream of light from my lantern, and that from Simson's taper, lay broad and clear, without a shadow, without the smallest break, across the entire breadth of the grass. I had ceased even to be alarmed, for my part. My heart was rent with pity and trouble – pity for the poor suffering human creature that moaned and pleaded so, and trouble for myself and my boy. God! if I could not find any help – and what help could I find? – Roland would die.

We were all perfectly still till the first outburst was exhausted, as I knew (by experience) it would be. Dr. Moncrieff, to whom it was new, was quite motionless on the other side of the wall, as we were in our places. My heart had remained almost at its usual beating during the voice. I was used to it, it did not rouse all my pulses as it did at first. But just as it threw itself sobbing at the door (I cannot use other words), there suddenly came something which sent the blood coursing through my veins and my heart into my mouth. It was a voice inside the wall – the minister's well-known voice. I would have been prepared for it in any kind of adjuration, but I was not prepared for what I heard. It came out with a sort of stammering, as if too much moved for utterance. 'Willie, Willie! Oh, God preserve us! is it you?'

These simple words had an effect upon me that the voice of the invisible creature had ceased to have. I thought the old man, whom I had brought into this danger, had gone mad with terror. I made a dash round to the other side of the wall, half crazed myself with the thought. He was standing where I had left him, his shadow thrown vague and large upon the grass by the lantern which stood at his feet. I lifted my own light to see his face as I rushed forward. He was very pale, his eyes wet and glistening, his mouth quivering with parted lips. He neither saw nor heard me. We that had gone through this experience before, had crouched towards each other to get a little strength to bear it. But he was not even aware that I was there. His whole being seemed absorbed in anxiety and tenderness. He held out his hands, which trembled, but it seemed to me with eagerness, not fear. He went on speaking all the time. 'Willie, if it is you – and it's you, if it is not a delusion of Satan – Willie, lad! why come ye here frighting them that know you not? Why came ye not to me?'

He seemed to wait for an answer. When his voice ceased, his countenance, every line moving, continued to speak. Simson gave me another terrible shock, stealing into the open doorway with his light, as much awe-stricken, as wildly curious, as I. But the minister resumed, without seeing Simson, speaking to someone else. His voice took a tone of expostulation—

'Is this right to come here? Your mother's gone with your name on her lips. Do you think she would ever close her door on her own lad? Do ye think the Lord will close the door, ye faint-hearted creature? No! – I forbid ye! Cry out no more to man. Go home, ye wandering spirit! Go home! Do you hear me – me that christened ye, that have struggled with ye, that have wrestled for ye with the

Lord?' Here the loud tones of his voice sank into tenderness. 'And her too, poor woman! poor woman! her you are calling upon. She's no here. You'll find her with the Lord. Go there and seek her, not here. Do you hear me, lad? go after her there. He'll let you in, though it's late. Man, take heart! if you will lie and sob and greet, let it be at Heaven's gate, and no your poor mother's ruined door.'

He stopped to get his breath, and the voice had stopped, not as it had done before, when its time was exhausted and all its repetitions said, but with a sobbing catch in the breath as if over-ruled. Then the minister spoke again: 'Are you hearing me, Will? Oh, laddie, you've liked the beggarly elements all your days. Be done with them now. Go home to the Father – the Father! Are you hearing me?' Here the old man sank down upon his knees, his face raised upwards, his hands held up with a tremble in them, all white in the light in the midst of the darkness. I resisted as long as I could, though I cannot tell why – then I, too, dropped upon my knees. Simson all the time stood in the doorway, with an expression in his face such as words could not tell, his under-lip dropped, his eyes wild, staring. It seemed to be to him, that image of blank ignorance and wonder, that we were praying. All the time the voice, with a low arrested sobbing, lay just where he was standing, as I thought.

'Lord,' the minister said – 'Lord, take him into Thy everlasting habitations. The mother he cries to is with Thee. Who can open to him but Thee? Lord, when is it too late for Thee, or what is too hard for Thee? Lord, let that woman there draw him inower! Let her draw him inower!'

I sprang forward to catch something in my arms that flung itself within the door. The illusion was so strong that I never paused till I felt my forehead graze against the wall and my hands clutch the ground – for there was nobody there to save from falling, as in my foolishness I thought. Simson held out his hand to me to help me up. He was trembling and cold, his lower lip hanging, his speech almost inarticulate. 'It's gone,' he said, stammering – 'it's gone!' We leant upon each other for a moment, trembling so much, both of us, that the whole scene trembled as if it were going to dissolve and disappear, and yet as long as I live I will never forget it – the shining of the strange lights, the blackness all round, the kneeling figure with all the whiteness of the light concentrated on its white venerable head and uplifted hands. A strange solemn stillness seemed to close all round us. By intervals a single syllable, 'Lord! Lord!' came from the old minister's lips. He saw none of us, nor thought of us. I never knew how long we stood, like sentinels guarding him at his prayers, holding our lights in a confused dazed way, not knowing what we did. But at last he rose from his knees and, standing up at his full height, raised his arms, as the Scotch manner is at the end of a religious service, and solemnly gave the apostolic benediction – to what? to the silent earth, the dark woods, the wide breathing atmosphere – for we were but spectators gasping an Amen!

It seemed to me that it must be the middle of the night, as we all walked back. It was in reality very late. Dr. Moncrieff put his arm into mine. He walked slowly, with an air of exhaustion. It was as if we were coming from a death bed. Something hushed and solemnized the very air. There was that sense of relief in it which there always is at the end of a deathstruggle. And Nature persistent, never daunted, came back in all of us, as we returned into the ways of life. We said nothing to each other, indeed, for a time, but when we got clear of the trees and reached the opening near the house, where we could see the sky, Dr. Moncrieff himself was the first to speak. 'I must be going,' he said, 'it's very late, I'm afraid. I will go down the glen, as I came.'

'But not alone. I am going with you, doctor.'

'Well, I will not oppose it. I am an old man, and agitation wearies more than work. Yes, I'll be thankful of your arm. To-night, Colonel, you've done me more good turns than one.'

I pressed his hand on my arm, not feeling able to speak. But Simson, who turned with us, and who had gone along all this time with his taper flaring, in entire unconsciousness, came to himself, apparently at the sound of our voices, and put out that wild little torch with a quick movement, as if of shame. 'Let me carry your lantern,' he said, 'it is heavy.' He recovered with a spring, and in a moment, from the awe-stricken spectator he had been, became himself, sceptical and cynical. 'I should like to ask you a question,' he said. 'Do you believe in Purgatory, Doctor? It's not in the tenets of the Chuch, as far as I know.'

'Sir,' said Dr. Moncrieff, 'an old man like me is sometimes not very sure what he believes. There is just one thing I am certain of – and that is the loving-kindness of God.'

'But I thought that was in this life. I am no theologian—'

'Sir,' said the old man again, with a tremor in him which I could feel going over all his frame, 'if I saw a friend of mine within the gates of hell, I would not despair, but his Father would take him by the hand still – if he cried like *you*.'

'I allow it is very strange – very strange. I cannot see through it. That there must be human agency, I feel sure. Doctor, what made you decide upon the person and the name?'

The minister put out his hand with the impatience which a man might show if he were asked how he recognized his brother. 'Tuts!' he said, in familiar speech – then more solemnly, 'how should I not recognize a person that I know better – far better – than I know you?'

'Then you saw the man?'

Dr. Moncrieff made no reply. He moved his hand again with a little impatient movement, and walked on, leaning heavily on my arm. And we went on for a long time without another word, threading the dark paths, which were steep and slippery with the damp of the winter. The air was very still – not more than enough to make a faint sighing in the branches, which mingled with the sound of the water to which we were descending. When we spoke again, it was about indifferent matters – about the height of the river, and the recent rains. We parted with the minister at his own door, where his old housekeeper appeared in great pertubation, waiting for him. 'Eh me, minister! the young gentleman will be worse?' she cried.

'Far from that – better. God bless him!' Dr. Moncrieff said.

I think if Simson had begun again to me with his questions, I should have pitched him over the rocks as we returned up the glen, but he was silent, by a good inspiration. And the sky was clearer than it had been for many nights, shining high over the trees, with here and there a star faintly gleaming through the wilderness of dark and bare branches. The air, as I have said, was very soft in them, with a subdued and peaceful cadence. It was real, like every natural sound, and came to us like a hush of peace and relief. I thought there was a sound in it as of the breath of a sleeper, and it seemed clear to me that Roland must be sleeping, satisfied and calm. We went up to his room when we went in. There we found the complete hush of rest. My wife looked up out of a doze, and gave me a smile. 'I think he is a great deal better, but you are very late,' she said in a whisper, shading the light with her hand that the doctor might see his patient. The boy had got back something like his own colour. He woke as we stood all round his bed. His eyes had the happy half-awakened look of childhood, glad to shut again, yet pleased with the interruption and glimmer of light. I stooped over him and kissed his forehead, which was moist and cool. 'All is well, Roland,' I said. He looked up at me with a glance of pleasure, and took my hand and laid his cheek upon it, and so went to sleep.

For some nights after, I watched among the ruins, spending all the dark hours up to midnight patrolling about the bit of wall which was associated with so many emotions, but I heard nothing, and saw nothing beyond the quiet course of Nature, nor, so far as I am aware, has anything been heard again. Dr. Moncreiff gave me the history of the youth, whom he never hesitated to name. I did not ask, as Simson did, how he recognized him. He had been a prodigal – weak, foolish, easily imposed upon, and 'led away,' as people say. All that we had heard had passed actually in life, the doctor said. The young man had come home thus a day or two after his mother died – who was no more than the housekeeper in the old house – and distracted with the news, had thrown himself down at the door and called upon her to let him in. The old man could hardly speak of it for tears. To me it seemed as if – heaven help us, how little do we know about anything! – a scene like that might impress itself somehow upon the hidden heart of Nature. I do not pretend to know how, but the repetition had struck me at the time as, in its terrible strangeness and incomprehensibility, almost mechanical – as if the unseen actor could not exceed or vary but was bound to re-enact the whole. One thing that struck me, however, greatly, was the likeness between the old minister and my boy in the manner of regarding those strange phenomena. Dr. Moncrieff was not terrified, as I had been myself, and all the rest of us. It was no 'ghost,' as I fear we all vulgarly considered it, to him but – a poor creature whom he knew under these conditions, just as he had known him in the flesh, having no doubt of his identity. And to Roland it was the same. This spirit in pain – if it was a spirit – this voice out of the unseen – was a poor fellow-creature in misery, to be succoured and helped out of his trouble, to my boy. He spoke to me quite frankly about it when he got better. 'I knew father would find some way,' he said. And this was when he was strong and well, and all idea that he would turn hysterical or become a seer of visions had happily passed away.

I must add one curious fact which does not seem to me to have any relation to the above, but which Simson made great use of, as the human agency which he was determined to find somehow. We had examined the ruins very closely at the time of these occurrences; but afterwards, when all was over, as we went casually about them one Sunday afternoon in the idleness of that unemployed day, Simson with his stick penetrated an old window which had been entirely blocked up with fallen soil. He jumped down into it in great excitement, and called me to follow. There we found a little hole – for it was more a hole than a room – entirely hidden under the ivy ruins, in which there was some quantity of straw laid in a corner, as if someone had made a bed there, and some remains of crusts about the floor. Someone had lodged there, and not very long before, he made out; and that this unknown being was the author of all the mysterious sounds we heard he was convinced. 'I told you it was human agency.' he said, triumphantly. He forgets, I suppose, how he and I stood with our lights seeing nothing, while the space between us was audibly traversed by something that could speak, and sob, and suffer. There is no argument with men of this kind. He is ready to get up a laugh against me on this slender ground. 'I was puzzled myself – I could not make it out – but I always felt convinced human agency was at the bottom of it. And here it is – and a clever fellow he must have been,' the doctor says.

Bagley left my service as soon as he got well. He assured me it was no want of respect; but he could not stand 'them kind of things,' and the man was so shaken and ghastly that I was glad to give him a present and let him go. For my own part, I made a point of staying out the time, two years, for which I had taken Brentwood; but I did not renew my tenancy. By that time we had settled, and found for ourselves a pleasant home of our own.

I must add that when the doctor defies me, I can always bring back gravity to his countenance, and a pause in his railing, when I remind him of the juniper bush. To me that was a matter of little importance. I could believe I was mistaken. I did not care about it one way or other; but on his mind the effect was different. The miserable voice, the spirit in pain, he could think of as the result of ventriloquism, or reverberation, or – anything you please: an elaborate prolonged hoax executed somehow by the tramp that had found a lodging in the old tower. But the juniper bush staggered him. Things have effects so different on the minds of different men.

THE SPECTRE BRIDEGROOM

Washington Irving

On the summit of one of the heights of the Odenwald, a wild and romantic tract of Upper Germany that lies not far from the confluence of the Maine and the Rhine, there stood, many, many years since, the castle of the Baron Von Landshort. It is now quite fallen to decay, and almost buried among beech-trees and dark firs; above which, however, its old watch-tower may still be seen struggling, like the former possessor I have mentioned, to carry a high head, and look down upon the neighbouring country.

The baron was a dry branch of the great family of Katzenellenbogen, and inherited the reliques of the property, and all the pride of his ancestors. Though the warlike disposition of his predecessors had much impaired the family possessions, yet the baron still endeavoured to keep up some show of former state. The times were peaceful, and the German nobles, in general, had abandoned their inconvenient old castles, perched like eagles' nests among the mountains, and had built more convenient residences in the valleys: still the baron remained proudly drawn up in his little fortress, cherishing, with hereditary inveteracy, all the old family feuds; so that he was on ill terms with some of his nearest neighbours, on account of disputes that had happened between their great-great-grandfathers.

The baron had but one child, a daughter; but Nature, when she wants but one child, always compensates by making it a prodigy; and so it was with the daughter of the baron. All the nurses, gossips and country cousins assured her father that she had not her equal for beauty in all Germany; and who should know better than they? She had, moreover, been brought up with great care under the superintendence of two maiden aunts, who had spent some years of their early life at one of the little German courts, and were skilled in all the branches of knowledge necessary to the education of a fine lady. Under their instructions she became a miracle of accomplishments. By the time she was eighteen she could embroider to admiration, and had worked whole histories of the saints in tapestry, with such strength of expression in their countenances, that they looked like so many souls in purgatory. She could read without great difficulty, and had spelled her way through several church legends, and almost all the chivalric wonders of the Heldenbuch. She had even made considerable proficiency in writing; could sign her own name without missing a letter, and so legibly that her aunts could read it without spectacles. She excelled in making little elegant good-for-nothing lady-like knickknacks of all kinds; was versed in the most abstruse dancing of the day; played a number of airs on the harp and guitar; and knew all the tender ballads of the Minnelieders by heart.

At the time of which my story treats, there was a great family gathering at the castle, on an affair of the utmost importance. It was to receive the destined bridegroom of the baron's daughter. A negotiation had been carried on between the father and an old nobleman of Bavaria, to unite the dignity of their houses by the marriage of their children. The preliminaries had been conducted with proper punctilio. The young people were betrothed without seeing each other; and the time was appointed for the marriage ceremony. The young Count Von Altenburg had been recalled from the army for the purpose, and was actually on his way to the baron's to receive his bride. Missives had even been received from him, from Würzburg, where he was accidentally detained, mentioning the day and hour when he might be expected to arrive.

The castle was in a tumult of preparation to give him a suitable welcome. The fair bride had been decked out with uncommon care. The two aunts had superintended her toilet, and quarrelled the whole morning about every article of her dress. The young lady had taken advantage of their contest to follow the bent of her own taste; and fortunately it was a good one. She looked as lovely as youthful bridegroom could desire; and the flutter of expectation heightened the lustre of her charms.

In the meantime the fatted calf had been killed; the forests had rung with the clamour of the huntsmen; the kitchen was crowded with good cheer; the cellars had yielded up whole oceans of *Rhein-wein* and *Ferne-wein;* and even the great Heidelberg tun had been laid under contribution. Everything was ready to receive the distinguished guest with *Saus und Braus* in the true spirit of German hospitality – but the guest delayed to make his appearance. Hour rolled after hour. The sun that had poured his downward rays upon the rich forests of the Odenwald, now just gleamed along the summits of the mountain. The baron mounted the highest tower, and strained his eyes in hopes of catching a distant sight of the count and his attendants. Once he thought he beheld them; the sound of horns came floating from the valley, prolonged by the mountain echoes. A number of horsemen were seen far below, slowly advancing along the road; but when they had nearly reached the foot of the mountain, they suddenly struck off in a different direction. The last ray of sunshine departed – the bats began to flit by in the twilight – the road grew dimmer and dimmer to the view; and nothing appeared stirring in it, but now and then a peasant lagging homeward from his labour.

When the old castle of Landshort was in this state of perplexity, a very interesting scene was transacting in a different part of the Odenwald.

The young Count Von Altenburg was tranquilly pursuing his route in that sober jog-trot in which a man travels towards matrimony when his friends have taken all the trouble and uncertainty of courtship off his hands, and a bride is waiting for him as certainly as a dinner at the end of his journey. He had encountered, at Würtzburg, a youthful companion in arms, with whom he had seen some service on the frontiers – Herman Von Starkenfaust, one of the stoutest hands and worthiest of German chivalry, who was now returning from the army. His father's castle was not far distant from the old fortress of Landshort, although an hereditary feud rendered the families hostile, and strangers to each other.

In the warm-hearted moment of recognition the young friends related all their past adventures and fortunes, and the count gave the whole history of his intended nuptials with a young lady whom he had never seen, but of whose charm he had received the most enrapturing descriptions.

As the route of the friends lay in the same direction, they agreed to perform the rest of their journey together; and that they might do it the more leisurely, set off from

Würzburg at an early hour, the count having given directions for his retinue to follow and overtake him.

They beguiled their wayfaring with recollections of their military scenes and adventures; but the count was apt to be a little tedious, now and then, about the reputed charms of his bride, and the felicity that awaited him.

In this way they entered among the mountains of the Odenwald and were traversing one of its most lonely and thickly wooded passes. It is well known that the forests of Germany have always been as much infested by robbers as its castles by spectres; and, at this time, the former were particularly numerous, from the hordes of disbanded soldiers wandering about the country. It will not appear extraordinary, therefore, that the cavaliers were attacked by a gang of these stragglers in the depth of the forest. They defended themselves with bravery, but were nearly overpowered when the count's retinue arrived to their assistance. At sight of them the robbers fled, but not until the count had received a mortal wound. He was slowly and carefully conveyed back to the city of Würzburg, and a friar summoned from a neighbouring convent, who was famous for his skill in administering to both soul and body; but half of his skill was superfluous; the moments of the unfortunate count were numbered.

With his dying breath he entreated his friend to repair instantly to the castle of Landshort and explain the fatal cause of his not keeping his appointment with his bride. Though not the most ardent of lovers, he was one of the most punctilious of men, and appeared earnestly solicitous that this mission should be speedily and courteously executed. 'Unless this is done,' said he, 'I shall not sleep quietly in my grave!' He repeated these words with peculiar solemnity. A request, at a moment so impressive, admitted no hesitation. Starkenfaust endeavoured to soothe him to calmness, promised faithfully to execute his wish, and gave him his hand in solemn pledge. The dying man pressed it in acknowledgement, but soon lapsed into delirium – raved about his bride – his engagement – his plighted word; ordered his horse, that he might ride to the castle of Landshort; and expired in the fancied act of vaulting into the saddle.

Starkenfaust bestowed a sigh, and a soldier's tear, on the untimely fate of his comrade; and then pondered on the awkward mission he had undertaken. His heart was heavy and his head perplexed; for he was to present himself an unbidden guest among hostile people and to damp their festivity with tidings fatal to their hopes. Still there were certain whisperings of curiosity in his bosom to see this far-famed beauty of Katzenellenbogen, so cautiously shut up from the world; for he was a passionate admirer of the sex, and there was a dash of eccentricity and enterprise in his character that made him fond of all singular adventure.

Previous to his departure he made all due arrangements with the holy fraternity of the convent for the funeral solemnities of his friend, who was to be buried in the cathedral of Würzburg, near some of his illustrious relatives; and the mourning retinue of the count took charge of his remains.

It is now high time we should return to the ancient family of Katzenellenbogen, who were impatient for their guest, and still more for their dinner; and to the worthy little baron whom we left airing himself on the watchtower.

Night closed in, but still no guest arrived. The baron descended from the tower in despair. The banquet, which had been delayed from hour to hour, could no longer be postponed. The meats were already overdone; the cook in an agony; and the whole household had the look of a garrison that had been reduced by famine. The baron was obliged reluctantly to give orders for the feast without the presence of the guest. All were seated at table, and just on the point of commencing, when the sound of a horn from without the gate gave notice of the approach of a stranger. Another long blast filled the old courts of the castle with echoes, and was answered by the warder from the walls. The baron hastened to receive his future son-in-law.

The drawbridge had been let down, and the stranger was before the gate. He was a tall gallant cavalier, mounted on a black steed. His countenance was pale, but he had a beaming, romantic eye, and an air of stately melancholy. The baron was a little mortified that he should have come in this simple, solitary style. His dignity for a moment was ruffled, and he felt disposed to consider it a want of proper respect for the important occasion, and the important family with which he was to be connected. He, however, pacified himself with the conclusion that it must have been youthful impatience which had induced him thus to spur on sooner than his attendants.

'I am sorry,' said the stranger, 'to break in upon you thus unseasonably—'

Here the baron interrupted him with a world of compliments and greetings; for, to tell the truth, he prided himself upon his courtesy and his eloquence. The stranger attempted, once or twice, to stem the torrent of words, but in vain, so he bowed his head and suffered it to flow on. By the time the baron had come to a pause, they had reached the inner court of the castle; and the stranger was again about to speak, when he was once more interrupted by the appearance of the female part of the family, leading forth the shrinking and blushing bride. He gazed on her for a moment as one entranced; it seemed as if his whole soul beamed forth in the gaze, and rested upon that lovely form. One of the maiden aunts whispered something in her ear; she made an effort to speak; her moist blue eye was timidly raised; gave a shy glance of inquiry on the stranger; and was cast again to the ground. The words died away; but there was a sweet smile playing about her lips, and a soft dimpling of the cheek, that showed her glance had not been unsatisfactory. It was impossible for a girl of the fond age of eighteen, highly predisposed for love and matrimony, not to be pleased with so gallant a cavalier.

The late hour at which the guest had arrived left no time for parley. The baron was peremptory, and deferred all particular conversation until the morning, and led the way to the untasted banquet.

It was served up in the great hall of the castle. Around the walls hung the hard-favoured portraits of the heroes of the house of Katzenellenbogen, and the trophies which they had gained in the field and in the chase. Hacked corslets, splintered jousting-spears and tattered banners were mingled with the spoils of sylvan warfare; the jaws of the wolf, and the tusks of the boar, grinned horribly among cross-bows and battle-axes, and a huge pair of antlers branched accidentally over the head of the youthful bridegroom.

The cavalier took but little notice of the company or the entertainment. He scarcely tasted the banquet, but seemed absorbed in admiration of his bride. He conversed in a low tone that could not be overheard – for the language of love is never loud; but where is the female ear so dull that it cannot catch the softest whisper of the lover? There was a mingled tenderness and gravity in his manner that appeared to have a powerful effect upon the young lady. Her colour came and went as she listened with deep attention. Now and then she made some blushing reply, and when his eye was turned away, she would steal a side-long glance at his romantic countenance, and heave a gentle sigh of tender happiness. It was evident that the young couple were completely enamoured. The aunts, who were deeply versed in the mysteries of the heart, declared that they had fallen in love with other at first sight.

The feast went on merrily, or at least noisily, for the guests were all blest with those keen appetites that attend upon light purses and mountain air. The baron told his best and longest stories, and never had he told them so well or with such great effect. If there was anything marvellous, his auditors were lost in astonishment; and if anything facetious, they were sure to laugh exactly in the right place. The baron, it is true, like most great men, was too dignified to utter any joke but a dull one; it was always enforced, however, by a bumper of excellent Hochheimer; and even a dull joke, at one's own table, served up with jolly old wine, is irresistible. Many good things were said by poorer and keener wits, that would not bear repeating, except on similar occasions; many sly speeches whispered in ladies' ears, that almost convulsed them with suppressed laughter; and a song or two roared out by a poor but merry and broad-faced cousin of the baron, that absolutely made the maiden aunts hold up their fans.

Amidst all this revelry the stranger guest maintained a most singular and unseasonable gravity. His countenance assumed a deeper cast of dejection as the evening advanced; and, strange as it may appear, even the baron's jokes seemed only to render him the more melancholy. At times he was lost in thought, and at times there was a perturbed and restless wandering of the eye that bespoke a mind but ill at ease. His conversations with the bride became more and more earnest and mysterious. Lowering clouds began to steal over the fair serenity of her brow, and tremors to run through her tender frame.

All this could not escape the notice of the company. Their gaiety was chilled by the unaccountable gloom of the bridegroom; their spirits were infected; whispers and glances were interchanged, accompanied by shrugs and dubious shakes of the head. The song and laugh grew less and less frequent; there were dreary pauses in the conversation, which were at length succeeded by wild tales and supernatural legends. One dismal story produced another still more dismal, and the baron nearly frightened some of the ladies into hysterics with the history of the goblin horseman that carried away the fair Leonora; a dreadful but true story, which has since been put into excellent verse, and is read and believed by all the world.

The bridegroom listened to this tale with profound attention. He kept his eyes steadily fixed on the baron, and, as the story drew to a close, began gradually to rise from his seat, growing taller and taller, until, in the baron's entranced eye, he seemed almost to tower into a giant. The moment the tale was finished, he heaved a deep sigh, and took a solemn farewell of the company. The baron was perfectly thunderstruck.

'What! going to leave the castle at midnight? Why, everything was prepared for his reception: a chamber was ready for him if he wished to retire.'

The stranger shook his head mournfully and mysteriously; 'I must lay my head in a different chamber to-night.'

There was something in this reply, and the tone in which it was uttered, that made the baron's heart misgive him; but he rallied his forces and repeated his hospitable entreaties. The stranger shook his head silently, but positively, at every offer; and, waving his farewell to the company, stalked slowly out of the hall. The maiden aunts were absolutely petrified – the bride hung her head, and a tear stole to her eye.

The baron followed the stranger to the great court of the castle, where the black charger stood pawing the earth, and snorting with impatience. When they had reached the portal, whose deep archway was dimly lighted by a cresset, the stranger paused and addressed the baron in a hollow tone tone of voice, which the vaulted roof rendered still more sepulchral. 'Now that we are alone,' said he, 'I will impart to you the reason of my going. I have a solemn, an indispensable engagement—'

'Why,' said the baron, 'cannot you send some one in your place?'

'It admits of no substitute – I must attend it in person – I must away to Würzburg Cathedral—'

'Ay,' said the baron, plucking up spirit, 'but not until to-morrow – to-morrow you shall take your bride there.'

'No! No!' replied the stranger, with tenfold solemnity, 'my engagement is with no bride – the worms! the worms expect me! I am a dead man – I have been slain by robbers – my body lies at Würzburg – at midnight I am to be buried – the grave is waiting for me – I must keep my appointment!'

He sprang on his black charger, dashed over the drawbridge, and the clattering of his horse's hoofs was lost in the whistling of the night blast.

The baron returned to the hall in the utmost consternation and related what had passed. Two ladies fainted outright, others sickened at the idea of having banqueted with a spectre. It was the opinion of some that this might be the wild huntsman famous in German legend. Some talked of mountain sprites, of wood demons, and of other supernatural beings, with which the good people of Germany have been so grievously harassed since time immemorial. One of the poor relations ventured to suggest that it might be some sportive evasion of the young cavalier, and that the very gloominess of the caprice seemed to accord with so melancholy a personage. This, however, drew on him the indignation of the whole company, and especially of the baron, who looked upon him as little better than an infidel; so that he was fain to abjure his heresy as speedily as possible, and come into the faith of the true believers.

But, whatever may have been the doubts entertained, they were completely put to an end by the arrival, next day, of regular missives, confirming the intelligence of the young count's murder, and his interment in Würzburg Cathedral.

The dismay at the castle may well be imagined. The baron shut himself up in his chamber. The guests, who had come to rejoice with him, could not think of abandoning him in his distress. They wandered about the courts, or collected in groups in the hall, shaking their heads and shrugging their shoulders at the troubles of so good a man; and sat longer than ever at table, and ate and drank more stoutly than ever, by way of keeping up their spirits. But the situation of the widowed bride was most pitiable. To have lost a husband before she had even embraced him – and such a husband! If the very spectre could be so gracious and noble, what must have been the living man! She filled the house with lamentations.

On the night of the second day of her widowhood she had retired to her chamber, accompanied by one of her aunts, who insisted on sleeping with her. The aunt, who was one of the best tellers of ghost stories in all Germany, had just been recounting one of her longest, and had fallen asleep in the very midst of it. The chamber was remote and overlooked a small garden. The niece lay pensively gazing at the beams of the rising moon, as they trembled on the leaves of an aspen-tree before the lattice. The castle clock had just tolled midnight, when a soft strain of music stole up from the garden. She rose hastily from her bed, and stepped lightly to the window. A tall figure stood among the shadows of the trees. As it raised its head, a beam of moonlight fell upon the countenance. Heaven and earth! she beheld the spectre bridegroom! A loud shriek at that moment burst from her ear, and her aunt, who had been awakened by the music, and had followed her silently to the window, fell into her arms. When she looked again the spectre had disappeared.

Of the two females, the aunt now required the most soothing, for she was perfectly beside herself with terror. As to the young lady, there was something, even in the spectre of her lover, that seemed endearing. There was still the semblance of manly beauty; and though the shadow of a man is but little calculated to satisfy the affections of a love-sick girl, yet, where the substance is not to be had, even that is consoling. The aunt declared she would never sleep in that chamber again; the niece, for once, was refractory, and declared as strongly that she would sleep in no other in the castle: the consequence was, that she had to sleep in it alone; but she drew a promise from her aunt not to relate the story of the spectre, lest she should be denied the only melancholy pleasure left her on earth – that of inhabiting the chamber over which the guardian shade of her lover kept its nightly vigils.

How long the good old lady would have observed this promise is uncertain, for she dearly loved to talk of the marvellous, and there is a triumph in being the first to tell a frightful story; it is, however, still quoted in the neighbourhood, as a memorable instance of female secrecy, that she kept it to herself for a whole week; when she was suddenly absolved from all further restraint by intelligence brought to the breakfast table one morning, that the young lady was not to be found. Her room was empty – the bed had not been slept in – the window was open, and the bird had flown.

The astonishment and concern with which the intelligence was received can only be imagined by those who have witnessed the agitation which the mishaps of a great man cause among his friends. Even the poor relations paused for a moment from the indefatigable labours of the trencher; when the aunt, who had at first been struck speechless, wrung her hands, and shrieked out, 'The goblin, the goblin! she's carried away by the goblin!'

In a few words she related the fearful scene of the garden, and concluded that the spectre must have carried off his bride. Two of the domestics corroborated the opinion, for they had heard the clattering of a horse's hoofs down the mounain about midnight, and had no doubt that it was the spectre on his black charger, bearing his way to the tomb. All present were struck with the direful probability; for events of the kind are extremely common in Germany, as many well-authenticated histories bear witness.

What a lamentable situation was that of the poor baron! What a heart-rending dilemma for a fond father, and a member of the great family of Katzenellenbogen! His only daughter had either been rapt away to the grave, or he was to have some wood-demon for a son-in-law, and perchance a troop of goblin grandchildren. As usual, he was completely bewildered, and all the castle in an uproar. The men were ordered to take horse, and to scour every road and path and glen of the Odenwald. The baron himself had just drawn on his jackboots, girded on his sword, and was about to mount his steed to sally forth on the doubtful quest, when he was brought to a pause by a new apparition. A lady was seen approaching the castle, mounted on a palfrey, attended by a cavalier on horseback. She galloped up to the gate, sprang from her horse, and, falling at the baron's feet, embraced his knees. It was his lost daughter, and her companion – the Spectre Bridegroom! The baron was astounded. He looked at his daughter, then at the spectre, and almost doubted the evidence of his senses. The latter, too, was wonderfully improved in his appearance, since his visit to the world of spirits. His dress was splendid, and set off a noble figure of manly symmetry. He was no longer pale and melancholy. His fine countenance was flushed with the glow of youth, and joy rioted in his large dark eye.

The mystery was soon cleared up. The cavalier (for in truth, as you must have known all the while, he was no goblin) announced himself as Sir Herman Von Starkenfaust. He related his adventure with the young count. He told how he had hastened to the castle to deliver the unwelcome tidings, but that the eloquence of the baron had interrupted him in every attempt to tell his tale; how the sight of the bride had completely captivated him, and that to pass a few hours near her, he had tacitly suffered the mistake to continue; how he had been sorely perplexed in what way to make a decent retreat, until the baron's goblin stories had suggested his eccentric exit; how, fearing the feudal hostility of the family, he had repeated his visits by stealth – had haunted the garden beneath the young lady's window – had wooed – had won – had borne away in triumph – and, in a word, had wedded the fair.

Under any other circumstances the baron would have been inflexible, for he was tenacious of paternal authority, and devoutly obstinate in all family feuds; but he loved his daughter; he had lamented her as lost; he rejoiced to find her still alive; and, though her husband was of a hostile house, yet, thank Heaven, he was not a goblin. There was something, it must be acknowledged, that did not exactly accord with his notions of strict veracity, in the joke the knight had passed upon him of his being a dead man; but several old friends present, who had served in the wars, assured him that every stratagem was excusable in love, and that the cavilier was entitled to especial privilege, having lately served as a trooper.

Matters, therefore, were happily arranged. The baron pardoned the young couple on the spot. The revels at the castle were resumed. The poor relations overwhelmed this new member of the family with loving kindness; he was so gallant, so generous – and so rich. The aunts, it is true, were somewhat scandalised that their system of strict seclusion and passive obedience should be so badly exemplified, but attributed it all to their negligence in not having the windows grated. One of them was particularly mortified at having her marvellous story marred, and that the only spectre she had ever seen should turn out a counterfeit; but the niece seemed perfectly happy at having found him substantial flesh and blood – and so the story ends.

LIGEIA

Edgar Allan Poe

And the will therein lieth, which dieth not. Who knoweth the mysteries of the will, with its vigour? For God is but a great will pervading all things by nature of its intentness. Man doth not yield him to the angels, nor unto death utterly, save only through the weakness of his feeble will. – *Joseph Glanvill*.

I cannot, for my soul, remember how, when, or even precisely where, I first became acquainted with the lady Ligeia. Long years have since elapsed, and my memory is feeble through much suffering. Or, perhaps, I cannot *now* bring these points to mind, because, in truth, the character of my beloved, her rare learning, her singular yet placid cast of beauty, and the thrilling and enthralling eloquence of her low musical language, made their way into my heart, by paces so steadily and stealthily progressive, that they have been unnoticed and unknown. Yet I believe that I met her first and most frequently in some large, old, decaying city near the Rhine. Of her family I have surely heard her speak. That it is of a remotely ancient date cannot be doubted. Ligeia! Ligeia! Buried in studies of a nature more than all else adapted to deaden impressions of the outward world, it is by that sweet word alone, by Ligeia, that I bring before mine eyes in fancy the image of her who is no more. And now, while I write, a recollection flashes upon me that I have *never known* the paternal name of her who was my friend and my betrothed, and who became the partner of my studies and finally the wife of my bosom. Was it a playful charge on the part of my Ligeia? or was it a test of my strength of affection, that I should institute no inquiries upon this point? or was it rather a caprice of my own, a wildly romantic offering on the shrine of the most passionate devotion? I but indistinctly recall the fact itself, what wonder that I have utterly forgotten the circumstances which originated or attended it? And indeed if ever that spirit which is entitled *Romance,* if ever she, the wan and the misty-winged *Ashtophet* of idolatrous Egypt, presided, as they tell, over marriages ill-omened, then most surely she presided over mine.

There is one dear topic, however, on which my memory fails me not. It is the *person* of Ligeia. In stature she was tall, somewhat slender, and in her latter days, even emaciated. I would in vain attempt to portray the majesty, the quiet ease of her demeanour, or the incomprehensible lightness and elasticity of her footfall. She came and departed as a shadow. I was never made aware of her entrance into my closed study, save by the dear music of her low sweet voice, as she placed her marble hand upon my shoulder. In beauty of face no maiden ever equalled her. It was the radiance of an opium dream, an airy and spirit-lifting vision more wildly divine than the phantasies which hovered about the slumbering souls of the daughters of Delos. Yet her features were not that of regular mould which we have been falsely taught to worship in the classical labours of the heathen. 'There is no exquisite beauty,' says Bacon, Lord Verulam, speaking truly of all the forms and *genera* of beauty, 'without some *strangeness* in the proportion.' Yet, although I saw that the features of Ligeia were not of a classical regularity, although I perceived that her loveliness was indeed 'exquisite,' and felt that there was much of 'strangeness' pervading it, yet I have tried in vain to detect the irregularity and to trace home my own perception of 'the strange.' I examined the contour of the lofty pale forehead – it was faultless; how cold indeed that the word when applied to a majesty so divine! the skin rivalled the purest ivory, the commanding extent and repose, the gentle prominence of the regions above the temples; and then the raven-black, the glossy, the luxuriant and naturally curling tresses, setting forth the full force of the Homeric epithet, 'hyacinthine!' I looked at the delicate outlines of the nose, and nowhere but in the graceful medallions of the Hebrews had I beheld a similar perfection. There were the same luxurious smoothness of surface, the same scarcely perceptible tendency to the aquiline, the same harmoniously curved nostrils speaking the free spirit. I regarded the sweet mouth. Here was indeed the triumph of all things heavenly, the magnificent turn of the short upper lip, the soft, voluptuous slumber of the under, the dimples which sported, and the colour which spoke, the teeth glancing back, with a brilliancy almost startling, every ray of the holy light which fell upon them in her serene and placid, yet most exultingly radiant of all smiles. I scrutinised the formation of the chin – and here, too, I found the gentleness of breadth, the softness and the majesty, the fulness and the spirituality of the Greek – the contour which the god Apollo revealed but in a dream to Cleomenes, the son of the Athenian. And then I peered into the large eyes of Ligeia.

For eyes we have no models in the remotely antique. It might have been, too, that in these eyes of my beloved lay the secret to which Lord Verulam alludes. They were, I must believe, far larger than the ordinary eyes of our own race. They were even fuller than the fullest of the gazelle eyes of the tribe of the valley of Nourjahad. Yet it was only at intervals – in moments of intense excitement – that this peculiarity became more than slightly noticeable in Ligeia. And at such moments was her beauty – the beauty of beings either above or apart from the earth – the beauty of the fabulous Houri of the Turk. The hue of the orbs was the most brilliant of black, and far over them hung jetty lashes of great length. The brows, slightly irregular in outline, had the same tint. The 'strangeness,' however, which I found in the eyes, was of a nature distinct from the formation, or the colour, or the brilliancy of the features, and must, after all, be referred to the *expression*. Ah, word of no meaning! behind whose vast latitude of mere sound we intrench our ignorance of so much of the spiritual. The expression of the eyes of Ligeia! How for long hours have I pondered upon it! How have I through the whole of a midsummer night struggled to fathom it! What was it – that something more profound than the well of Democritus – which lay far within the pupils of my beloved? What *was* it? I was possessed with a passion to discover. Those eyes! those large, those shining, those divine orbs! they became to me twin stars of Leda, and I to them devoutest of astrologers.

There is no point among the many incomprehensible anomalies of the science of mind more thrillingly exciting than the fact – never, I believe, noticed in the schools –

that in our endeavours to recall to memory something long forgotten, we often find ourselves *upon the very verge* of remembrance, without being able in the end to remember. And thus how frequently, in my intense scrutiny of Ligeia's eyes, have I felt approaching the full knowledge of their expression – felt it approaching – yet not quite be mine – and so at length entirely depart! And (strange, oh strangest mystery of all!) I found in the commonest objects of the universe a circle of analogies to that expression. I mean to say that, subsequently to the period when Ligeia's beauty passed into my spirit, there dwelling as in a shrine, I derived, from existences in the material world, a sentiment such as I felt always around, within me, by her large and luminous orbs. Yet not the more could I define that sentiment, or analyse, or even steadily view it. I recognised it, let me repeat, sometimes in the survey of a rapidly-growing chrysalis, a stream of running water. I have felt it in the ocean, in the falling of a meteor. I have felt it in the glances of unusually aged people. And there are one or two stars in heaven (one especially, a star of the sixth magnitude, double and changeable, to be found near the large star in Lyra) in a telescopic scrutiny of which I have been made aware of the feeling. I have been filled with it by certain sounds from stringed instruments, and not unfrequently by passages from books. Among innumerable other instances, I well remember something in a volume of Joseph Glanvill, which (perhaps merely from its quaintness – who shall say?) never failed to inspire me with the sentiment: 'And the will therein lieth, which dieth not. Who knoweth the mysteries of the will, with its vigour? For God is but a great will pervading all things by nature of its intentness. Man doth not yield him to the angels, nor unto death utterly, save only through the weakness of his feeble will.'

Length of years and subsequent reflection have enabled me to trace, indeed, some remote connection between this passage in the English moralist and a portion of the character of Ligeia. An *intensity* in thought, action, or speech, was possibly in her a result, or at least an index, of that gigantic volition which, during our long intercourse, failed to give other and more immediate evidence of its existence. Of all the women whom I have ever known, she, the outwardly calm, the ever-placid Ligeia, was the most violent a prey to the tumultuous vultures of stern passion. And of such passion I could form no estimate, save by the miraculous expansion of those eyes which at once so delighted and appalled me, by the almost magical melody, modulation, distinctness, and placidity of her very low voice, and by the fierce energy (rendered doubly effective by contrast with her manner of utterance) of the wild words which she habitually uttered.

I have spoken of the learning of Ligeia: it was immense – such as I have never known in woman. In the classical tongues was she deeply proficient, and as far as my own acquaintance extended in regard to the modern dialects of Europe, I have never known her at fault. Indeed, upon any theme of the most admired, because simply the most abtruse of the boasted erudition of the academy, have I *ever* found Ligeia at fault? How singularly, how thrillingly, this one point in the nature of my wife has forced itself, at this late period only, upon my attention! I said her knowledge was such as I have never known in woman, but where breathes the man who has traversed, and successfully, *all* the wide areas of the moral, physical, and mathematical science? I saw not then what I now clearly perceive, that the acquisitions of Ligeia were gigantic, were astounding; yet I was sufficiently aware of her infinite supremacy to resign myself, with a child-like confidence, to her guidance through the chaotic world of metaphysical investigation at which I was most busily occupied during the earlier years of our marriage. With how vast a triumph – with how vivid a delight – with how much of all that is ethereal in hope, did I *feel*, as she bent over me in studies but little sought – but less known – that delicious vista by slow degrees expanding before me, down whose long, gorgeous, and all untrodden path, I might at length pass onward to the goal of a wisdom too divinely precious not to be forbidden!

How poignant, then, must have been the grief with which, after some years, I beheld my well-grounded expectations take wings to themselves and fly away! Without Ligeia I was but as a child groping benighted. Her presence, her readings alone, rendered vividly luminous the many mysteries of the transcendentalism in which we were immersed. Wanting the radiant lustre of her eyes, letters, lambent and golden, grew duller than Saturnian lead. And now those eyes shone less and less frequently upon the pages over which I pored. Ligeia grew ill. The wild eyes blazed with a too – too glorious effulgence: the pale fingers became of the transparent waxen hue of the grave; and the blue veins upon the lofty forehead swelled and sank impetuously with the tides of the most gentle emotion. I saw that she must die – and I struggled desperately in spirit with the grim Azrael. And the struggles of the passionate wife were, to my astonishment, even more energetic than my own. There had been much in her stern nature to impress me with the belief that to her, death would have come without its terrors, but not so. Words are impotent to convey any idea of the fierceness of resistance with which she wrestled with the Shadow. I groaned in anguish at the pitiable spectacle. I would have soothed, I would have reasoned; but in the intensity of her wild desire for life – for life – *but* for life – solace and reason were alike the uttermost of folly. Yet not until the last instance, amid the most convulsive writhings of her fierce spirit, was shaken the external placidity of her demeanour. Her voice grew more gentle – grew more low – yet I would not wish to dwell upon the wild meaning of the quietly uttered words. My brain reeled as I hearkened, entranced, to a melody more than mortal – to assumptions and aspirations which mortality had never before known.

That she loved me I should not have doubted; and I might have been easily aware that, in a bosom such as hers, love would have reigned no ordinary passion. But in death only was I fully impressed with the strength of her affection. For long hours, detaining my hand, would she pour out before me the overflowing of a heart whose more than passionate devotion amounted to idolatry. How had I deserved to be so blessed by such confessions? – how had I deserved to be so cursed with the removal of my beloved in the hour of her making them? But upon this subject I cannot bear to dilate. Let me say only, that in Ligeia's more than womanly abandonment to love, alas! all unmerited, all unworthily bestowed, I at length recognised the principle of her longing, with so wildly earnest a desire, for the life which was now fleeing so rapidly away. It is this wild longing – it is this eager vehemence of desire for life – *but* for life – that I have no power to portray – no utterance capable of expressing.

At high noon of the night in which she departed, beckoning me peremptorily to her side, she bade me repeat certain verses composed by herself not many days before. I obeyed her. They were these :—

> Lo! 'tis a gala night
>   Within the lonesome latter years!
> An angel throng, bewinged, bedight
>   In veils, and drowned in tears,
> Sit in a theatre, to see
>   A play of hopes and fears,
> While the orchestra breathes fitfully
>   The music of the spheres.
>
> Mimes, in the form of God on high,
>   Mutter and rumble low,
> And hither and thither fly;
>   Mere puppets they, who come and go
> At bidding of vast formless things
>   That shift the scenery to and fro,
> Flapping from out their Condor wings
>   Invisible Woe!
>
> That motley drama! – oh, be sure
>   It shall not be forgot!
> With its Phantom chased for evermore,
>   By a crowd that seize it not,
> Through a circle that ever returneth in
>   To the self-same spot;
> And much of Madness, and more of Sin
>   And Horror, the soul of the plot!
>
> But see, amid the mimic rout
>   A crawling shape intrude!
> A blood-red thing that writhes from out
>   The scenic solitude!
> It writhes! – it writhes! – with mortal pangs
>   The mimes become its food,
> And the seraphs sob at vermin fangs
>   In human gore inbued.
>
> Out – out are the lights – out all!
>   And over each quivering form,
> The curtain, a funeral pall,
>   Comes down with the rush of a storm –
> And the angels, all pallid and wan,
>   Uprising, unveiling, affirm
> That the play is the tragedy, 'Man,'
>   And its hero, the Conqueror Worm.

'O God!' half-shrieked Ligeia, leaping to her feet and extending her arms aloft with a spasmodic movement, as I made an end of these lines – 'O God! O Divine Father! shall these things be undeviatingly so? shall this conqueror be not once conquered? Are we not part and parcel in Thee? Who – who knoweth the mysteries of the will with its vigour? Man doth not yield him to the angels, *nor unto death utterly,* save only through the weakness of his feeble will.'

And now, as if exhausted with emotion, she suffered her white arms to fall, and returned solemnly to her bed of death. And as she breathed her last sighs there came mingled with them a low murmur from her lips. I bent to them my ear, and distinguished, again, the concluding words of the passage in Glanvill :— *'Man doth not yield him to the angels, nor unto death utterly, save only through the weakness of his feeble will.'*

She died, and I, crushed into the very dust with sorrow, could no longer endure the lonely desolation of my dwelling in the dim and decaying city by the Rhine. I had no lack of what the world calls wealth. Ligeia had brought me far more, very far more, than ordinarily falls to the lot of mortals. After a few months therefore of weary and aimless wandering, I purchased, and put in some repair, an abbey which I shall not name, in one of the wildest and least frequented portions of fair England. The gloomy and dreary grandeur of the building, the almost savage aspect of the domain, the many melancholy and time-honoured memories connected with both, had much in unison with the feelings of utter abandonment which had driven me into that remote and unsocial region of the country. Yet, although the external abbey, with its verdant decay hanging about it, suffered but little alteration, I gave way, with a child-like perversity, and perchance with a faint hope of alleviating my sorrows, to a display of more than regal magnificence within. For such follies, even in childhood, I had imbibed a taste, and now they came back to me as if in the dotage of grief. Alas, I feel how much even of incipient madness might have been discovered in the gorgeous and fantastic draperies, in the solemn carvings of Egypt, in the wild cornices and furniture, in the Bedlam patterns of the carpets of tufted gold! I had become a bounden slave in the trammels of opium, and my labours and my orders had taken a colouring from my dreams. But these absurdities I must not pause to detail. Let me speak only of that one chamber, ever accursed, whither in a moment of mental alienation I led from the altar as my bride – as the successor of the unforgotten Ligeia – the fair-haired and blue-eyed Lady Rowena Trevanion of Tremaine.

There is no individual portion of the architecture and decoration of that bridal chamber which is not now visibly before me. Where were the souls of the haughty family of the bride, when through thirst of gold, they permitted to pass the threshold of an apartment *so* bedecked, a maiden and a daughter so beloved? I have said that I minutely remember the details of the chamber, yet I am sadly forgetful on topics of deep moment, and here there was no system, no keeping, in the fantastic display, to take hold upon the memory. The room lay in a high turret of the castellated abbey, was pentagonal in shape, and of capacious size. Occupying the whole southern face of the pentagon was the sole window, an immense sheet of unbroken glass from Venice, – a single pane, and tinted of a leaden hue, so that the rays of either the sun or moon passing through it fell with a ghastly lustre on the objects within. Over the upper portion of this huge window extended the trellis-work of an aged vine which clambered up the massy walls of the turret. The ceiling, of gloomy-looking oak, was excessively lofty, vaulted, and elaborately fretted with the wildest and most grotesque specimens of a semi-Gothic, semi-Druidical device. From out the most central recess of this melancholy vaulting, suspended by a single chain of gold with long links, a huge censer of the same metal, Saracenic in pattern, and with many perforations so contrived that there writhed in and out, as if endued with a serpent vitality, a continual succession of parti-coloured fires.

Some few ottomans and golden candelabra, of Eastern figure, were in various stations about, and there was the couch, too, the bridal couch, of an Indian model, and low, and sculptured of solid ebony, with a pall-like canopy above. In each of the angles of the chamber stood on end a gigantic sarcophagus of black granite, from the tombs of the kings over against Luxor, with their aged lids full of immemorial sculpture. But in the draping of the apartment lay, alas! the chief phantasy of all. The lofty walls, gigantic in height, even unproportionately so, were hung from summit to foot in vast folds with a heavy and massive-looking tapestry – tapestry of a material which was found alike as a carpet on the floor, as a covering for the ottomans and the ebony bed, as a canopy for the bed, and as the gorgeous volutes of the curtains which partially shaded the window. The material was the richest cloth of gold. It was spotted all over, at irregular intervals, with arabesque figures about a foot in diameter, and wrought upon the cloth in patterns of the most jetty black. But these figures partook of the true character of the arabesque only when regarded from a single point of view. By a contrivance now common, and indeed traceable to a very remote period of antiquity, they were made changeable in every aspect. To one entering the room they both bore the appearance of simple monstrosities, but upon a farther advance this appearance gradually departed, and, step by step, as the visitor moved his station in the chamber, he saw himself surrounded by an endless succession of the ghastly forms which belong to the superstition of the Norman, or arise in the guilty slumbers of the monk. The phantasmagoric effect was vastly heightened by the artificial introduction of a strong continual current of wind behind the draperies, giving a hideous and uneasy animation to the whole.

In halls such as these, in a bridal chamber such as this, I passed with the Lady of Tremaine the unhallowed hours of the first month of our marriage, passed them with but little disquietude. That my wife dreaded the fierce moodiness of my temper, that she shunned me, and loved me but little, I could not help perceiving, but it gave me rather pleasure than otherwise. I loathed her with a hatred belonging more to demon than to man. My memory flew back (oh, with what intensity of regret!) to Ligeia, the beloved, the august, the beautiful, the entombed. I revelled in recollections of her purity, of her wisdom, of her lofty, ethereal nature, of her passionate, her idolatrous love. Now, then, did my spirit fully and freely burn with more than all the fires of her own. In the excitement of my opium dreams (for I was habitually fettered in the shackles of the drug) I would call aloud upon her name during the silence of the night, or among the sheltered recesses of the glens by day, as if, through the wild eagerness, the solemn passion, the consuming ardour of my longing for the departed, I could restore her to the pathway she had abandoned – ah, *could* it be for ever? upon the earth.

About the commencement of the second month of the marriage, the Lady Rowena was attacked with sudden illness, from which her recovery was slow. The fever which consumed her rendered her nights uneasy; and in her perturbed state of half-slumber she spoke of sounds and of motions in and about the chamber of the turret, which I concluded had no origin save in the distemper of her fancy, or perhaps in the phantasmagoric influences of the chamber itself. She became at length, convalescent – finally, well. Yet but a brief period elapsed, ere a second more violent disorder again threw her upon a bed of suffering : and from this attack her frame, at all times feeble, never altogether recovered. Her illnesses were, after this epoch, of alarming character, and of more alarming recurrence, defying alike the knowledge and the great exertions of her physicians. With the increase of the chronic disease which had thus, apparently, taken too sure hold upon her constitution to be eradicated by human means, I could not fail to observe a similar increase in the nervous irritation of her temperament, and in her excitability by trivial causes of fear. She spoke again, and now more frequently and pertinaciously, of the sounds – of the slight sounds – and of the unusual motions among the tapestries, to which she had formerly alluded.

One night, near the closing in of September, she pressed this distressing subject with more than usual emphasis upon my attention. She had just awakened from an unquiet slumber, and I had been watching, with feelings half of anxiety, half of terror, the workings of her emaciated countenance. I sat by the side of her ebony bed, upon one of those ottomans of India. She partly arose, and spoke, in an earnest low whisper, of sounds which she *then* heard, but which I could not hear – of motions which she *then* saw, but which I could not perceive. The wind was rushing hurriedly behind the tapestries, and I wished to show her (what, let me confess it, I could not *all* believe) that those almost inarticulate breathings, and those very gentle variations of the figures upon the wall, were but the natural effects of that customary rushing of the wind.

But a deadly pallor, overspreading her face, had proved to me that my exertions to reassure her would be fruitless. She appeared to be fainting, and no attendants were within call. I remembered where was deposited a decanter of light wine which had been ordered by her physicians, and hastened across the chamber to procure it. But, as I stepped beneath the light of the censer, two circumstances of a startling nature attracted my attention. I felt that some palpable although invisible object had passed lightly by my person; and I saw that there lay upon the golden carpet, in the very middle of the rich lustre thrown from the censer, a shadow – a faint, indefinite shadow of angelic aspect – such as might be fancied for the shadow of a shade. But I was wild with the excitement of an immoderate dose of opium, and heeded these things but little, nor spoke of them to Rowena. Having found the wine, I recrossed the chamber, and pouring out a gobletfull, which I held to the lips of the fainting lady. She had now partially recovered, however, and took the vessel herself, while I sank upon an ottoman near me, with my eyes fastened upon her person. It was then that I became distinctly aware of the gentle footfall upon the carpet, and near the couch; and in a second thereafter, as Rowena was in the act of raising the wine to her lips, I saw, or may have dreamed that I saw, fall within the goblet, as if from invisible springs in the atmosphere of the room, three or four large drops of a brilliant and ruby coloured fluid. If this I saw – not so Rowena. She swallowed the wine unhesitatingly, and I forebore to speak to her of a circumstance which must, after all, I considered, have been but the suggestion of a vivid imagination, rendered morbidly active by the terror of the lady, by the opium, and by the hour.

Yet I cannot conceal it from my own perception that, immediately subsequent to the fall of the ruby-drops, a rapid change for the worse took place in the disorder of my wife; so that, on the third subsequent night, the hands of her menials prepared her for the tomb, and on the fourth I sat alone, with her shrouded body, in that fantastic chamber which had received her as my bride. Wild visions, opium-engendered, flitted shadow-like, before me. I gazed with unquiet eye upon the sarcophagi in the angles of the room, upon the varying figures of the drapery, and upon the writhing of the parti-coloured fires in the censer overhead. My eyes then fell, as I called to mind the circumstances of a former night, to the spot beneath the glare of the censer, where I had seen the faint traces of the shadow. It was there, however, no longer; and breathing with great freedom, I turned my glances to the pallid and rigid figure upon the bed. Then rushed upon me a thousand memories of Ligeia, and then came back upon my heart, with the turbulent violence of a flood, the whole of that unutterable woe with which I had regarded *her* thus enshrouded. The night waned; and still, with a bosom full of bitter thoughts of the one only and supremely beloved, I remained gazing upon the body of Rowena.

It might have been midnight, or perhaps earlier, or later, for I had taken no note of time, when a sob, low, gentle, but very distinct, startled me from my reverie. I *felt* that it same from the bed of ebony – the bed of death. I listened in an agony of superstitious terror – but there was no repetition of the sound. I strained my vision to detect any motion in the corpse, but there was not the slightest perceptible. Yet I could not have been deceived. I *had* heard the noise, however faint, and my soul was awakened within me. I resolutely and perseveringly kept my attention riveted upon the body. Many minutes elapsed before any circumstance occurred tending to throw light upon the mystery. At length it became evident that a slight, a very feeble, and barely noticeable tinge of colour had flushed up within the cheeks, and along the sunken small veins of the eyelids. Through a species of unutterable horror and awe, for which the language of morality has no sufficiently energetic expression, I felt my heart cease to beat, my limbs grow rigid where I sat. Yet a sense of duty finally operated to restore my self-possession. I could no longer doubt that we had been precipitate in our preparations – that Rowena still lived. It was necessary that some immediate exertion be made; yet the turret was altogether apart from the portion of the abbey tenanted by the servants – there was none within call – I had no means of summoning them to my aid without leaving the room for many minutes – and this I could not venture to do. I therefore struggled alone in my endeavours to call back the spirit still hovering. In a short period it was certain, however, that a relapse had taken place; the colour disappeared from both eyelid and cheek; leaving a wanness even more than that of marble; the lips became doubly shrivelled and pinched up in the ghastly expression of death; a repulsive clamminess, and coldness overspread rapidly the surface of the body; and all the usual rigorous stiffness immediately supervened. I fell back with a shudder upon the couch from which I had been so startingly aroused, and again gave myself up to passionate waking visions of Ligeia.

An hour thus elapsed, when (could it be possible?) I was a second time aware of some vague sound issuing from the region of the bed. I listened – in extremity of horror. The sound came again – it was a sigh. Rushing to the corpse, I saw – distinctly saw – a tremor upon the lips. In a minute afterwards they relaxed, disclosing a bright line of the pearly teeth. Amazement now struggled in my bosom with the profound awe which had hitherto reigned there alone. I felt that my vision grew dim, that my reason wandered; that it was only by a violent effort that I at length succeeded in nerving myself to the task which duty thus once more had pointed out. There was now a partial glow upon the forehead and upon the cheek and throat; a perceptible warmth pervaded the whole frame; there was even a slight pulsation at the heart. The lady *lived;* and with redoubled ardour I betook myself to the task of restoration. I chafed and bathed the temples and the hands, and used every exertion which experience, and no little medical reading, could suggest. But in vain. Suddenly, the colour fled, the pulsation ceased, the lips resumed the expression of the dead, and, in an instant afterwards, the whole body took upon itself the icy chilliness, the livid hue, the intense rigidity, the sunken outline, and all the loathsome peculiarities of that which has been for many days a tenant of the tomb.

And again I sank into visions of Ligeia – and again (what marvel that I shudder while I write?) – *again* there reached my ears a low sob from the region of the ebony bed. But why shall I minutely detail the unspeakable horrors of that night? Why shall I pause to relate how, time after time, until near the period of the grey dawn, this hideous drama of revivification was repeated; how each terrific relapse was only into a sterner and apparently more irredeemable death; how each agony wore the aspect of a struggle with some invisible foe; and how each struggle was succeeded by I know not what of wild change in the personal appearance of the corpse? Let me hurry to a conclusion.

The greater part of the fearful night had worn away, and she who had been dead, once again stirred – and now more vigorously than hitherto, although arousing from a dissolution more appalling in its utter hopelessness than any. I had long ceased to struggle or to move, and remained sitting rigidly upon the ottoman, a helpless prey to a whirl of violent emotions, of which extreme awe was perhaps the least terrible, the least consuming. The corpse, I repeat, stirred, and now more vigorously than before. The hues of life flushed up with unwonted energy into the countenance – the limbs relaxed – and, save that the eyelids were yet pressed heavily together, and that the bandages and draperies of the grave still imparted their charnel character to the figure, I might have dreamed that Rowena had indeed shaken off, utterly, the fetters of death. But if this idea was not, even then, altogether adopted, I could at least doubt no longer, when arising from the bed, tottering, with feeble steps, with closed eyes, and with the manner of one bewildered in a dream, the thing that was enshrouded advanced bodily and palpably into the middle of the apartment.

I trembled not – I stirred not – for a crowd of uttrable fancies connected with the air, the stature, the demeanour of the figure, rushing hurriedly through my brain, had paralysed – and chilled me into stone. I stared not – but gazed upon the apparation. There was a mad disorder in my thoughts – a tumult unappeasable. Could it, indeed, be the *living* Rowena who confronted me? Could it indeed be Rowena *at all* – the fair haired, the blue-eyed Lady Rowena Trevanion of Tremaine? Why, *why* should I doubt it? The bandage lay heavily about the mouth – but then might it not be the mouth of the breathing Lady of Tremaine? And the cheeks – there were the roses as in her noon of life – yes, these might indeed be the fair cheeks of the living Lady of Tremaine. And the chin, with its dimples, as in health, might it not be hers? – but *had she then grown taller since her malady?* What inexpressible madness seized upon me with that thought?

One bound, and I had reached her feet! Shrinking from my touch, she let fall from her head, unloosened, the ghastly cerements which had confined it, and there streamed forth, into the rushing atmosphere of the chamber, huge masses of long and dishevelled hair; *it was blacker than the raven wings of midnight!* And now slowly opened *the eyes* of the figure which stood before me. 'Here then, at least,' I shrieked aloud, 'can I never – can I never be mistaken – these are the full, and the black, and the wild eyes – of my lost love – of the Lady – of the LADY LIGEIA.'

CLARIMONDE

(La Morte Amoureuse)

Théophile Gautier

Brother, you ask me if I have ever loved. Yes. My story is a strange and terrible one; and though I am sixty-six years of age, I scarcely dare even now to disturb the ashes of that memory. To you I can refuse nothing; but I should not relate such a tale to any less experienced mind. So strange were the circumstances of my story, that I can scarcely believe myself to have ever actually been a party to them. For more than three years I remained the victim of a most singular and diabolical illusion. Poor country priest though I was, I led every night in a dream – would to God it had been all a dream! – a most worldly life, a damning life, a life of Sardanapalus. One single look too freely cast upon a woman well-nigh caused me to lose my soul; but finally by the grace of God and the assistance of my patron saint, I succeeded in casting out the evil spirit that possessed me. My daily life was long interwoven with a nocturnal life of a totally different character. By day I was a priest of the Lord, occupied with prayer and sacred things; by night, from the instant that I closed my eyes I became a young nobleman, a connoisseur of women, dogs and horses; gambling, drinking and blaspheming, and when I awoke at early daybreak, it seemed to me, on the other hand, that I had been sleeping, and had only dreamed that I was a priest. Of this somnambulistic life there now remains to me only the recollection of certain scenes and words which I cannot banish from my memory; but although I never actually left the walls of my presbytery, one would think to hear me speak that I were a man who, weary of all worldly pleasures, had become a religious, seeking to end a tempestuous life in the service of God, rather than a humble seminarist who had grown old in this obscure curacy, situated in the depths of the woods and even isolated from the life of the century.

Yes, I have loved as none in the world ever loved –

with an insensate and furious passion – so violent that I am astonished it did not cause my heart to burst asunder. Ah, what nights – what nights!

From my earliest childhood I had felt a vocation to the priesthood, so that all my studies were directed with that idea in view. Up to the age of twenty-four my life had been only a prolonged novitiate. Having completed my course of theology I successfully received all the minor orders, and my superiors judged me worthy, in spite of my youth, to pass the last awful degree. My ordination was fixed for Easter week.

I had never gone into the world. My world was confined by the walls of the college and the seminary. I knew in a vague sort of way that there was something called Woman, but I never permitted my thoughts to dwell on such a subject, and I lived in a state of perfect innocence. Twice a year only I saw my infirm and aged mother, and in those visits were comprised my sole relations with the outer world.

I regretted nothing; I felt not the least hesitation at taking the last irrevocable step; I was filled with joy and impatience. Never did a betrothed lover count the slow hours with more feverish ardour; I slept only to dream that I was saying Mass; I believed there could be nothing in the world more delightful than to be a priest; I would have refused to be a king or a poet in preference. My ambition could conceive of no loftier aim.

I tell you this in order to show you that what happened to me could not have happened in the natural order of things, and to enable you to understand that I was the victim of an inexplicable fascination.

At last the great day came. I walked to the church with a step so light that I fancied myself sustained in air, or that I had wings upon my shoulders. I believed myself an angel, and wondered at the sombre and thoughtful faces of my companions, for there were several of us. I had passed all the night in prayer, and was in a condition wellnigh bordering on ecstasy. The bishop, a venerable old man, seemed to be God the Father leaning over his Eternity, and I beheld Heaven through the vault of the temple.

You well know the details of that ceremony – the benediction, the communion under both forms, the anointing of the palms of the hands with the Oil of Catechumens and then the holy sacrifice concelebrated with the bishop.

Ah, truly spake Job when he declared that the imprudent man is one who hath not made a covenant with his eyes! I accidentally lifted my head, which until then I had kept down, and beheld before me, so close that it seemed that I could have touched her – although she was actually a considerable distance from me and on the farther side of the sanctuary railing – a young woman of extraordinary beauty, and attired with royal magnificence. It seemed as though scales had suddenly fallen from my eyes. I felt like a blind man who unexpectedly recovers his sight. The bishop, so radiantly glorious but an instant before, suddenly vanished away, the tapers paled upon their golden candlesticks like stars in the dawn and a vast darkness seemed to fill the whole church. The young woman appeared in bright relief against the background of that darkness, like some angelic revelation. She seemed herself radiant, and radiating light rather than receiving it.

I lowered my eyelids, firmly resolved not to open them again, that I might not be influenced by external objects, for distraction had gradually taken possession of me until I hardly knew what I was doing.

In another minute, nevertheless, I reopened my eyes, for through my eyelashes I still beheld her, all sparkling with prismatic colours, and surrounded with such a purple penumbra as one beholds in gazing at the sun.

Oh, how beautiful she was! The greatest painters, who followed ideal beauty into heaven itself, and thence brought back to earth the true portrait of the Madonna, never in their delineations even approached that wildly beautiful reality which I saw before me. Neither the verses of the poet nor the palette of the artist could convey any conception of her. She was rather tall, with a form and bearing of a goddess. Her hair, of a soft blonde hue, was parted in the midst and flowed back over her temples in two rivers of rippling gold; she seemed a diademed queen. Her forehead, bluish-white in its transparency, extended its calm breadth above the arches of her eyebrows, which by a strange singularity were almost black, and admirably relieved the effect of sea-green eyes of unsustainable vivacity and brilliancy. What eyes! With a single flash they could have decided a man's destiny. They had a life, a limpidity, an ardour, a light that I have never seen in human eyes; they shot forth rays like arrows, which I could distinctly *see* enter my heart. I know not if the fire which illumined them came from heaven or from hell, but assuredly it came from one or the other. That woman was either an angel or a demon, perhaps both. Assuredly she never sprang from Eve, our common mother. Teeth of the most lustrous pearl gleamed in her smile, and at every inflection of her lips little dimples appeared in the satiny rose of her adorable cheeks. There was a delicacy and pride in the regal outline of her nostrils bespeaking noble blood. Agate gleams played over the smooth lustrous skin of her half-bare shoulders, and strings of great blonde pearls – almost equal to her neck in beauty of colour – descended upon her bosom. From time to time she elevated her head with the undulating grace of a startled serpent or peacock, thereby imparting a quivering motion to the high lace ruff which surrounded it like a silver trellis-work.

She wore a robe of orange-red velvet, and from her wide ermine-lined sleeves there peeped forth patrician hands of infinite delicacy, and so ideally transparent that, like the fingers of Aurora, they permitted the light to shine through them.

All these details I can recollect at this moment as plainly as though they were of yesterday, for notwithstanding I was greatly troubled at the time, nothing escaped me; the faintest touch of shading, the little dark speck at the point of the chin, the almost imperceptible down at the corners of the lips, the velvety floss upon the brow, the quivering shadows of the eyelashes upon the cheeks, I could notice everything with astonishing lucidity of perception.

And gazing I felt opening within me gates that had until then remained closed; outlets long obstructed became all clear, permitting glimpses of unfamiliar perspectives within; life suddenly made itself visible to me under a totally novel aspect. I felt as though I had just been born into a new world and a new order of things. A frightful anguish began to torture my heart as with red-hot pincers. Every successive minute seemed to me at once but a second and yet a century. Meanwhile the ceremony was proceeding, and I shortly found myself transported far from that world of which my newly born desires were furiously besieging the entrance. Nevertheless I answered 'Yes' when I wished to say 'No,' though all within me protested against the violence done to my soul by my tongue. Some occult power seemed to force the words from my throat against my will. Thus it is, perhaps, that so many young girls walk to the altar firmly resolved to refuse in a startling manner the husband imposed upon them, and that yet not one ever fulfils her intention. Thus it is, doubtless, that so many poor novices take the veil, though they have resolved to tear it into shreds at the moment when called upon to utter the vows. One dares not thus cause so great a scandal to all present, nor deceive the expectation of so many people. All those eyes, all those wills seem to weigh down upon you like a cope of lead; and, moreover, measures have been so well taken, everything has been so thoroughly arranged beforehand and after a fashion so evidently irrevocable, that the will yields to the weight of circumstances and utterly breaks down.

As the ceremony proceeded the features of the fair unknown changed their expression. Her look had at first been one of caressing tenderness; it changed to an air of disdain and of mortification, as though at not having been able to make itself understood.

With an effort of will sufficient to have uprooted a mountain, I strove to cry out that I would not be a priest, but I could not speak; my tongue seemed nailed to my palate, and I found it impossible to express my will by the least syllable of negation. Though fully awake, I felt like one under the influence of a nightmare, who vainly strives to shriek out the one word upon which life depends.

She seemed conscious of the martyrdom I was undergoing, and, as though to encourage me, she gave me a look replete with divinest promise. Her eyes were a poem; their very glance was a song.

She said to me :

'If thou wilt be mine, I shall make thee happier than God himself in His paradise. The angels themselves will be jealous of thee. Tear off that funeral shroud in which thou art about to wrap thyself. I am Beauty, I am Youth, I am Life. Come to me! Together we shall be Love. Can Jehovah offer thee aught in exchange? Our lives will flow on like a dream, in one eternal kiss.

'Fling forth the wine of that chalice, and thou art free. I will conduct thee to the Unknown Isles. Thou shalt sleep in my bosom upon a bed of massy gold under a silver pavilion, for I love thee and would take thee away from thy God, before whom so many noble hearts pour forth floods of love which never reach even the steps of His throne!'

These words seemed to float to my ears in a rhythm of infinite sweetness, for her look was actually sonorous, and the utterances of her eyes were re-echoed in the depths of my heart as though living lips had breathed them into my life. I felt myself willing to renounce God, and yet my tongue mechanically fulfilled all the formalities of the ceremony. The fair one gave me another look, so beseeching, so despairing that keen blades seemed to pierce my heart, and I felt my bosom transfixed by more swords than those of Our Lady of Sorrows.

All was consummated; I had become a priest.

Never was deeper anguish painted on human face than upon hers. The maiden who beholds her affianced lover suddenly fall dead at her side, the mother bending over the empty cradle of her child, Eve seated at the threshold of the gate of Paradise, the miser who finds a stone substituted for his stolen treasure, the poet who accidentally permits the only manuscript of his finest work to fall into the fire, could not wear a look so despairing, so inconsolable. All the blood had abandoned her face, leaving it whiter than marble; her beautiful arms hung lifeless on either side of her body as though their muscles had suddenly relaxed, and she sought the support of a pillar, for her yielding limbs almost betrayed her. As for myself, I staggered towards the door of the church, livid as death, my forehead bathed with a sweat bloodier than that of Calvary; I felt as though I were being strangled; the vault seemed to have flattened down upon my shoulders, and it seemed to me that my head alone sustained the whole weight of the dome.

As I was about to cross the threshold a hand suddenly caught mine – a woman's hand! I had never till then touched the hand of any woman. It was cold as a serpent's skin, and yet its impress remained upon my wrist, burnt there as though branded by a glowing iron. It was she. 'Unhappy man! Unhappy man! What hast thou done?'

she exclaimed in a low voice, and immediately disappeared in the crowd.

The aged bishop passed by. He cast a severe and scrutinising look upon me. My face presented the wildest aspect imaginable; I blushed and turned pale alternately; dazzling lights flashed before my eyes. A companion took pity on me. He seized my arm and led me out. I could not possibly have found my way back to the seminary unassisted. At the corner of the street, while the young priest's attention was momentarily turned in another direction, a negro page, fantastically garbed, approached me, and without pausing on his way slipped into my hand a little pocket-book with gold-embroidered corners, at the same time giving me a sign to hide it. I concealed it in my sleeve, and there kept it until I found myself alone in my cell. Then I opened the clasp. There were only two leaves within, bearing the words, 'Clarimonde. At the Concini Palace.' So little acquainted was I at this time with the things of this world that I had never heard of Clarimonde, celebrated as she was, and I had no idea as to where the Concini Palace was situated. I hazarded a thousand conjectures, each more extravagant than the last; but, in truth, I cared little whether she were a great lady or a courtesan, so that I could but see her once again.

My love, although the growth of a single hour, had taken imperishable root. I did not even dream of attempting to tear it up, so fully was I convinced such a thing would be impossible. That woman had completely taken possession of me. One look from her had sufficed to change my very nature. She had breathed her will into my life, and I no longer lived in myself, but in her and for her. I gave myself up to a thousand extravagances. I kissed the place upon my hand which she had touched, and I repeated her name over and over again for hours in succession. I only needed to close my eyes in order to see her distinctly as though she were actually present; and I reiterated to myself the words she had uttered in my ear at the church porch: 'Unhappy man! Unhappy man! What hast thou done?' I comprehended at last the full horror of my situation, and the funereal and awful restraints of the state into which I had just entered became clearly revealed to me. To be a priest! – that is, to be chaste, never to love, to observe no distinction of sex or age, to turn from the sight of all beauty, to put out one's own eyes, to hide for ever crouching in the chill shadows of some church or cloister, to visit none but the dying, to watch by unknown corpses, and ever bear about with one the black soutane as a garb of mourning for oneself, so that your very dress might serve as a pall for your coffin.

And I felt life rising within me like a subterranean lake, expanding and overflowing; my blood leaped fiercely through my arteries; my long-restrained youth suddenly burst into active being, like the aloe which blossoms but once in a hundred years, and then bursts into blossom with a clap of thunder.

What could I do in order to see Clarimonde once more? I had no pretext to offer for desiring to leave the seminary, not knowing any person in the city. I would not even be able to remain there for more than a short time, and was only waiting my assignment to the curacy which I must thereafter occupy. I tried to remove the bars of the window; but it was at a fearful height from the ground, and I found that as I had no ladder it would be useless to think of escaping thus. And, furthermore, I could descend thence only by night in any event, and afterward how should I be able to find my way through the inextricable labyrinth of streets? All these difficulties, which to many would have appeared altogether insignificant, were gigantic to me, a poor seminarist who had fallen in love only the day before for the first time, without experience, without money, without attire.

'Ah!' cried I to myself in my blindness, 'were I not a priest I could have seen her every day; I might have been her lover, her spouse. Instead of being wrapped in this dismal shroud of mine I would have had garments of silk and velvet, golden chains, a sword and fair plumes like other handsome young cavaliers. My hair, instead of being dishonoured by the tonsure, would flow down upon my neck in waving curls; I would have a fine waxed moustache; I would be a gallant.' But one hour passed before an altar, a few hastily articulated words, had for ever cut me off from the number of the living, and I had myself sealed down the stone of my own tomb; I had with my own hand bolted the gate of my prison!

I went to the window. The sky was beautifully blue; the trees had donned their spring robes; nature seemed to be making parade of an ironical joy. The *Place* was filled with people, some going, others coming; young beaux and young belles were sauntering in couples towards the groves and gardens; merry youths passed by, cheerily trolling refrains of drinking songs – it was all a picture of vivacity, life, animation, gaiety, which formed a bitter contrast with my mourning and my solitude. On the steps of the gate sat a young mother playing with her child. She kissed its little rosy mouth, and performed, in order to amuse it, a thousand divine little puerilities such as only mothers know how to invent. The father standing at a little distance smiled gently upon the charming group, and with folded arms seemed to hug his joy to his heart. I could not endure that spectacle. I closed the window with violence, and flung myself on my bed, my heart filled with frightful hate and jealousy, and gnawed my fingers and my bedcovers like a tiger that has passed days without food.

I know not how long I remained in this condition, but at last, while writhing on the bed in a fit of spasmodic fury, I suddenly perceived the Abbé Sérapion, who was standing erect in the centre of the room, watching me attentively. Filled with shame of myself, I let my head fall upon my breast and covered my face with my hands.

'Romuald, my friend, something very extraordinary is going on within you,' observed Sérapion, after a few moments' silence; 'your conduct is altogether inexplicable. You – always so quiet, so pious, so gentle – you to rage in your cell like a wild beast! Take heed, brother – do not listen to the suggestions of the devil. The Evil Spirit, furious that you have consecrated yourself for ever to the Lord, is prowling around you like a ravening wolf and making a last effort to obtain possession of you. Instead of allowing yourself to be conquered, my dear Romuald, make to yourself a cuirass of prayers, a buckler of mortifications and combat the enemy like a valiant man; you will then assuredly overcome him. Virtue must be proved by temptation, and gold comes forth purer from the hands of the assayer. Fear not. Never allow yourself to become discouraged. The most watchful and steadfast souls are at moments liable to such temptation. Pray, fast and meditate and the Evil Spirit will depart from you.'

The words of the Abbé Sérapion restored me to myself, and I became a little more calm. 'I came,' he continued, 'to tell you that you have been appointed to the curacy of C———. The priest who had charge of it has just died, and Monseigneur the Bishop has ordered me to have you installed there at once. Be ready, therefore, to start to-morrow.' I responded with an inclination of the head, and the Abbé retired. I opened my breviary and began reading some prayers, but the letters became confused and blurred under my eyes, the thread of the ideas entangled itself hopelessly in my brain, and the volume at last fell from my hands without my being aware of it.

To leave to-morrow without having been able to see her again, to add yet another barrier to the many already interposed between us, to lose for ever all hope of being able to meet her, except, indeed, through a miracle! Even to write to her, alas! would be impossible, for by whom could I despatch my letter? With my sacred character of priest, to whom could I dare unbosom myself, in whom could I confide? I became a prey to the bitterest anxiety.

Then suddenly recurred to me the words of the Abbé Sérapion regarding the artifices of the devil; and the strange character of the adventure, the supernatural beauty of Clarimonde, the phosphoric light of her eyes, the burning imprint of her hand, the agony into which she had thrown me, the sudden change wrought within me when all my piety vanished in a single instant – these and other things clearly testified to the work of the Evil One, and perhaps that satiny hand was but the glove which concealed his claws. Filled with terror at these fancies, I again picked up the breviary which had slipped from my knees and fallen upon the floor, and once more gave myself up to prayer.

Next morning Sérapion came to take me away. Two mules freighted with our miserable valises awaited us at the gate. He mounted one, and I the other as well as I knew how.

As we passed along the streets of the city, I gazed attentively at all the windows and balconies in the hope of seeing Clarimonde, but it was yet early in the morning, and the city had hardly opened its eyes. Mine sought to penetrate the blinds and window-curtains of all the palaces before which we were passing. Sérapion doubtless attributed this curiosity to my admiration of the architecture, for he slackened the pace of his animal in order to give me time to look around me. At last we passed the city gates and began to mount the hill beyond. When we arrived at its summit I turned to take a last look at the place where Clarimonde dwelt. The shadow of a great cloud hung over all the city; the contrasting colours of its blue and red roofs were lost in the uniform half-tint, through which here and there floated upward, like white flakes of foam, the smoke of freshly kindled fires. By a singular optical effect one edifice, which surpassed in height all the neighbouring buildings that were still dimly veiled by the vapours, towered up, fair and lustrous with the gilding of a solitary beam of sunlight – although actually more than a league away it seemed quite near. The smallest details of its architecture were plainly distinguishable – the turrets, the platforms, the window-casements and even the swallow-tailed weather vanes.

'What is that palace I see over there, all lighted up by the sun?' I asked Sérapion. He shaded his eyes with his hand, and having looked in the direction indicated, replied; 'It is the ancient palace which the Prince Concini has given to the courtesan Clarimonde. Awful things are done there!'

At that instant, I know not yet whether it was a reality or an illusion, I fancied I saw gliding along the terrace a shapely white figure, which gleamed for a moment in passing and as quickly vanished. It was Clarimonde.

Oh, did she know that at that very hour, all feverish and restless – from the height of the rugged road which separated me from her and which, alas! I could never more descend – I was directing my eyes upon the palace where she dwelt, and which a mocking beam of sunlight seemed to bring nigh to me, as though inviting me to enter therein as its lord? Undoubtedly she must have known it, for her soul was too sympathetically united with mine not to have felt its least emotional thrill, and that subtle sympathy it must have been which prompted her to climb – although clad only in her nightdress – to the summit of the terrace, amid the icy dews of the morning.

The shadow gained the palace, and the scene became to the eye only a motionless ocean of roofs and gables, amid which one mountainous undulation was distinctly visible. Sérapion urged his mule forward, my own at once followed at the same gait, and a sharp angle in the road at last hid the city of S—— for ever from my eyes, as I was destined never to return thither. At the close of a weary three days' journey through dismal country fields, we caught sight of the cock upon the steeple of the church of which I was going to take charge, peeping above the trees, and after having followed some winding roads fringed with thatched cottages and little gardens, we found ourselves in front of the façade, which certainly possessed few features of magnificence. A porch ornamented with some mouldings, and two or three pillars rudely hewn from sandstone; a tiled roof with counterforts of the same sandstone as the pillars, that was all. To the left lay the cemetery, overgrown with high weeds, and having a great iron cross rising up in its centre; to the right stood the presbytery under the shadow of the church. It was a house of the most extreme simplicity and frigid cleanliness. We entered the enclosure. A few chickens were picking up some oats scattered upon the ground; accustomed, seemingly, to the black habit of ecclesiastics, they showed no fear of our presence and scarcely troubled themselves to get out of our way. A hoarse, wheezy barking fell upon our ears, and we saw an aged dog running towards us.

It was my predecessor's dog. He had dull bleared eyes, grizzled hair, and every mark of the greatest age to which a dog can possibly attain. I patted him gently, and he proceeded at once to march along beside me with an air of satisfaction unspeakable. A very old woman, who had been the housekeeper of the former curé, also came to meet us, and after having invited me into a little back parlour, asked whether I intended to retain her. I replied that I would take care of her, and the dog, and the chickens, and all the furniture her master had bequeathed her at his death. At this she became fairly transported with joy, and the Abbé Sérapion at once paid her the price which she asked for her little property.

As soon as my installation was over, the Abbé Sérapion returned to the seminary. I was, therefore, left alone, with no one but myself to look to for aid and counsel. The thought of Clarimonde again began to haunt me, and in spite of all my endeavours to banish it, I always found it present in my meditations. One evening, while promenading in my little garden along the walks bordered with box-plants, I fancied that I saw through the elm-trees the figure of a woman, who followed my every movement, and that I beheld two sea-green eyes gleaming through the foliage; but it was only an illusion, and on going round to the other side of the garden, I could find nothing except a footprint on the sanded walk – a footprint so small that it seemed to have been made by the foot of a child. The garden was enclosed by very high walls. I searched every nook and corner of it, but could discover no one there. I have never succeeded in fully accounting for this circumstance, which, after all, was nothing compared with the strange things which happened to me afterward.

For a whole year I lived thus, filling all the duties of my calling with the most scrupulous exactitude, praying and fasting, exhorting and lending aid to the sick, and bestowing alms even to the extent of frequently depriving myself of the very necessaries of life. But I felt a great aridness within me, and the sources of grace seemed closed against me. I never found that happiness which should spring from the fulfilment of a holy mission; my thoughts were far away, and the words of Clarimonde were ever upon my lips like an involuntary refrain. Oh, brother, meditate well on this! Through having but once lifted my eyes to look upon a woman, through one fault apparently so venial, I have for years remained a victim to the most miserable agonies, and the happiness of my life has been destroyed for ever.

I will not longer dwell upon those defeats, or on those inward victories invariably followed by yet more terrible falls, but will at once proceed to the facts of my story. One night my door-bell was long and violently rung. The aged housekeeper arose and opened to the stranger, and the figure of a man, whose complexion was deeply bronzed, and who was richly clad in a foreign costume, with a poniard at his girdle, appeared under the rays of Barbara's lantern. Her first impulse was one of terror, but the stranger reassured her, and stated that he desired to see me at once on matters relating to my holy calling. Barbara invited him upstairs, where I was on the point of retiring. The stranger told me that his mistress, a very noble lady, was lying on the point of death, and desired to see a priest. I replied that I was prepared to follow him, took with me the sacred articles necessary for extreme unction, and descended in all haste. Two horses black as night itself stood without the gate, pawing the ground with impatience, and veiling their chests with long streams of smoky vapour exhaled from their nostrils. He held the stirrup and aided me to mount upon one; then, merely laying his hand upon the pommel of the saddle, he vaulted on the other, pressed the animal's sides with his knees, and loosened rein. The horse bounded forward with the velocity of an arrow. Mine, of which the stranger held the bridle, also started off at a swift gallop, keeping up with his companion. We devoured the road. The ground flowed backwards beneath us in a long streaked line of pale grey, and the black silhouettes of the trees seemed fleeing by us on either side like an army in rout. We passed through a forest so profoundly gloomy that I felt my flesh creep in the still darkness with superstitious fear. The showers of bright sparks which flew from the stony road under the ironshod feet of our horses, remained glowing in our wake like a fiery trail; and had anyone at that hour beheld us both – my guide and myself – he must have taken us for two spectres riding upon nightmares. Witch-fires ever and anon flitted across the road before us, and the night-birds shrieked fearsomely in the depth of the woods beyond, where we beheld at intervals the phosphorescent eyes of wild cats. The manes of the horses became more and more dishevelled, the sweat streamed over their flanks and their breath came through their nostrils hard and fast. But when he found them slacking pace, the guide reanimated them by uttering a strange, guttural, unearthly cry, and the gallop began again with fury. At last the whirlwind race ceased; a huge black mass pierced through with many bright points of light suddenly rose before us, the hoofs of our horses echoed louder upon a strong wooden drawbridge, and we rode under a great vaulted archway which darkly yawned between two enormous towers. Some great excitement evidently reigned in the castle. Servants with torches were crossing the courtyard in every direction, and, above, lights were ascending and descending from landing to landing. I obtained a confused glimpse of vast masses of architecture – columns, arcades, flights of steps, stairways – a royal voluptousness and elfin magnificence of construction worthy of fairyland. A negro page – the same who had before brought me the tablet from Clarimonde, and whom I instantly recognised

– approached to aid me in dismounting, and the majordomo, attired in black velvet with a gold chain about his neck, advanced to meet me, supporting himself upon an ivory cane. Tears were falling from his eyes and streaming over his cheeks and white beard. 'Too late!' he cried, sorrowfully shaking his venerable head. 'Too late, sir priest! But if you have not been able to save the soul, come at least to watch by the poor body.'

He took my arm and conducted me to the deathchamber. I wept not less bitterly than he, for I had learned that the dead one was none other than that Clarimonde whom I had so deeply and so wildly loved. A *prie-dieu* stood at the foot of the bed; a bluish flame flickering in a bronze patera filled all the room with a wan, deceptive light, here and there bringing out in the darkness at intervals some projection of furniture or cornice. In a chiselled urn upon the table there was a faded white rose, whose leaves – except one that still held – had all fallen, like odorous tears, to the foot of the vase. A broken black mask, a fan and disguises of every variety, which were lying on the arm-chairs, bore witness that death had entered suddenly and unannounced into that sumptuous dwelling. Without daring to cast my eyes upon the bed, I knelt down and began to repeat the Psalms for the Dead, with exceeding fervour, thanking God that he had placed the tomb between me and the memory of this woman, so that I might thereafter be able to utter her name in my prayers as a name for ever sanctified by death. But my fervour gradually weakened, and I fell insensible into a reverie. That chamber bore no semblence to a chamber of death. In lieu of the odours which I had been accustomed to breathe during such funereal vigils, a languorous vapour of Oriental perfume – I know not what amorous odour of woman – softly floated through the tepid air. That pale light seemed rather a twilight gloom contrived for voluptuous pleasures, than a substitute for the yellow-flickering watch-tapers which shine by the side of corpses. I thought upon the strange destiny which enabled me to meet Clarimonde again at the very moment when she was lost to me for ever, and a sigh of regretful anguish escaped from my breast. Then it seemed to me that some one behind me had also sighed, and I turned round to look. It was only an echo. But in that moment my eyes fell upon the bed of death which they had till then avoided. The red damask curtains, decorated with large flowers worked in embroidery, and looped up with gold bullion, permitted me to behold the fair maid, lying at full length, with hands joined upon her bosom. She was covered with a linen wrapping of dazzling whiteness, which formed a strong contrast with the gloomy purple of the hangings, and was of so fine a texture that it concealed nothing of her body's charming form, and allowed the eye to follow those beautiful outlines – undulating like the neck of a swan – which even death had not robbed of their supple grace. She seemed an alabaster statue executed by some skilful sculptor to place upon the tomb of a queen, or rather, perhaps, like a slumbering maiden over whom the silent snow had woven a spotless veil.

I could no longer maintain my constrained attitude of prayer. The air of the alcove intoxicated me, that febrile perfume of half-faded roses penetrated my very brain, and I began to pace restlessly up and down the chamber, pausing at each turn before the bier to contemplate the graceful corpse lying beneath the transparency of its shroud. Wild fancies came thronging to my brain. I thought to myself that she might not, perhaps, be really dead; that she might only have feigned death for the purpose of bringing me to her castle, and then declaring her love. At one time I even thought I saw her foot move under the whiteness of the coverings, and slightly disarrange the long, straight folds of the winding sheet.

And then I asked myself: 'Is this indeed Clarimonde? What proof have I that it is she? Might not that black page have passed into the service of some other lady? Surely, I must be going mad to torture and afflict myself thus!' But my heart answered with a fierce throbbing: 'It is she; it is she indeed!' I approached the bed again and fixed my eyes with redoubled attention upon the object of my incertitude. Ah, must I confess it? That exquisite perfection of bodily form, although purified and made sacred by the shadow of death, affected me more voluptuously than it should have done, and that repose so closely resembled slumber that one might well have mistaken it for such. I forgot that I had come here to perform a funeral ceremony; I fancied myself a young bridegroom entering the chamber of the bride, who all modestly hides her fair face and through coyness seeks to keep herself wholly veiled. Heartbroken with grief, yet wild with hope, shuddering at once with fear and pleasure, I bent over her and grasped the corner of the sheet. I lifted it back, holding my breath all the while through fear of waking her. My arteries throbbed with such violence that I felt them hiss through my temples, and the sweat poured from my forehead in streams, as though I had lifted a mighty slab of marble. There, indeed, lay Clarimonde, even as I had seen her at the church on the day of my ordination. She was not less charming than then. With her, death seemed but a last coquetry. The pallor of her cheeks, the less brilliant carnation of her lips, her long eyelashes lowered and relieving their strange fringe against the white skin, lent her an unspeakable seductive aspect of melancholy chastity and mental suffering; her long loose hair, still intertwined with some little blue flowers, made a shining pillow for her head, and veiled the nudity of her shoulders with its thick ringlets; her beautiful hands, purer, more diaphanous than the Host, were crossed on her bosom in an attitude of pious rest and silent prayer, which served to counteract all that might have proved otherwise too alluring – even after death – in the exquisite roundness and ivory polish of her bare arms from which the pearl bracelets had not yet been removed. I remained long in mute contemplation, and the more I gazed, the less I could persuade myself that life had really abandoned that beautiful body for ever. I do not know whether it was an illusion or a reflection of the lamplight, but it seemed to me that blood was again beginning to circulate under the lifeless pallor, although she remained all motionless. I laid my hand lightly on her arm; it was cold, but no colder than her hand on the day when it touched mine at the portals of the church. I resumed my position, bending my face above her, and bathing her cheeks with the warm dew of my tears. Ah, what bitter feelings of despair and helplessness, what agonies unutterable did I endure in that long watch! Vainly did I wish that I could have gathered all my life into one mass that I might give it all to her, and breathe into her chill form the flame which devoured me. The night advanced, and feeling the moment of eternal separation approach, I could not deny myself the last sad sweet pleasure of imprinting a kiss upon the dead lips of her who had been my only love. . . . Oh, miracle! A faint breath mingled itself with my breath, and the mouth of Clarimonde responded to the passionate pressure of mine. Her eyes unclosed, and lighted up with something of their former brillancy; she uttered a long sigh, and uncrossed her arms, passed them around my neck with a look of ineffable delight. 'Ah, it is thou, Romuald!' she murmured in a voice languishingly sweet as the last vibrations of a harp. 'What ailed thee, dearest? I waited so long for thee that I am dead; but we are now betrothed; I can see thee and visit thee. Adieu, Romuald, adieu! I love thee. That is all I wished to tell thee, and I give thee back the life which thy kiss for a moment recalled. We shall soon meet again.'

Her head fell back, but her arms still encircled me, as though to retain me still. A furious whirlwind suddenly burst in the window, and entered the chamber. The last remaining leaf of the white rose for a moment palpitated at the extremity of the stalk like a butterfly's wing, then it detached itself and flew forth through the open casement, bearing with it the soul of Clarimonde. The lamp was extinguished, and I fell insensible upon the bosom of the beautiful dead.

When I came to myself again I was lying on the bed in my little room at the presbytery, and the old dog of the former curé was licking my hand which had been hanging down outside the covers. Barbara, all trembling with age and anxiety, was busying herself about the room, opening and shutting drawers, and emptying powders into glasses. On seeing me open my eyes, the old woman uttered a cry of joy, the dog yelped and wagged his tail, but I was still so weak that I could not speak a single word or make the slightest motion. Afterwards I learned that I had lain thus for three days, giving no evidence of life beyond the faintest respiration. Those three days do not reckon in my life, nor could I ever imagine whither my spirit had departed during those three days; I have no recollection of aught relating to them. Barbara told me that the same coppery-complexioned man who came to seek me on the night of my departure from the presbytery, had brought me back the next morning in a closed litter, and departed immediately afterwards. When I became able to collect my scattered thoughts, I reviewed within my mind all the circumstances of that fateful night. At first I thought I had been the victim of some magical illusion, but ere long the recollection of other circumstances, real and palpable in themselves, came to forbid that supposition. I could not believe that I had been dreaming, since Barbara as well as myself had seen the strange man with his two black horses, and described with exactness every detail of his figure and apparel. Nevertheless it appeared that none knew of any castle in the neighbourhood answering to the description of that in which I had again found Clarimonde.

One morning I found the Abbé Sérapion in my room. Barbara had advised him that I was ill, and he had come with all speed to see me. Although this haste on his part testified to an affectionate interest in me, yet his visit did not cause me the pleasure which it should have done. The Abbé Sérapion had something penetrating and inquisitorial in his gaze which made me feel very ill at ease. His presence filled me with embarrassment and a sense of guilt. At the first glance he divined my interior trouble, and I hated him for his clairvoyance.

While he inquired after my health in hypocritically honeyed accents, he constantly kept his two great yellow lion-eyes fixed upon me, and plunged his look into my soul like a sounding lead. Then he asked me how I directed my parish, if I was happy in it, how I passed the leisure hours allowed me in the intervals of pastoral duty, whether I had become acquainted with many of the inhabitants of the place, what was my favourite reading and a thousand other such questions. I answered these inquiries as briefly as possible, and he, without ever waiting for my answers, passed rapidly from one subject of query to another. That conversation had obviously no connection with what he actually wished to say. At last, without any premonition, but as though repeating a piece of news which he had recalled on the instant, and feared might otherwise be forgotten subsequently, he suddenly said, in a clear vibrant voice, which rang in my ears like the trumpets of the Last Judgment:

'The great courtesan Clarimonde died a few days ago, at the close of an orgy which lasted eight days and eight nights. It was something infernally splendid. The abominations of the banquets of Belshazzar and Cleopatra were re-enacted there. Good God, what age are we living in? The guests were served by swarthy slaves who spoke an unknown tongue, and who seemed to me to be veritable demons. The livery of the very least among them would have served for the gala dress of an emperor. There have always been very strange stories told of this Clarimonde, and all her lovers came to a violent or miserable end. They used to say that she was a ghoul, a female vampire; but I believe she was none other than Beelzebub himself.'

He ceased to speak and began to regard me more attentively than ever, as though to observe the effect of his words upon me. I could not refrain from starting when I heard him utter the name of Clarimonde, and this news of her death, in addition to the pain it caused me by reason of its coincidence with the nocturnal scenes I had witnessed, filled me with an agony and terror which my face betrayed, despite my utmost endeavours to appear composed. Sérapion fixed an anxious and severe look upon me, and then observed: 'My son, I must warn you that you are standing with foot raised upon the brink of an abyss; take heed lest you fall therein. Satan's claws are long, and tombs are not always true to their trust. The tombstone of Clarimonde should be sealed down with a triple seal, for, if report be true, it is not the first time she has died. May God watch over you, Romuald!'

And with these words the Abbé walked slowly to the door. I did not see him again at that time, for he left for S— almost immediately.

I became completely restored to health and resumed my accustomed duties. The memory of Clarimonde and the words of the old Abbé were constantly in my mind; nevertheless no extraordinary event had occurred to verify the funeral predictions of Sérapion, and I had begun to believe that his fears and my own terrors were over-exaggerated, when one night I had a strange dream. I had hardly fallen asleep when I heard my bed-curtains drawn apart, as their rings slid back upon the curtain rod with a sharp sound. I rose up quickly upon my elbow, and beheld the shadow of a woman standing erect before me. I recognised Clarimonde immediately. She bore in her hand a little lamp, shaped like those which are placed in tombs, and its light lent her fingers a rosy transparency, which extended itself by lessening degrees even to the opaque and milkly whiteness of her bare arm. Her only garment was the linen winding-sheet which had shrouded her when lying upon the bed of death. She sought to gather its folds over her bosom as though ashamed of being so scantily clad, but her little hand was not equal to the task. She was so white that the colour of the drapery blended with that of her flesh under the pallid rays of the lamp. Enveloped with this subtle tissue which betrayed all the contour of her body, she seemed more like a marble statue than a woman endowed with life. But dead or living, statue or woman, shadow or body, her beauty was still the same, only that the green light of her eyes was less brilliant, and her mouth, once so warmly crimson, was only tinted with a faint tender rosiness, like that of her cheeks. The little blue flowers which I had noticed entwined in her hair were withered and dry, and had lost nearly all their leaves, but this did not prevent her from being charming – so charming that notwithstanding the strange character of the adventure, and the unexplainable manner in which she had entered my room, I felt not ever for a moment the least fear.

She placed the lamp on the table and seated herself at the foot of my bed; then bending towards me, she said, in that voice at once silvery clear and yet velvety in its sweet softness, such as I never heard from any lips save hers:

'I have kept thee long in waiting, dear Romuald, and it must have seemed to thee that I had forgotten thee. But I come from afar off, very far off, and from a land whence no other has ever yet returned. There is neither sun nor moon in that land whence I come: all is but space and shadow; there is neither road nor pathway: no earth for the foot, no air for the wing; and nevertheless behold me here, for Love is stronger than Death and must conquer him in the end. Oh, what sad faces and fearful things I have seen on my way hither! What difficulty my soul, returned to earth through the power of will alone, has had in finding its body and reinstating itself therein! What terrible efforts I had to make ere I could lift the ponderous slab with which they had covered me! See, the palms of my poor hands are all bruised! Kiss them, sweet love, that they may be healed!' She laid the cold palms of her hands upon my mouth, one after the other. I kissed them, indeed, many times, and she the while watched me with a smile of ineffable affection.

I confess to my shame that I had entirely forgotten the advice of the Abbé Sérapion and the sacred office wherewith I had been vested. I had fallen without resistance, and at the first assault. I had not even made the least effort to repel the tempter. The fresh coolness of Clarimonde's skin penetrated my own, and I felt voluptuous tremors pass over my whole body. Poor child! in spite of all I saw afterwards, I can hardly yet believe she was a demon; at least she had no appearance of being such, and never did Satan so skilfully conceal his claws and horns. She had drawn her feet up beneath her, and squatted down on the edge of the couch in an attitude full of negligent coquetry. From time to time she passed her little hand through my hair and twisted it into curls, as though trying how a new style of wearing it would become my face. I abandoned myself to her hands with the most guilty pleasure, while she accompanied her gentle play with the prettiest prattle. The most remarkable fact was that I felt no astonishment whatever at so extraordinary an adventure, and as in dreams one finds no difficulty in accepting the most fantastic events as simple facts, so all these circumstances seemed to me perfectly natural in themselves.

'I loved thee long ere I saw thee, dear Romuald, and sought thee everywhere. Thou wast my dream, and I first saw thee in the church at the fatal moment. I said at once, "It is he!" I gave thee a look into which I threw all the love I ever had, all the love I now have, all the love I shall ever have for thee – a look which would have damned a cardinal or brought a king to his knees at my feet in view of all his court. Thou remainedst unmoved, preferring thy God to me!

'Ah, how jealous I am of that God whom thou didst love and still lovest more than me!

'Woe is me, unhappy one that I am! I can never have thy heart all to myself, I whom thou didst recall to life with a kiss – dead Clarimonde, who for thy sake bursts asunder the gates of the tomb, and comes to consecrate to thee a life which she has resumed only to make thee happy!'

All her words were accompanied with the most impassioned caresses, which bewildered my sense and my reason to such an extent, that I did not fear to utter a frightful blasphemy for the sake of consoling her, and to declare that I loved her as much as God.

Her eyelids rekindled and shone like chrysoprases. 'In truth? – in very truth? – as much as God!' she cried, flinging her beautiful arms around me. 'Since it is so, thou wilt come with me; thou wilt follow me withersoever I desire. Thou wilt cast away thy ugly black habit. Thou shalt be the proudest and most envied of cavaliers; thou shalt be my lover! To be the acknowledged lover of Clarimonde, who has refused even a Pope, that will be something of which to feel proud! Ah, the fair, unspeakable happy existence, the beautiful golden life we shall live together! And when shall we depart?'

'To-morrow! To-morrow!' I cried in my delirium.

'To-morrow, then, so let it be!' she answered. 'In the meanwhile I shall have opportunity to change my toilet, for this is a little too light and in nowise suited for a journey. I must go forthwith to notify all my friends who believe me dead, and mourn for me as deeply as they are capable of doing. The money, the dresses, the carriages – all will be ready. I shall call for thee at this same hour. Adieu, dear heart!' And she lightly touched my forehead with her lips. The lamp went out, the curtains closed again, and all became dark; a leaden, dreamless sleep fell on me and held me unconscious until the morning following.

I awoke later than usual, and the recollection of this singular adventure troubled me during the whole day. I finally persuaded myself that it was a mere vapour of my heated imagination. Nevertheless its sensations had been so vivid that it was difficult to persuade myself that they were not real, and it was not without some presentiment of what was going to happen that I got into bed at last, after having prayed God to drive far from me all thoughts of evil, and to protect the chastity of my slumber.

I soon fell into a deep sleep, and my dream was continued. The curtains again parted, and I beheld Clarimonde, not as on the former occasion, pale in her pale winding-sheet, with the violets of death upon her cheeks, but gay, sprightly, jaunty, in a superb travelling dress of green velvet, trimmed with gold lace, and looped up on either side to allow a glimpse of satin petticoat. Her blonde hair escaped in thick ringlets from beneath a broad black felt hat, decorated with white feathers whimsically twisted into various shapes. In one hand she held a little riding whip terminated by a golden whistle. She tapped me lightly with it, and exclaimed: 'Well, my fine sleeper, is this the way you make your preparations? I thought I should find you up and dressed. Arise quickly, we have no time to lose.'

I leaped out of bed at once.

'Come, dress yourself, and let us go,' she continued, pointing to a little package she had brought with her. 'The horses are becoming impatient of delay and champing their bits at the door. We ought to have been by this time at least ten leagues distant from here.'

I dressed myself hurriedly, and she handed me the articles of apparel herself one by one, bursting into laughter from time to time at my awkwardness, as she explained to me the use of a garment when I had made a mistake. She hurriedly arranged my hair, and this done, held up before me a little pocket mirror of Venetian crystal, rimmed with silver filigree-work, and playfully asked: 'How dost find thyself now? Wilt engage me for thy valet de chambre?'

I was no longer the same person, and I could not even recognise myself. I resembled my former self no more than a finished statue resembles a block of stone. My old face seemed but a coarse daub of the one reflected in the mirror. I was handsome, and my vanity was sensibly tickled by the metamorphosis. That elegant apparel, that richly embroidered vest had made of me a totally different personage, and I marvelled at the power of transformation owned by a few yards of cloth cut after a certain pattern. The spirit of my costume penetrated my very skin, and within ten minutes more I had become something of a coxcomb.

In order to feel more at ease in my new attire, I took several turns up and down the room. Clarimonde watched me with an air of maternal pleasure, and appeared well satisfied with her work. 'Come, enough of this child's-play! Let us start, Romuald, dear. We have far to go, and we may not get there in time.' She took my hand and led me forth. All the doors opened before her at a touch, and we passed by the dog without awakening him.

At the gate we found Margheritone waiting, the same swarthy groom who had once before been my escort. He held the bridles of three horses, all black like those which bore us to the castle – one for me, one for him, one for Clarimonde. Those horses must have been Spanish genets born of mares fecundated by a zephyr, for they were fleet as the wind itself, and the moon, which had just risen at our departure to light us on the way, rolled over the sky like a wheel detached from her own chariot. We beheld her on the right leaping from tree to tree, and putting herself out of breath in the effort to keep up with us. Soon we came upon a level plain where, hard by a clump of trees, a carriage with four vigorous horses awaited us. We entered it, and the postilions urged their animals into a mad gallop. I had one arm around Clarimonde's waist, and one of her hands clasped in mine; her head leaned upon my shoulder, and I felt her bosom, half bare, lightly pressing against my arm. I had never known such intense happiness. In that hour I had forgotten everything, and I no more remembered ever having been a priest than I remembered what I had been doing in my mother's womb, so great was the fascination which the evil spirit exerted upon me. From that night my nature seemed in some sort to have become halved, and there were two men within me, neither of whom knew the other. At one moment I believed myself a priest who dreamed nightly that he was a gentleman, at another that I was a gentleman who dreamed he was a priest. I could no longer distinguish the dream from the reality, nor could I discover where the reality began or where ended the dream. The exquisite young lord and libertine railed at the priest, the priest loathed the dissolute habits of the young lord. Two spirals entangled and confounded the one with the other, yet never touching, would afford a fair representation of this bicephalic life which I lived. Despite the strange character of my condition, I do not believe that I ever inclined, even for a moment to madness. I always retained with extreme vividness all the perceptions of my two lives. Only there was one absurd fact which I could not explain to myself – namely, that the consciousness of the same individuality existed in two men so opposite in character.

It was an anomaly for which I could not account – whether I believed myself to be the curé of the little village of C—, or *Il Signor Romualdo,* the titled lover of Clarimonde.

Be that as it may, I lived, at least I believed that I lived, in Venice. I have never been able to discover rightly how much of an illusion and how much of reality there was in this fantastic adventure. We dwelt in a great palace on the Canaleio, filled with frescoes and statues, and containing two Titians in the noblest style of the great master, which were hung in Clarimonde's chamber. It was a palace worthy of a king. We had each our gondola, our *barcarolli* in family livery, our music hall and our special poet. Clarimonde always lived upon a magnificent scale; there was something of Cleopatra in her nature. As for me, I had the retinue of a prince's son, and I was regarded with as much reverential respect as though I had been of the family of one of the twelve Apostles or the four Evangelists of the Most Serene Republic. I would not have turned aside to allow even the Doge to pass, and I do not believe that since Satan fell from heaven, any creature was ever prouder or more insolent than I. I went to the Ridotto, and played with a luck which seemed absolutely infernal. I received the best of all society – the sons of ruined families, women of the theatre, shrewd knaves, parasites, hectoring swashbucklers. But notwithstanding the dissipation of such a life, I always remained faithful to Clarimonde. I loved her wildly. She would have excited satiety itself, and chained inconstancy. To have Clarimonde was to have twenty mistresses; aye, to possess all women : so mobile, so varied of aspect, so fresh in new charms was she all in herself – a very chameleon of a woman, in sooth. She made you commit with her the infidelity you would have committed with another, by donning to perfection the character, the attraction, the style of beauty of the woman who appeared to please you. She returned my love a hundredfold, and it was in vain that the young patricians and even the Ancients of the Council of Ten made her the most magnificent proposals. A Foscari even went so far as to offer to espouse her. She rejected all his overtures. Of gold she had enough. She wished no longer for anything but love – a love youthful, pure, evoked by herself, which should be a first and last passion. I would have been perfectly happy but for a cursed nightmare which recurred every night, and in which I believed myself to be a poor village curé, practising mortification and penance for my excesses during the day. Reassured by my constant association with her, I never thought further of the strange manner in which I had become acquainted with Clarimonde. But the words of the Abbé Sérapion concerning her recurred often in my memory, and never ceased to cause me uneasiness.

For some time the health of Clarimonde had not been so good as usual; her complexion grew paler day by day. The physicians who were summoned could not comprehend the nature of her malady and knew not how to treat it. They all prescribed some insignificant remedies, and never called a second time. Her paleness, nevertheless, visibly increased, and she became colder and colder, until she seemed almost as white and dead as upon that memorable night in the unknown castle. I grieved with anguish unspeakable to behold her thus slowly perishing; and she, touched by my agony, smiled upon me sweetly and sadly with the fateful smile of those who feel that they must die.

One morning I was seated at her bedside, and breakfasting from a little table placed close at hand, so that I might not be obliged to leave her for a single instant. In the act of cutting some fruit I accidentally inflicted rather a deep gash on my finger. The blood immediately gushed forth in a little purple jet, and a few drops spurted upon Clarimonde. Her eyes flashed, her face suddenly assumed an expression of savage and ferocious joy such as I had never before observed in her. She leaped out of her bed with animal agility – the agility as it were of an ape or a cat – and sprang upon my wound, which she began to suck with an air of unutterable pleasure. She swallowed the blood in little mouthfuls, slowly and carefully, like a connoisseur tasting a wine from Xeres or Syracuse. Gradually her eyelids half-closed, and the pupils of her green eyes became oblong instead of round. From time to time she paused in order to kiss my hand, then she would again press her lips to the wound in order to coax forth a few more drops. When she found that the blood would no longer come, she arose with eyes liquid and brilliant, rosier than a May dawn; her face full and fresh, her hand warm and moist – in fine, more beautiful than ever, and in the most perfect health.

'I shall not die! I shall not die!' she cried, clinging to my neck, half-mad with joy. 'I can love thee yet for a long time. My life is thine. My life is thine, and all that is of me comes from thee. A few drops of thy rich and noble blood, more precious and more potent than all the elixirs of the earth, have given me back life.'

This scene long haunted my memory, and inspired me with strange doubts in regard to Clarimonde; and the same evening, when slumber had transported me to my presbytery, I beheld the Abbé Sérapion, graver and more anxious of aspect than ever. He gazed attentively at me, and sorrowfully exclaimed: 'Not content with losing your soul, you now desire also to lose your body. Wretched young man, into how terrible a plight have you fallen!' The tone in which he uttered these words powerfully affected me, but in spite of its vividness even that impression was soon dissipated, and a thousand other cares erased it from my mind. At last one evening, while looking into a mirror whose traitorous position she had not taken into account, I saw Clarimonde in the act of emptying a powder into the cup of spiced wine which she had long been in the habit of preparing after our repasts. I took the cup feigned to carry it to my lips, and then placed it on the nearest article of furniture as though intending to finish it at my leisure. Taking advantage of a moment when the fair one's back was turned, I threw the contents under the table, after which I retired to my chamber and went to bed, fully resolved not to sleep, but to watch and discover what should come of all this mystery. I did not have to wait long. Clarimonde entered in her nightdress, and having removed her apparel, crept into bed and lay down beside me. When she felt assured that I was asleep, she bared my arm, and drawing a gold pin from her hair, began to murmur in a low voice:

'One drop, only one drop! One ruby at the end of my needle. . . . Since thou lovest me yet, I must not die! . . . Ah, poor love! His beautiful blood, so brightly purple, I must drink it. Sleep, my only treasure! Sleep, my god, my child! I will do thee no harm; I will only take of thy life what I must to keep my own from being for ever extinguished. But that I love thee so much, I could well resolve to have other lovers whose veins I could drain; but since I have known thee all other men have become hateful to me. . . . Ah, the beautiful arm! How round it is! How white it is! How shall I ever dare to prick this pretty blue vein!' And while thus murmuring to herself she wept, and I felt her tears raining on my arm as she clasped it with her hands. At last she took the resolve, slightly punctured me with her pin and began to suck up the blood which oozed from the place. Although she swallowed only a few drops, the fear of weakening me soon seized her, and she carefully tied a little band around my arm, afterwards rubbing the wound with an unguent which immediately cicatrised it.

Further doubts were impossible. The Abbé Sérapion was right. Notwithstanding this positive knowledge, however, I could not cease to love Clarimonde, and I would gladly of my own accord have given her all the blood she required to sustain her factitious life. Moreover, I felt but little fear of her. The woman seemed to plead with me for the vampire, and what I had already heard and seen sufficed to reassure me completely. In those days I had plenteous veins, which would not have been so easily exhausted as at present; and I would not have thought of bargaining for my blood, drop by drop. I would rather have opened myself the veins of my arm and said to her: 'Drink, and may my love infiltrate itself throughout thy body together with my blood!' I carefully avoided ever making the least reference to the narcotic drink she had prepared for me, or to the incident of the pin, and we lived in the most perfect harmony.

Yet my priestly scruples began to torment me more than ever, and I was at a loss to imagine what new penance I could invent in order to mortify and subdue my flesh. Although these visions were involuntary and though I did not actually participate in anything relating to them, I could not dare to touch the body of Christ with hands so impure and a mind defiled by such debauches whether real or imaginary. In an effort to avoid falling under the influence of these wearisome hallucinations, I strove to prevent myself from being over come by sleep. I held my eyelids open with my fingers, and stood for hours together leaning upright against the wall, fighting sleep with all my might; but the dust of drowsiness invariably gathered upon my eyes at last, and finding all resistance useless, I would have to let my arms fall in the extremity of despairing weariness, and the current of slumber would again bear me away to the perfidious shores. Sérapion addressed me with the most vehement exhortations, severely reproaching me for my softness and want of fervour. Finally, one day when I was more wretched than usual, he said to me: 'There is but one way by which you can obtain relief from this continual torment, and though it is an extreme measure it must be made use of; violent diseases require violent remedies. I know where Clarimonde is buried. It is necessary that we shall disinter her remains, and that you shall behold in how pitable a state the object of your love is. Then you will no longer be tempted to lose your soul for the sake of a corpse ready to crumble into dust. That will assuredly restore you to yourself.' For my part, I was so tired of this double life that I at once consented, desiring to ascertain beyond a doubt whether a priest or a gentleman had been the victim of delusion. I had become fully resolved either to kill one of the two men within me for the benefit of the other, or else to kill both, for so terrible an existence could not last long and be endured. The Abbé Sérapion provided himself with a mattock, a lever and a lantern, and at midnight we made our way to the cemetery of —, the location and place of which were perfectly familiar to him. After having directed the rays of the dark lantern upon the inscriptions of several tombs, we came at last upon a great slab, half concealed by huge weeds and devoured by mosses and parasitic plants, whereupon we deciphered the opening lines of the epitaph:

> Here lies Clarimonde
> Who was famed in her lifetime
> As the fairest of women.[1]

'It is here without a doubt,' muttered Sérapion, and placing his lantern on the ground, he forced the point of

[1] Ici gît Clarimonde
Qui fut de son vivant
La plus belle du monde

The broken beauty of the lines is unavoidably lost in the translation.

the lever under the edge of the stone and began to raise it. The stone yielded, and he proceeded to work with the mattock. Darker and more silent than the night itself, I stood by and watched him do it, while he, bending over his dismal toil, streamed with sweat, panted and his hard-coming breath seemed to have the harsh tone of a death-rattle. It was a weird scene, and had any persons from without beheld us, they would assuredly have taken us rather for profane wretches and shroud-stealers than for priests of God. There was something grim and fierce in Sérapion's zeal which lent him the air of a demon rather than of an apostle or an angel, and his great aquiline face, with all its stern features brought out in strong relief by the lantern-light, had something fearsome in it which enhanced the unpleasant fancy. An icy sweat came out upon my forehead in huge beads. Within the depths of my own heart I felt that the act of the austere Sérapion was an abominable sacrilege; and I could have prayed that a triangle of fire would issue from the entrails of the dark clouds heavily rolling above us, to reduce him to cinders. The owls which had been nestling in the cypress trees, startled by the gleam of the lantern, flew against it from time to time, striking their dusty wings against its panes, and uttering plaintive cries of lamentation; wild foxes yelped in the far darkness, and a thousand sinister noises detached themselves from the silence. At last Sérapion's mattock struck the coffin itself, making its planks re-echo with a deep sonorous sound, with that terrible sound nothingness utters when stricken. He wrenched apart and tore up the lid, and I beheld Clarimonde, pallid as a figure of marble, with hands joined; her white winding-sheet made but one fold from her head to her feet. A little crimson drop sparkled like a speck of dew at one corner of her colourless mouth. Sérapion, at this spectacle, burst into fury: 'Ah, thou art here, demon! Impure courtesan! Drinker of blood and gold!' And he flung holy water upon the corpse and the coffin, over which he traced the sign of the cross with his sprinkler. Poor Clarimonde had no sooner been touched by the blessed spray than her beautiful body crumpled into dust, and became only a shapeless and frightful mass of cinders and half-calcined bones.

'Behold your mistress, my Lord Romuald!' cried the

inexorable priest, as he pointed to these sad remains. 'Will you be easily tempted after this to promenade on the Lido or at Fusina with your beauty?' I covered my face with my hands; a vast ruin had taken place within me. I returned to my presbytery, and the noble Lord Romuald, the lover of Clarimonde, separated himself from the poor priest with whom he had kept such strange company so long. But once only, the following night, I saw Clarimonde. She said to me, as she had said the first time at the portals of the church: 'Unhappy man! Unhappy man! What hast thou done? Wherefore hast thou hearkened to that imbecile priest? Wert thou not happy? And what harm had I ever done thee that thou shouldst violate my poor tomb, and lay bare the miseries of my nothingness? All communication between our souls and our bodies is henceforth ever broken. Adieu! Thou wilt yet regret me!' She vanished, and I never saw her any more.

Alas! she spoke truly indeed. I have regretted her more than once, and I regret her still. My soul's peace has been very dearly bought. The love of God was not too much to replace such a love as hers. And this, brother, is the story of my youth. Never gaze upon a woman, and walk abroad only with eyes ever fixed upon the ground; for however chaste and watchful one may be, the error of a single moment is enough to make one lose eternity.

(Translated from the French by George Saintsbury)

All Sphere Books are available at your bookshop or
newsagent, or can be ordered from the following address:

Sphere Books, Cash Sales Department,
P.O. Box 11, Falmouth, Cornwall.

Please send cheque or postal order (no currency), and allow
7p per copy to cover the cost of postage and packing
in U.K. or overseas.